MW01155989

NIGHTSHADE

ALSO BY MICHAEL CONNELLY

Fiction

The Black Echo

The Black Ice

The Concrete Blonde

The Last Coyote

The Poet

Trunk Music

Blood Work

Angels Flight

Void Moon

A Darkness More Than Night

City of Bones

Chasing the Dime

Lost Light

The Narrows

The Closers

The Lincoln Lawyer

Echo Park

The Overlook

The Brass Verdict

The Scarecrow

Nine Dragons

The Reversal

The Fifth Witness

The Drop

The Black Box

The Gods of Guilt

The Burning Room

The Crossing

The Wrong Side of Goodbye

The Late Show

Two Kinds of Truth

Dark Sacred Night

The Night Fire

Fair Warning

The Law of Innocence

The Dark Hours

Desert Star

Resurrection Walk

The Waiting

Nonfiction

Crime Beat

Ebooks

Suicide Run

Angle of Investigation

Mulholland Dive

The Safe Man

Switchblade

NIGHTSHADE

A Novel

MICHAEL CONNELLY

LITTLE, BROWN AND COMPANY
New York Boston London

Copyright © 2025 by Hieronymus, Inc.

Hachette Book Group supports the right to free expression and the value of copyright. The purpose of copyright is to encourage writers and artists to produce the creative works that enrich our culture.

The scanning, uploading, and distribution of this book without permission is a theft of the author's intellectual property. If you would like permission to use material from the book (other than for review purposes), please contact permissions@hbgusa.com. Thank you for your support of the author's rights.

Little, Brown and Company
Hachette Book Group
1290 Avenue of the Americas, New York, NY 10104
littlebrown.com

First Edition: May 2025

Little, Brown and Company is a division of Hachette Book Group, Inc. The Little, Brown name and logo are trademarks of Hachette Book Group, Inc.

The publisher is not responsible for websites (or their content) that are not owned by the publisher.

The Hachette Speakers Bureau provides a wide range of authors for speaking events. To find out more, go to hachettespeakersbureau.com or email hachettespeakers@hbgusa.com.

Little, Brown and Company books may be purchased in bulk for business, educational, or promotional use. For information, please contact your local bookseller or the Hachette Book Group Special Markets Department at special.markets@hbgusa.com.

ISBN 9780316588485 (hc) / 9780316589567 (lp) / 9780316595179 (signed) / 9780316595162 (B&N signed)
LCCN 2025933146

Printing 1, 2025

LSC-H

Printed in the United States of America

For Callie

NIGHTSHADE

1

THE MARINE LAYER was as thick as cotton and had formed a thousand-foot wall that shrouded the entrance to the harbor. The *Adjourned* was late and Stilwell waited for it in his John Deere Gator by the fuel dock behind the Casino. The harbor was almost empty, the red-and-orange mooring balls floating free in lines across the glass surface. Stilwell knew that as soon as the layer burned off, the weekenders would start arriving. The harbormaster's office had reported that it would be at full capacity for the first big weekend of summer. Stilwell was ready for it.

He heard another cart pull up behind his. An electric. Soon the seat next to Stilwell was taken by Lionel McKey.

"Good morning, Sergeant," he said. "I thought I might find you here. Waiting for the *Adjourned*?"

"What can I do for you, Lionel?" Stilwell asked.

"Anything new to say about the mutilations up at the preserve? I've got about four hours till my deadline."

"*Mutilation,* not mutilations. One mutilation. It's still under investigation and I've got nothing new to report at this time. When I do, you'll be the first to know."

"Is that a promise?"

"It's a promise."

His answer was punctuated by a foghorn from somewhere inside the layer. Stilwell knew by the tone that it was the Catalina Express about to come through the shroud. He wanted to be over there to watch the arrivals as he did most free mornings, counting the number of tourists who came believing that the Casino was a gambling house only to learn that it was a grand ballroom and movie theater. But meeting the *Adjourned* was more important this morning than counting fools.

"So what are you putting in the paper about it?" he asked.

"Well, not much," McKey said. "I don't want to look like an idiot, you know."

"I think that's wise."

"Why, because you know something?"

"No, but I mean, use your common sense, Lionel. You really think it was a close encounter of the green kind?"

"No, not really."

"Well, there you go. What time's your deadline?"

"Two."

"If anything changes before then, I'll be sure to let you know."

"Okay, thanks. I'll be at the *Call*."

"And I've got your numbers."

"Have a good weekend."

"If I can. It'll be busy."

"For sure."

McKey hopped out of the Gator and went back to his cart. As he drove off, Stilwell saw the *Catalina Call* logo of linked *C*s painted on the side panel.

A few seconds later the prow of the Express poked through the fog layer and headed toward the ferry landing on the other side of the harbor.

Following in its wake fifty yards behind was the *Adjourned*. It had been a smart move using the bigger vessel as a lead through the layer instead of coming in blind. The Express had the most modern navigational tools at the fingertips of its captain and crew.

The *Adjourned* was a forty-year-old Viking 35. Judge Harrell kept it clean and well maintained. It was white with distinctive blue trim and matching canvas over the salon's windows. Stilwell watched it cut down the first mooring lane, past the floating dock behind the Black Marlin Club, and come to the last orange ball. Harrell cut the engines and used a gaff to hook the line under the ball. He was wearing a wet suit, which told Stilwell he would not need a dinghy pickup. The judge quickly moored the boat, then climbed over the stern to the fantail and jumped into the cold water.

Stilwell got out of the cart and went to the storage box on the back. He unlocked it and got two green-and-white-striped towels out and draped one of them over the passenger seat. By the time he had it in place, Harrell was climbing up the ladder onto the fuel dock.

Stilwell threw him the other towel.

"Looked like some thick stuff out there, Judge," he said.

"Trojan-horsed on the tail of the Express," Harrell said.

Before getting into the Gator, he toweled off the wet suit and draped the towel over his head.

"I saw that," Stilwell said. "Smooth move."

"Anyway, sorry to be late," Harrell said. "I called Mercy and she's cued everything up."

Harrell took a seat in the cart on the towel Stilwell had spread.

"Yes, sir," Stilwell said. "Just a few D-and-Ds and a wobbler."

"Tell me about the wobbler," the judge said.

Stilwell circled the Casino and headed toward the justice center in town.

"Well, technically, it's a burglary of an occupied dwelling with a firearm enhancement," Stilwell said. "But the dwelling is occupied by the suspect's ex-girlfriend, and he claims he was stealing back his Glock because he was afraid of leaving it with her, like she might harm herself with it."

"How noble," Harrell said. "You know this man?"

"Kermit Henderson, born and raised here. Works up at the golf course running mowers and doing general maintenance. The girlfriend is Becki Trower, another local. I was thinking maybe you work a deal like you did with Sean Quinlan and we get some maintenance done around the sub. Especially since Sean is coming off his time."

"Okay, we'll hear him out. If that's all you've got, I might get some fishing in later."

"There's also this."

Stilwell leaned forward, reached into his back pocket, and pulled out the document he had printed earlier that morning and folded lengthwise to fit. He handed it to the judge, who unfolded it and started to read.

"Search warrant," Harrell said.

He got quiet as he read the summary and probable cause statement. Then he shook his head, not because he disagreed with anything he had read but because it made him angry.

"You got a pen?" he said.

Stilwell took the pen out of his shirt pocket and handed it to Harrell. The judge scribbled his signature on the appropriate line and handed the pen and the warrant back to Stilwell.

"I gave up a long time ago trying to understand why people do what they do to each other," Harrell said. "But cruelty to animals still gets to me. If this guy did what you suspect, then he better find a good lawyer and hope I don't get the case."

"I hear you," Stilwell said. "I'm the same."

A few minutes later they were at the justice complex on

Sumner Avenue. Stilwell and Harrell went into the sheriff's sub-station, where the judge kept his clothes and black robe in a locker. Stilwell unlocked the holding facility so that Harrell could use the shower and get dressed for court. Kermit Henderson, unable to make bail, was in one of the cells. He watched the judge go by, leaving wet footprints on the gray linoleum.

Stilwell saw no sign of Sean Quinlan. He texted him to tell him to mop the jail after the judge was finished showering and getting dressed. It would be Quinlan's final duty, as the judge was set to release him from probation.

Stilwell went into the courtroom and saw that Monika Juarez was already in place at the prosecution table. Mercy Chapa was at the clerk's desk for her one-morning-a-week gig. The rest of the time she was manager, dispatcher, and general overseer of the sheriff's substation, and Stilwell's right hand.

Juarez was a small woman with brown skin. Her hair was in black ringlets that framed her thin face but did not fully hide the whitish scar that ran along the left side of her jaw. Stilwell had never asked her about it but thought that however she got it, it probably had something to do with why she'd become a prosecutor. She was about thirty and assigned to the superior court in Long Beach. Like Judge Harrell, she came to Catalina once a week to handle the island's cases, but she preferred to come over the night before on the Express, stay at the Zane Grey at county expense, and then go directly to court in the morning.

"The judge is getting ready," Stilwell told her. "He'll probably start with Henderson. After that, it's the misdemeanors. Will you need me for those?"

"No, they look pretty routine," Juarez said.

"I picked up the judge and talked to him about Henderson. I think he's going to offer him probation if he'll take over maintenance around here for a few months."

"He's got a gun charge."

"Technically, yeah. But he was stealing the gun. His own gun. He didn't bring it with him."

"And you believe that?"

"I do because the victim — his ex — acknowledged in an interview I conducted that she had his gun and wouldn't give it back after she kicked him out. Her statement is in there."

"I didn't see that yet. I just started looking at the file."

That told Stilwell she hadn't done her homework the night before at the ZG. "Well, you'll get to it. I'll let you read and I'll see how the judge is doing."

What Stilwell really wanted to do was execute the search warrant Harrell had signed. He went back over to the sheriff's side of the building and saw Ralph Lampley in the bullpen, eating a blueberry muffin at the desk he shared with the other deputies. Lampley had the longest-running assignment to the Catalina substation. This was because the sheriff's department had deemed him a liability in high-crime districts on the mainland. Though only twenty-eight years old, he had already been involved in two shooting deaths while on patrol in mainland Los Angeles County. Both had drawn wrongful-death lawsuits, currently being litigated, in which tens of millions of dollars were at stake. The department had cleared him in internal investigations because to do otherwise would make the lawsuits indefensible, so Lampley was allowed to keep his badge but was transferred to the Catalina Island unit, where it was thought he'd likely keep his weapon holstered. The rumor was that as soon as the lawsuits were adjudicated or settled, he would be fired.

"Lamp, why aren't you out and about?" Stilwell asked.

"Because frickin' Fernando didn't bother charging my wheels," Lampley said. "So I'm waiting for at least a half a charge before I hit the street."

He was talking about the electric UTV cart he shared with the night-shift deputy. Normally, Stilwell would have been annoyed with Angel Fernando for failing to charge the cart when he'd finished his shift that morning. It was the third time this month. Fernando was the newest import from the mainland, where they didn't patrol in electric golf carts, and he had a habit of forgetting to charge at the end of shift. Instead of dwelling on Fernando's lack of attention to the routines of his job, Stilwell saw an opportunity to get himself out of the station.

"Okay, then, can you finish up there and handle court this morning?" he asked Lampley. "I've got to go serve a search warrant, and I need someone to take Kermit into court once the judge is on the bench."

Lampley spoke with his mouth full of muffin. "Yeah, I can do that," he said. "Is that warrant for the mutilation case?"

"Yes," Stilwell said. "But keep it to yourself."

"Cool. You go, Sarge. I can handle court."

"Shouldn't take long. Once you get a decent charge, check with the judge and see if he wants a ride back to his boat after court."

"Will do."

Stilwell left the sub, making a mental note to remind Fernando once again to leave the patrol cart charging at the end of shift. As the detective sergeant assigned to the Avalon substation, Stilwell was the commanding officer on the island. With that distinction came a host of administrative and scheduling duties he reluctantly accepted. Having to remind a veteran deputy to plug in his golf cart at the end of his shift was not one of his favorites.

2

STILWELL DROVE OUT to the industrial district south of town. Next to the desalination plant was a warren of warehouses, among them the cart barn used by Island Mystery Tours. The main garage door was open and Stilwell parked the Gator in front of it so no vehicle could leave. A man in a greasy blue jumpsuit stepped out of the shadows of one of the cart bays, and Stilwell guessed he had probably been sleeping back there. His hair was matted on one side. He looked as though he had not shaved in a week, and the bloodshot eyes behind his glasses indicated he was hungover.

"Hey, what's up?" he asked.

"I'm Sergeant Stilwell with the sheriff's office," Stilwell said. "I have a search warrant for these premises."

"Search warrant? What the fuck?"

"What's your name, sir?"

The man pointed to an oval patch on the left side of his jump-suit. "Henry."

"Henry what?"

"Gaston."

"Well, Henry, here is the warrant, and I'm going to need you to step aside and let me enter the premises."

Stilwell handed him the document signed earlier by the judge. Gaston held the paper at arm's length to read it, even though he was wearing glasses.

"Says you're looking for animal blood," he said. "That's crazy. Ain't no blood here."

"Either way, I'm going to search," Stilwell said. "The judge signed and authorized it this morning."

"You're that new guy they put in charge at the substation, huh?"

"If by 'new,' you mean a year ago, then, yeah, that would be me."

"You know I'm going to have to call Baby Head about this."

Stilwell moved to the back of the Gator and unlocked the storage compartment. He took out a set of disposable gloves, a flashlight, and the bottle of Bluespray he kept in the kit he'd put together when he'd worked homicide on the mainland.

"You can call anybody you want," he said to Gaston as he was gathering it all. "But I'm going to conduct the court-ordered search now."

He closed the compartment and walked directly toward Gaston even though there was plenty of room in the garage entry to go around him. Intimidated by the move, Gaston stepped back and out of the way. He pulled a cell phone from his pocket and started making a call.

Stilwell entered the garage and saw that the left side was lined with empty charging bays. All the tour carts were presumably in use or at least down at the harbor ready for the arrival of tourists coming in off the boats. The right side of the garage was where carts were repaired or cannibalized for parts. There were two six-seaters in various stages of disassembly. One was on a lift because it had no wheels. The other was in need of bodywork, as its fiberglass front was splintered — it appeared to have been driven into something.

In the rear right corner of the garage was an L-shaped work-bench with tools hanging on a pegboard behind it. This drew Stil-well's attention and he walked around the two broken carts to take a look. Gaston had followed him into the barn and was standing in the center, talking to somebody on his phone.

"He's got a warrant to search the place," he said. "I couldn't stop him."

Stilwell scanned the pegboard until his eyes came to a hand-saw with a long blade and a blue plastic handle.

"Uh, right now he's in the back by the tools," Gaston said. "You going to come over?"

Stilwell pulled out his phone and took a photo of the handsaw where it was hanging on the board. He then put on his gloves and took down the saw. Under the beam of the flashlight, he studied the blade carefully. It did not take him long to determine that it was new. There were no scratches on its stainless-steel surface and no corrosion from the salt air, and its teeth were pristine, showing no sign that they had ever cut even a stick of butter.

The saw's plastic handle, however, was old and marked by time and use. It was only the blade that was new.

"That's a pipe saw," Gaston said. "We use it mostly on fiber-glass and PVC."

He had come up behind Stilwell. He was no longer on the phone.

"You cut anything else with it?" Stilwell asked.

"Just stuff with the carts," Gaston said. "We customize. Some-times we cut 'em clean in half and make two four-seaters into an eight-seater or a six-pack. Like that."

"Doesn't look like anybody's been cutting with this one lately. Blade looks brand-new. You change it recently, Henry?"

"Uh, no."

"You sure?"

"Course I'm sure."

"Do me a favor and close the garage and turn off the overhead lights."

"How come?"

"Because if you don't, I will, and I might hit the wrong switch."

"All right."

Gaston went to do as he was told. Stilwell looked again at the saw. The blade was about eighteen inches long and had very small teeth — right for a smooth cut through fiberglass and PVC pipes. It was secured to the handle by two wing nuts. He used his thumb and forefinger to turn the nuts and detach the blade. Gaston pulled down on a chain attached to a pulley at the top of the garage door and it started to descend.

Once Stilwell had the blade separated, he put the handle on the workbench and studied one side and then the other in his flashlight's beam. The overhead lights went out and the garage dropped into darkness save for Stilwell's flashlight and some daylight that leaked in under the corrugated roof's eaves.

Stilwell sprayed one side of the saw handle with the chemical in the bottle, a compound that emitted a whitish-blue glow in the presence of hemoglobin. He then turned off the flashlight and waited and watched.

"What's going on?" Gaston called from the darkness.

"I'm conducting a presumptive test for blood," Stilwell said.

That brought only silence from the space where Gaston stood.

A minute went by and nothing happened. Stilwell flicked on the flashlight, turned the saw handle over, and sprayed the new side with the chemical. While he had the light on, he swept the beam across the garage to locate Gaston. He had moved away from the garage door and was now standing ten feet behind Stilwell, trying to see what he was doing.

"Stay right there for me, Henry," he said.

"How come?" Gaston said. "I work here. I'm entitled to be anywhere I want."

"I need to know where you are when the lights are off. Don't fuck with me. You won't want that."

"Fine. I'm staying right here. Whatever makes you happy."

"Thank you."

Stilwell turned the light off and looked at the workbench. The holes in the saw handle where the blade had been attached were filled with a pale blue phosphorescent glow. It meant that blood had most likely seeped into the holes and so had not been washed away during cleaning.

"You can turn the lights on, Henry," Stilwell said.

Gaston went back to the switch and the overhead lights came on. Stilwell approached the garage door holding the saw handle in a gloved hand.

"Open it," he said.

Gaston pulled down on the chain, and the garage door began to rise.

"What's that mean, *presumpive*?" he asked.

"*Presumptive,*" Stilwell corrected. "It means it looks like there was blood but the lab will have to confirm."

"So you're taking that?"

"Under the authority of the search warrant, yes. Who were you talking to on the phone, Henry?"

"I called Baby Head at the booth. He's on his way."

"Not going to make a difference. I'm still taking it."

Stilwell walked out to the UTV and took an evidence bag from the storage compartment. He placed the saw handle in it, sealed it, and used a red marker to write the date, time, and search warrant number on it. He put the bag in the storage compartment and locked it with a key.

He moved to the cart's seat and grabbed the clipboard from

the shelf below the dashboard. Gaston was standing in the garage doorway, watching.

"I'm writing you a receipt for the handle I'm taking," he said.

"What's that do?" Gaston said.

"Documents chain of evidence."

" 'Chain of evidence'?"

"A record of who has handled evidence and where it's gone."

"Evidence of what?"

"You know what, Henry? It's not like Baby Head went out there and cut up the buffalo himself. He's too clever for that. I'm guessing he had someone do it. I'll be sending this saw handle to the lab in overtown. If the blood on it matches that mutilated buffalo's, I'll be back. Those are protected animals, and killing one — that's a felony. We're going to have a big weekend, and I'll probably be running my ass off with drunk-and-disorderlies. I'm thinking about taking Tuesday off to recoup and then I'll get this to the lab Wednesday or Thursday. I figure from there, it will take a few weeks for the lab to get to it. Homicides of humans take priority. But once I deliver it, there's no turning back. So what I'll do is give you till then — Wednesday — to come in, talk to me, and work something out. After that, it will be out of my hands."

He took the receipt from the clipboard, pulled off the yellow copy, and got out of the cart. He walked over and handed it to Gaston.

"Wednesday, Henry," he said.

The whole thing was a bluff. Stilwell knew that the lab would apply negative priority to his DNA request. He'd be lucky to get results before the end of the year.

"Baby Head ain't going to allow this shit," Gaston said. "He knows people."

"Yeah, so do I," Stilwell said.

Stilwell got in the John Deere, turned the key, and backed

away from the barn. In the street, he put it in forward but was blocked when another cart pulled in front of him. It was a six-seater from Island Mystery Tours, the green papier-mâché alien lying chest-down on the roof, its three-fingered hands grasping the sides as if holding on for dear life.

Oscar "Baby Head" Terranova, the owner-manager of the franchise, jumped out and approached him.

"What the hell are you doing, Stilwell?" he asked angrily.

"I'm pretty sure Henry already told you on the phone," Stilwell said. "He's got a copy of the search warrant and the receipt. You can figure it out from there."

There was a line of sweat forming on Baby Head's smoothly shaved scalp. He had a tattoo of a diamond ring on his neck below his left ear and a full sleeve of tats on his right arm depicting skulls, flowers, and a three-digit number Stilwell didn't recognize but guessed was the area code of his place of origin.

"You're barking up the wrong tree, man," he said.

"Maybe so," Stilwell said. "It wouldn't be the first time and it won't be the last."

"I know about you, man. We all know about you. You were on thin ice when you got here, and now you're about to drop right through. Hope you got your water wings on."

"Can you move your cart now, sir? I need to get back to the station."

"Fuck you."

Terranova jumped back in his cart and pinned the pedal. The cart drove up and into the cart barn, forcing Gaston to move quickly to get out of the way.

Stilwell headed back to town, stopping briefly atop Mount Ada to take in the beauty of the mountains and the crescent-shaped harbor below. The Casino looked like a cupcake with red icing.

Several boats had already come in since he'd picked up the judge earlier.

Arriving back at the sub, Stilwell saw Lampley about to head out in his freshly charged patrol cart. He pulled up next to him.

"How'd it go?" Lampley asked.

"I found blood on a saw handle," Stilwell said. "I'll get it to the lab and see what happens."

"Don't hold your breath on that."

"I won't. You handle court?"

"Yeah, it went quick."

"What happened with Kermit?"

"Harrell gave him three months' community service. Told him to work it off in the sub."

"Perfect. I'll make a to-do list and put it on the board. Everybody can add to it."

"Okay."

"Where are you going now?"

"Just doing the circuit. No calls yet. The calm before the storm."

"Copy that."

Stilwell threw him a mock salute and pulled his cart into its assigned parking space. Before he got to the door of the substation, he took a call from the harbormaster's office.

"It's Tash. We need you over here on the skiff dock right away."

Tash Dano was the assistant harbormaster. Stilwell had met her on his rounds when he was first assigned to the island. He had met with everybody in any position of power or authority in the small community, from the mayor of Avalon down to the assistant harbormaster. Most were standoffish because deputies assigned to Catalina seemed to come and go quickly; they left as soon as they were rehabilitated in the eyes of the mainland command staff. The island was known as a way station for the department's freaks and fuckups and therefore it was not worth the residents' investment of time to get to know any of its personnel. Tash was different. She had invited Stilwell to lunch and even gave him her own tour of the island. She had lived there her entire life and had no plans to leave. Stilwell immediately liked her.

"What's up over there?" he asked.

"You know Abbott, the scraper?" she asked.

"I know who he is. First name is Denzel, right?"

"Right. He just called and said there's a body down there under the *Aurora*. He said it's got an anchor chain wrapped around it. A human body. He couldn't tell male or female."

It took Stilwell a few moments to understand what Tash was saying. He got regular updates on what boats were moored in the harbor. He remembered that the *Aurora* was a seagoing yacht registered out of Venezuela. It had entered the harbor two days earlier and moored on the fourth line of buoys, where the big boats were staged.

"Okay, I'm on my way," Stilwell said. "Tell Abbott to meet me at the skiff dock."

"Will do," Tash said.

"And Tash, when's the *Aurora* staying till?"

"Today. They're leaving today."

"What time?"

"Anytime. They have the ball till sixteen hundred but can shove off whenever they want."

"We might have to do something about that. I'll probably want to hold them in port if what Abbott says he saw is true."

"You want me to call the Coast Guard in? They could stop them."

"I want to confirm the body before we start calling in the troops."

"Gotcha. How you going to do that?"

"I'm going to have Abbott take me down."

"Oh."

"Problem?"

"No. Just be careful."

"Copy that. I will."

Stilwell went into the sub to get his wet suit.

3

THE WATER WAS cold. It felt like ice poking into his ears as he descended. Most of his body was insulated by the wet suit he'd kept from his days on the sheriff's dive team, but his feet, his scalp, and his ears were exposed to the chill.

Stilwell felt a sense of déjà vu as he went down. The cold. The sound of his own measured breathing in the mask. The slow motion and silence of things underwater.

He followed Denzel Abbott down, both tethered by the hookahs connected to the compressor up on the hull scraper's skiff. The air piped through the hose was foul, stale, and oily in Stilwell's mouth and lungs. He fought back nausea as he sank with the help of the weight belt borrowed from Abbott.

The sun had burned away the marine layer by the time Stilwell got back to the harbor after Tash Dano's call. Abbott told him that he had been scraping barnacles off the *Aurora* when the glint of shiny metal caught his eye from twenty-five yards away. He went farther down to investigate and was repelled by what he saw. He was pretty sure it was a body wrapped in something black and anchored, but he did not go closer to determine further details.

They went into the water about thirty feet off the *Aurora*'s stern. Rays of light shot through the tall branches of the kelp forest rising from the bottom, otherworldly strands of green leaves languidly reaching for sunlight and swaying in the current like a line of dancers in sync. Stilwell could now see a reflection off a polished metal anchor.

They moved through the shadow of the *Aurora*'s hull as they dropped farther into the depths of the harbor. The body — if it was a body — was thirty feet down. It was as Abbott had described: A human figure bloated and bursting from an opening in what looked like a large black bag that was wrapped in braided anchor line and a heavy galvanized chain. The chain extended three feet down to an anchor snagged on a coral outcropping. Long dark hair had come through the opening in the black plastic and floated free in the current. Stilwell could see that it was attached to a white scalp. As he approached, he realized that it looked like a macabre balloon arrangement buffeted by the bottom current of the harbor.

Stilwell wore diving gloves he had retrieved with his wet suit from his locker at the sub. He used a finger to spread the drawstring opening in the black bag until he could see a face. It was waxy and misshapen from bloating caused by decomp gases. It was almost unrecognizable as human, but he knew from his experiences in the blue world that it was indeed a person.

He noticed a streak of purple dye in the dark hair and guessed he was looking at the remains of a woman. There were fissure lines in the face that could have been caused by decomposition, postmortem sea-life predation, or injury sustained prior to death. The image brought back memories of victims he had seen as a body-recovery diver — horrors he'd thought he'd put behind him. In the vernacular, they were called floaters or sinkers, depending on the circumstances — words used to dehumanize and compartmentalize what was seen in the murky depths. But Stilwell

21

couldn't forget them. The girl at the bottom of Lake Piru, with eyes cast up toward the light and a god that hadn't saved her. The man in the suit and tie, his sunglasses still in place, with concrete blocks tied to his feet at the Bouquet Reservoir. The baby in the back seat of the car driven intentionally down the boat ramp at Castaic Lake. All found in the depths of a blue world that was calm and quiet and yet so deadly.

He could tell that this one had been in the water a while. Four days, at least. His eyes left the blanched eyes of the dead woman and moved down the chain to the anchor that had kept the body from floating to the surface. It was a plow anchor that had caught snugly on the coral ledge.

Stilwell knew the stages of decomposition in cold water. The body had been weighted and submerged. It had been anchored to the bottom until microorganisms in the intestines began creating gases, leading to bloat and buoyancy that started to lift the body despite the weight of the anchor and chain. Whoever had dropped the woman into the water had not anticipated these changes.

The body and the anchor chain would become buoyant enough to move easily with the currents, skipping across the coral and kelp beds until it finally rose to the surface or was snagged by something on the bottom. Stilwell had once recovered a body from Apollo Lake that had gotten entangled with an old washing machine that had been dumped off a boat. This anchor's snag on the coral ledge was only temporary. Stilwell knew it could loosen and break free with the change of current in the next outgoing tide.

He noted that the anchor wasn't from a large boat like the *Aurora*. He guessed its weight at twelve pounds. The stainless steel that had initially caught Abbott's eye was for show. It wasn't an anchor galvanized against corrosion and stored in a boat compartment. It most likely sat on rubber rollers on the prow, shining clean and on display, attached to a windlass that would drop and raise it at the push of a button from the boat's helm. The anchor hadn't come from a working boat. It was from a pleasure boat, maybe a sailboat. The kinds of vessels that filled the harbor every weekend.

He had seen enough. He needed to move to the surface to get the gas fumes out of his lungs and to call out the dive team as well as the homicide unit and coroner's investigators. This would not be his case and he was glad for that.

He turned and saw Abbott standing on the bottom several feet away from the body. His eyes were wide and scared behind his dive mask. Stilwell unsnapped his weight belt and turned back to the body. He wrapped the belt around the anchor, hoping to keep the body from wandering with the current should its mooring break loose from the ledge. He had not checked the tide chart that morning and wasn't sure when the current would change direction. He wanted to make sure the body did not surface in the harbor on the first day of Memorial Day weekend.

Stilwell's lungs were now burning from fuel-contaminated air. He pointed to the surface and Abbott nodded and started up. Stilwell followed, and they broke surface on either side of Abbott's skiff. Stilwell threw an arm over the side and yanked his mask off. He gulped in clean air and looked across the boat at Abbott, who held on to the other side.

"You've got a leak in your compressor," he said.

"I know," Abbott said. "I didn't think it was that bad."

"No, it's bad. I'm going to get a seven-point-oh headache out of it."

"Sorry, man. I guess I'm just used to it."

"Don't worry about it."

"So, what happens now? You going to just leave it where it is?"

"For now. I'll call out the recovery team as soon as I get to my phone. You'll get your weight belt back once they recover the body."

"I'm not worried about it."

Abbott hoisted himself over the side and into the skiff, causing it to rock violently. Stilwell was almost clipped on the chin when the rail rose. He waited until the boat calmed and then pulled himself up and over the side as well.

"Look who we got waitin' on us," Abbott said.

Stilwell turned to look back at the skiff dock and saw Tash Dano standing next to Lionel McKey. With them was Doug Allen, the four-term mayor of Avalon.

"News travels fast," Abbott said.

Stilwell nodded.

"Here we go," he whispered to himself.

4

THE MAYOR HAD his hands on his hips as he stood at the skiff dock and waited for them. Tash and Lionel stood slightly apart from Allen. Abbott ran the bow up on the landing, and Stilwell stepped off, a green-and-white towel draped over his shoulders.

"You need me anymore?" Abbott asked.

Stilwell turned to him. "The detectives from the mainland will probably want a statement," he said. "We can call you. Are you going home or back under?"

"Home," Abbott said. "No work after seeing that."

Stilwell nodded. He understood. He turned back, and Tash came forward and away from the reporter.

"Do we hold the *Aurora*?" she asked quietly. "They want to go."

"They can go," Stilwell said. "What's down there's been in the water longer than they've been here. Remind them to stay at idle speed till they're out of the harbor. I don't want to churn up the bottom."

"Will do," Tash said.

McKey came over to him next. "Is there a body?" he asked.

Before Stilwell could answer, the mayor spoke.

"Wait a minute," Allen said. "Wait just a minute. We're not saying anything for publication yet. Sergeant Stilwell, I need to speak with you privately before any public statement is made."

"Okay," Stilwell said. "For now."

"You need to go back up to the pier," Allen said to McKey.

"This is a public dock, Mayor," McKey said. "I have just as much right to be here as you do."

"Whatever," Allen said. "Sergeant, can you step over here?"

The two men walked to the opposite side of the floating dock, where they would not be overheard.

"Did you confirm a body is down there?" Allen whispered urgently.

"I did," Stilwell whispered back.

"So what happens now? I don't want that thing bobbing up on the surface in front of the Express. What are you going to do?"

"I'm going to call out the homicide unit and dive team. It's not going to come to the surface until we bring it up."

"Homicide . . . are you saying this is a murder?"

"The body's in some kind of a drawstring bag and weighted with an anchor and chain. That says homicide to me."

Allen took a step closer to Stilwell and raised his whisper to an urgent tone: "Look, you need to understand something here. The ferries are full, and every ball in the harbor is reserved. This is our second-biggest weekend of the year, after July Fourth, and I don't want this harbor turned into a crime scene circus."

"I get it, Mr. Mayor. But we're going to conduct the investigation that is warranted. We'll do our best to shield the body recovery from the public. There are ways to do that. But if you're suggesting we leave it down there till this place clears out Monday, you are —"

"Of course I'm not suggesting that. What I'm saying is that murder is bad for business. Be discreet. And don't tell that reporter anything until he's past deadline. He can put it in next week's edition for all I care. Not tomorrow's."

"I'll do what I can. Now I have to go make those calls."

Stilwell stepped away and headed toward the gangway to the pier.

"And Sergeant?"

He turned.

"Yes?" he asked impatiently.

"I received a complaint about you this morning," Allen said. "From one of our business owners. Oscar Terranova."

"Really? That was fast."

"You searched his business?"

"I had a warrant signed by Judge Harrell. It was all perfectly legal."

"He said you were heavy-handed."

"I don't know what that means. I had a search warrant for the place. I searched it. Baby Head showed up afterward and he wasn't happy. But that was it."

"Okay, understood. Can I ask what it was about?"

"No, you can't, Mayor. It's an open investigation. I can't talk about it."

"I was born and raised on this island, Sergeant. I've been mayor for sixteen years. You'll probably come and go like all the deputies assigned here before you. But I'll be here. I love this place and I want to protect it. I don't like surprises, especially when they may negatively affect the reputation of this beautiful island."

He gestured toward the water in the direction of where the body was anchored.

"I understand that," Stilwell said.

"Good," Allen said. "We're on the same page, then."

Stilwell nodded and turned rather than arguing with the mayor's conclusion. He saw that McKey remained on the dock, but

Tash was up on the pier and heading back to the harbormaster's office.

"I can't talk to you yet," Stilwell said as he attempted to pass the reporter.

"What do you mean?" McKey said. "Is there a body down there or not?"

"I can't say anything yet. Talk to Abbott. He can tell you what he saw. I can't."

"You're letting the mayor tell you what to do?"

"No. That's how it would be whether he was here or not. I'm following sheriff's department procedure, and you know it."

He left McKey there and went up the gangway to the pier. Several people were watching from the railing. Stilwell recognized most of them as locals who worked in the souvenir stalls on the pier. Word had spread quickly that there was something in the water.

He crossed Crescent and walked up Sumner to the sub. He went directly into the locker room, peeled off the wet suit, took a quick shower, and then put his work clothes and sidearm back on. His windowless office, the size of a walk-in closet, was off the bullpen, and from there he made the calls, starting with the homicide unit. It was a number he knew by heart. He didn't recognize the voice that answered and asked to speak to the captain.

"Corum."

"Cap, it's Stil. We've got a homicide out here. A body in the harbor. Looks like a female."

"A floater?"

"She's thirty feet under, held down by an anchor."

"And this is confirmed?"

"I went down, saw it myself. It's probably been in the water four days or so, judging by the decomp. Hard to tell, though, with the water temps in the low sixties. You need the divers and one of your teams out here."

"Jesus Christ — on a Friday."

"Yeah, I already got the mayor on my ass because this place is going to fill to the brim today. Murder is bad for business."

"Okay, listen, Ahearn and Sampedro have the up. I've gotta send them. Are you going to play nice with them?"

"Do I have a choice?"

"No, you don't."

"Then send 'em. I can hold their hands if I have to."

That brought a long silence from Corum. Stilwell thought about the last time he had encountered Rex Ahearn. It was when he had gone into the homicide unit on a Sunday morning to clean out his desk. He was surprised to find Ahearn there and it had gotten ugly pretty quickly. And physical.

"You know, Stil, I don't think I want you holding their hands," Corum said. "Just point 'em in the right direction and let them do their job."

"Well, their job is to solve the case, Cap. So good luck getting them to do that."

"I'm not going to get into that with you, Detective Sergeant."

Corum's invoking his full and formal rank made Stilwell realize that he had gone a step too far. He tried to recover.

"Captain, will your people set up the recovery team and the coroner's, or you want me to handle that?"

"No, we'll handle it. Your job now is to protect the crime scene as best you can. We'll take it from there."

"Copy that."

Corum disconnected without another word. Stilwell wished he had not brought up his grievances with Ahearn and Sampedro. He put the thought aside and stepped out of his office. Mercy Chapa was now at her desk in the substation. She was in her early fifties, with gray hair she didn't bother dyeing. It fit with her role as the unofficial mother hen of the substation. She handled all duties not related to direct law enforcement.

"Mercy, can you get Lampley up on the radio and tell him to meet me at the skiff dock?"

"Sure. I think he just drove Kermit up to the golf course."

"Well, tell him to get over to the dock. I'll meet him there."

"Right away, Sergeant."

Stilwell pulled a fresh radio out of the charger station on the wall next to Mercy's desk.

"Have there been any missing person reports that I wasn't told about?" he asked. "Any at all?"

"No," Mercy said. "You get all the reports."

"Right. Do you happen to know of anybody in town who has long dark hair with a purple streak? You know, like a purple dye?"

"Um, no. Is there really a body out there in the water?"

"There is. But I don't want you talking to anybody about it."

"I don't tell anybody about work. Is it a girl?"

"A female, yes, I'm pretty sure. You haven't heard about anybody not showing up for work or school or anything like that? Maybe somebody who supposedly went to overtown but didn't come back on schedule?"

Mercy was third generation on the island and Stilwell had learned early in his assignment to the Catalina sub that she had vast connections in the community.

"No, nothing."

"Okay. Well, let me know if you hear anything."

"Of course."

"I'll be out at the harbor waiting for the homicide team."

5

THE RECOVERY TEAM had come by boat and brought a coroner's investigator with them. The divers were in the water by the time the sheriff's helicopter flew in from the mainland, circled the harbor, and put down next to the Casino. Stilwell sent Lampley to pick up Ahearn and Sampedro, electing to spend as little time with them as possible.

It was late in the day and the harbor was now almost at capacity with vessels of various sizes moored side by side along three lines of buoys. Tash Dano had managed to keep the fourth line of balls open. She had called Stilwell and told him she was keeping the final boats with reservations out in the bay until he gave the all-clear. He told her that the investigation would move on from the harbor by dusk.

Stilwell was surprised to see only Ahearn walking down the pier with Lampley to the skiff dock gangway. Sampedro had apparently stayed behind on the mainland. Ahearn turned and started plodding down the gangway. He was in a suit and tie and therefore drew the attention of many of the tourists on the pier.

The tide was running out of the harbor now and the water level had dropped four feet since that morning. The gangway and skiff dock floated freely with the tide, and the four-foot drop put the gangway at a sharp downward angle. Ahearn was a large white man with wide shoulders and a thick neck supporting a round head. He picked up dangerous momentum as he came down. Stilwell stepped back, not wanting to get in the way.

The gangway had ribbed rubber matting to guard against slippage, but the deck of the skiff dock had recently been replaced with fiberboard and was slick with moisture from the lapping of harbor waters. The moment Ahearn's hard-soled dress shoes hit the deck, he went into a full skid. His feet shot out from under him, his arms pinwheeled, and he landed on his back. His silky suit greased his slide across the six feet of remaining deck, and he went into the water between two Zodiac inflatables.

"Shit!" Lampley yelled as he came down the gangway behind him.

Stilwell moved quickly to the edge of the deck, ready to rescue Ahearn, but he popped up between the two boats, immediately reacting to the cold Pacific water.

"Motherfuck!"

Stilwell leaned down and offered his hand and Lampley did the same, but Ahearn was too angry and embarrassed to accept help. He slapped their hands away.

"Get the fuck away!"

Stilwell and Lampley stepped back, raising their hands in surrender, and watched as the big man hoisted his upper body up over the edge of the deck. His dark suit and slicked-back hair made him look like one of the seals that often sunned on the deck in the mornings. He dragged himself out of the water and rolled onto his back, seemingly exhausted by the effort.

"Goddamn it!" he yelled. "I bet you loved that, Stillborn."

"Actually, no," Stilwell said. "Because now we have to worry about you getting dry clothes instead of working the case."

"Fuck off."

"Sure."

Stilwell turned to Lampley, whose eyes were wide with what he had just witnessed.

"When he's up, take him to the sub," he said. "Get him a hot shower and some clothes out of the court closet—if anything fits. I'll stay here. Call me when he's ready and I'll come over if the recovery team is finished."

Ahearn was pulling a wet wallet out of his back pocket.

"Jesus Christ," he said. "You could have warned me, Stillborn."

"You mean about wearing your Men's Wearhouse oxfords on a boat dock?" Stilwell said. "Yeah, I guess I could have."

Ahearn slowly started to get up, dripping water from every thread of his suit. He immediately slipped again and went down to one knee.

"Goddamn it, help me up!"

Lampley offered him a hand and Ahearn grabbed it and intentionally tried to pull him down, but the young deputy was able to hold his ground. Ahearn let go and got up on his own. He looked up at the pier and saw several tourists aiming their phones at the skiff dock.

"Great," he said. "All I need. I want every one of those phones collected and the videos deleted."

"That's not going to happen," Stilwell said. "Just go to the substation, get a shower, and put warm clothes on. We'll talk then." He looked at Lampley and nodded toward the gangway. "Take him," he said.

Lampley held out his hand to help Ahearn get to the gangway, but the detective slapped it away and crossed the deck with tiny steps, looking like someone on a pair of ice skates for the first time. Once he got to the rubber matting of the gangway, he was safe. He turned and looked back at Stilwell as if to say something but then thought better of it and headed up the ramp. He kept one hand on the railing but held the other up, offering his middle finger to anyone still videoing his embarrassment.

Stilwell watched them go until his phone started to buzz with a call from Tash Dano. She had seen Ahearn's deck slide from the harbor control tower.

"Wow, that was embarrassing," she said. "Was that the man from homicide?"

"It was," Stilwell said. "Couldn't have happened to a nicer guy. What's up, Tash?"

"Does that guy's splash delay things? How long until I can bring the last boats in from the bay? It'll be dark soon and they're getting a little pissed off sitting out there."

"Hold on."

Stilwell put the phone in his shirt pocket and then took the radio off his belt. It was set to the dive team's frequency, so there was no need for him to speak in code to the topside deputy, Gary Saunders, whom Stilwell had known for years.

"Gary, how long we talking now?"

He waited for a return voice on the radio.

"Uh, yeah, they're bringing her up. They already bagged her and we have the curtain up, so no worry on the lookie-loos. We'll get her on here and then we're done. Chuck already did a floor search. There's nothing. She was dropped somewhere else, probably in the bay, and the tide brought her in here."

"Roger that. What I thought."

"The weight belt is yours?"

"I borrowed it."

"Okay, we'll bring it to you."

"Thank you."

"Hey, was that A-Hole I saw slide into the water?"

That was one of the popular nicknames for Rex Ahearn. The other was a play on both his names: King A-Hole.

"It was," Stilwell said.

"I guess it couldn't have happened to a nicer guy," Saunders said.

"What I said."

"That's sure to go viral. A lot of people with phones up on the pier."

"I saw."

"Okay, we'll finish up here and drop by your twenty."

"Copy. Out."

Stilwell pulled his phone and relayed the information to Tash.

"Anything you can do to hurry them would be good," she said.

"They have to get back to the mainland with it," Stilwell said. "I'm sure they want to get there before dark."

"Okay."

"Hey, Tash, while I've got you, you remember seeing anyone around here with long dark hair with a streak of purple dye in it? A woman?"

"Hmm."

She went silent for a long moment before continuing.

"Something about that seems really familiar but I can't place her. I don't think it's a local. I know all the locals. But I think I remember seeing a girl with hair like that somewhere."

"A girl?"

"I mean a woman. She was older."

"If you can remember where or anything else, let me know."

"That's the person in the water?"

"Yes. Age unknown at the moment."

"Right. So sad."

"Yeah."

They disconnected. Stilwell sat down on a fiberglass equipment box at the end of the dock and watched the recovery operation from afar. Saunders had put up a privacy tent over the back deck of the dive boat. Stilwell knew that this was where they would place the body for the trip back across the bay.

The divers soon surfaced and lifted a submergible body bag onto the fantail of the dive boat. Saunders and a coroner's investigator Stilwell didn't recognize grabbed the straps on the bag and moved it through the gunwale door, onto the rear deck of the boat, and out of sight. Next the coiled rope, chain, and anchor were handed up by the divers, followed by the weight belt Stilwell had wrapped around the anchor.

The two recovery divers climbed up the drop ladder and onto the boat. The ladder went up and soon Stilwell heard the twin 150 engines come to life. Saunders went to the bow and pulled up the anchor and then the boat started moving at idle speed toward the skiff dock.

Stilwell called the harbormaster's office.

"Tash, you can start bringing the rest of the boats in."

"Perfect. They'll be happy."

"Did you tell them why there was a delay?"

"Uh, no."

"Good. I gotta go."

He disconnected, grabbed the front rail of the dive boat as it came to the dock, and gently brought it to a stop.

Saunders came forward with the dive belt Stilwell had borrowed from Abbott and handed it over the rail. "Do me a favor, Gary," Stilwell said. "Let me get a look at the anchor and chain."

"You got it," Saunders said.

He stepped back so that Stilwell could climb onto the boat. They went back to the stern, where the anchor, chain, and rope were on the deck next to the yellow body bag. Stilwell took out his phone and took separate photos of each item.

"Can we turn it to see if there's a manufacturer's mark?" he asked.

With a gloved hand, Saunders turned the anchor on the deck to show the other side. Imprinted on the polished metal was a manufacturer's brand.

"It's a Hold Fast," he said. "They make 'em by the thousands."

Stilwell was looking at the body bag. Even with bloating, the contents seemed small.

"You want a look?" Saunders asked.

"No, I saw it down below," Stilwell said. "That was enough."

"Yeah, she's ripe."

"Well, you guys can go. I'm sure Ahearn will be in touch."

"Then we're out of here."

Stilwell retraced his steps to the skiff dock, then used his foot to push the prow of the dive boat away. He himself almost slipped on the new decking. As the boat headed toward the mouth of the harbor, Stilwell's phone started to buzz. It was Lampley.

"Sarge, you coming back here?" he asked. "Detective Ahearn is getting dressed."

"Yeah, we're done here," Stilwell said. "I'm on my way to the sub."

6

AHEARN, IN THE office at the sub, was clad in a tight-fitting Hawaiian shirt and khakis that were three inches too short and only accentuated by the shower sandals he was wearing. It was the best Lampley could do with clothes usually reserved for detainees arrested with inappropriate or insufficient clothing for an appearance in court. Ahearn held up a phone when he saw Stilwell enter.

"Look at this shit," he said. "It's already on Instagram. I'm totally fucked."

"Does it identify you by name?" Stilwell asked.

"Not yet."

"Then you're not fucked. Do you want to talk about the case or about social media?"

Ahearn handed the phone to Lampley. His had obviously gone into the water with him.

"Yeah, I want to talk about the case," he said. "What's the status out there?"

"The body's on the boat and headed to Long Beach," Stilwell said.

"Good, then I can get the fuck out of here. This place—you

landed in a real dump out here, Stillborn, you know that? I mean, look at it. It's full of fuckups, old farts, and fiascoes."

"That's cool on the alliteration, but I kind of like it here. You sure you don't want to talk to the hull scraper who found the body or the harbormaster or anybody else before you go?"

"In this outfit, no. I'll just wait on the reports from you. Get them to me by, let's say, tomorrow morning at eight."

"Not a problem."

Stilwell was not going to let Ahearn get under his skin. He'd learned a lot since that Sunday morning at the homicide bureau. He looked over at Lampley, who was sitting at his desk acting like he was looking at something on his computer screen. Mercy was doing the same thing at her desk.

He turned his eyes back to Ahearn.

"Where's your partner?"

"Waiting at the Port of Long Beach, but you don't need to worry about that. This is not your case, Stillborn. You know that, right?"

"Once you make an ID — if you do actually make an ID — you'll need eyes and ears out here. There's no need to hold grudges, Ahearn. You won. You kept your job and I got shipped out here. Let's just put it behind us and do the work."

"Fuck you, man. Your complaint is still in my jacket. It's not going anywhere and I'll never get promoted. I'll never have my own squad. All because you got your head up your ass about a case that nobody ever gave a shit about."

"Except for me."

"Yeah, boo-hoo and fuck you. I'm out of here, and I'm telling you now, don't get any ideas. I find out you're working my case, and this time it won't be a transfer you get. It'll be sayonara, baby."

Stilwell raised his arms, palms out, in a hands-off gesture.

"I don't work homicide anymore," he said.

"That's right," Ahearn said. "You're the sheriff of shit town and it's going to stay that way for a long time."

"When you need something from out here, I'd prefer it if you let Sampedro make the call. It will work best that way, for both of us."

"With pleasure."

He lifted a plastic trash bag off a table. Stilwell guessed that it contained his clothes and shoes.

"How are you getting back?" Stilwell asked.

"The chopper's on its way," Ahearn said. "Maybe you can get Lampshade here to ride me over there in one of your little go-carts."

"We call them UTVs — utility task vehicles."

"And I call that pathetic."

"Maybe. Lampley, take him where he wants to go."

Lampley got up from his desk to carry out the mission. Stilwell said nothing as Ahearn headed for the door.

"Fuck you very much, Stillborn," he said over his shoulder.

Once Ahearn was out, Stilwell looked over at Mercy, who had been silent and unmoving behind her desk.

"So, what do you think, Mercy?" he asked.

"I think he's an asshole," she said. "He's the one who's pathetic."

"You know how to read 'em."

"What happened between you two?"

"That's a long story. We had a difference of opinion on a case and it didn't go well after that."

"That's too bad."

"Well, it got me out here, didn't it? Sometimes the place you don't want to be turns out to be the place you should be."

"I agree. I've never wanted to leave here."

"I'm getting that way myself."

"That's a good thing."

"I'm going over to the harbormaster's. You need me, get me over there."

"Will do."

Stilwell went out to the parking lot, and the first thing he saw was the open storage box on the back of his John Deere. He studied the cheap lock and saw that the box had been pried open. He checked the contents but nothing appeared to be missing. With his hands he was able to bend the metal tongue back into place so he could relock the box.

He got in the cart and started toward the pier. On the way he called Mercy and asked her if she had a number for Henry Gaston in her contacts file. Over the years working at the sub, Mercy had accumulated four index-card boxes containing contact information for residents of the island who'd had interactions with the sheriff's department, whether for reporting or committing a crime. Stilwell assumed that Gaston would be in one of the boxes for the latter reason.

By the time he parked at the pier, Mercy had texted him a cell phone number for Gaston. Stilwell sat in the cart and made the call.

"Hello?"

"Nice try, Henry."

"Who's this?"

"Stilwell."

"Stilwell? What are you talking about?"

"You know what I'm talking about. You saw me put the saw handle in the lockbox on my cart. You tried to get it back."

"No, I don't know what you mean."

"You were too late. I'd already put it in the evidence safe at the sub."

"I'm tellin' ya, I have no idea what you're talking about."

"You still have until Wednesday to come see me. After that,

it'll be out of my hands. You'll have to get yourself a good lawyer from overtown."

That brought silence.

"You still there, Henry?" Stilwell asked.

"I'm hanging up," Gaston said.

"I hope to see you."

"Man, don't even talk about me snitching. That could get me killed."

Stilwell smiled. Gaston had made an admission of sorts. "All the more reason to come in," he said.

"Never happen," Gaston said.

Gaston disconnected. Stilwell called Mercy back.

"Mercy, what was Gaston in your cards for?" he asked.

"A couple disorderlies," Mercy said. "Operating a vehicle while impaired, and in 2015 he got charged with receiving stolen property."

"Conviction?"

"And probation."

"Good to know. Thanks."

Stilwell disconnected and thought about Gaston. The conviction on his record was too old to have a probation tail, but he knew it could still be useful in dealing with Gaston the following week, when Stilwell was sure he would come in to make a deal.

He walked down the dock, surveying the harbor. All four mooring lanes appeared to be at capacity now. He saw several parties already beginning on the decks of the smaller boats and in the salons of the yachts. The holiday weekend was underway.

The harbormaster's tower was at the end of the pier, its upper-level windows lit from within. Stilwell could see Tash up there at the control desk. At the door, he punched in the numbers on the combination lock and entered.

He went up one flight to the control room, which was octagonal, with windows all around giving views of all mooring lanes and slips as well as the pier and the mountains that ringed the harbor. Tash was standing at the control counter holding a radio mic to her mouth.

"Sorry, *Delilah,* we're full up," she said. "All rental and owner moorings are spoken for at this time. I can offer you a mooring at Descanso or Hamilton until something opens up in the harbor."

Stilwell knew she was talking about the mooring lines available outside the protection of the harbor. He also knew that the capacity of the inner harbor was 360 boats of various sizes. When they were all taken, the town was full and busy. Shopkeepers, restaurateurs, and hoteliers were pleased, Mayor Allen was happy, and all was well.

Supposedly.

Stilwell waited while Tash radioed instructions to the harbor patrol boat to lead *Delilah* to a mooring off Descanso Beach. When she was finished, he approached the desk.

"Tash."

"Hey. Any news on the body?"

She whispered the word *body* as though saying it louder might create a panic in the harbor.

"Nothing yet. You thought of anybody with a purple streak in her hair?"

"No, not yet."

"I know you're super-busy, but how long would it take to pull together a list of what boats were in the harbor last weekend through Tuesday?"

"Why?"

"I'm guessing that body was in the water four or five days. That would take us back to last weekend. I'd like to know who was in the harbor then and the next few days after."

"I thought the investigation was being handled by the over-town sheriffs."

"It is, yeah, but they're going to need all the help they can get. Do you want me to talk to Dennis about getting records?"

Dennis Lafferty was the harbormaster and her boss. He was probably down in his office under the control room.

"No, I can do it. Just that today is busy. Maybe in the morning when people are still in their bunks?"

"That would be fine. Thanks."

"I'll do my best to pull it together. I feel so bad about that girl. It's horrible."

"Yeah. It is."

"I could see them from up here when they pulled her out. She was already in a body bag."

"Yeah, they do that when the recovery is in a public place with people watching."

"Did you ever do it that way?"

"On the dive team? Yeah. A few times. Oddly, there's something peaceful about it. When you're underwater, I mean."

Tash said nothing in response and Stilwell wondered if he had said something weird. She didn't know much about his time on the sheriff's dive team. It wasn't something he liked to talk about.

"Okay," he said. "I guess I'll let you get back to it."

"No, I...uh, it just seems so weird," Tash said. "Her being down there for...how long did you say?"

"Probably four days. Maybe longer. The tide brought her into the harbor. It's probably a case that has nothing to do with this place."

"But then why are you asking about a girl with a purple streak in her hair?"

"Force of habit, I guess. But I'll be standing down on this. Let A-Hole handle it from overtown."

"A-Hole?"

"What they call Ahearn over on the sheriff's homicide team."

"I wonder if you had anything to do with that."

"Could have. I'll talk to you later, Tash."

"Yes, see you later."

Stilwell nodded, hesitated, then headed for the steps.

7

STILWELL WOKE SATURDAY morning with a headache firing on all pistons behind his eyes. He didn't know whether to blame the fumes he had inhaled during the dive the day before or the two fingers of Knob Creek he had put down after finally getting off work the night before.

He went into the kitchen and put a pot of coffee on to brew, then went to the front door. It was seven a.m. and he had received no calls from the sub during the night, so he took that as a sign that all was quiet.

The *Catalina Call* was on the front porch. Stilwell picked it up and sat on one of the Adirondacks as he unfolded it. A photo of the sheriff's dive boat with the tented back deck was the center image on the front page. The headline was big and bold: HARBOR HOMICIDE: BOUND BODY RECOVERED. Stilwell smiled slightly as he thought about Mayor Allen unfolding the paper to the same image and words. He guessed that the editor of the *Call* had not gotten the message that murder was bad for business.

The story carried Lionel N. McKey's byline, and most of its details had been supplied by an interview with Denzel Abbott.

The sheriff's department officially declined to comment, which Stilwell believed would put him in the clear with the mayor.

The *Call* was tabloid-size, and the splash of the photo and story on the harbor homicide left room for only two other articles on the front page. One focused on the town council receiving a first look at design plans to build a giant Ferris wheel on the pier that would be lighted in neon and visible at night all the way from the mainland. Though billed as a project that would boost tourism to the island, it was a controversial proposal. Polling by the *Call* revealed significant opposition from Avalon residents. It had become common to see signs on lawns and in windows that said TURN THE WHEEL DOWN! And this was before any real plans had even been seen.

The last story on the page was another McKey-authored piece on the mystery surrounding the mutilation of a buffalo on the mountain preserve three nights earlier. The animal had been cleanly beheaded and the head remained missing. The mystery tapped into the island's long history of supposed UFO and USO sightings. With no official update from Stilwell on the investigation, McKey had turned to a chorus of self-proclaimed extraterrestrial experts who were eager to plant the idea of alien mischief at the preserve. "Look, they've been coming to Catalina since forever," said Jack Sprague from the Center for the Study of Unidentified Submersible Objects. "They're in the air and water. This doesn't surprise me at all."

Other so-called alien experts were quoted as well, though none offered an opinion, scientific or otherwise, as to why the aliens would want a buffalo's head.

Stilwell was about to turn to the continuation of the story inside the paper when he heard the front door open behind him.

"Coffee should be ready," he said.

"I've gotta go," Tash Dano said. "I'll get some at the tower."

"You sure?"

"I'm sure. Anything in there about the body?"

Stilwell stood up to show her the front page.

"The mayor didn't get to Denzel Abbott," he said. "He told McKey everything."

"Oh, man," Tash said. "His Honor's not going to be happy about that."

"Well, on the other hand, there's an alien story on the front page. That should be good enough to get a boatload or two of true believers to come out and spend their money."

"Aliens cancel out murders. Nice. You have any extraterrestrial suspects yet?"

"I have suspects. But they're more of the terrestrial kind."

"Hmm, too bad."

She was already dressed for the day in khaki cargo pants and a black polo with the harbormaster badge embroidered on it. Tash was a beauty in Stilwell's opinion. She was a lean and tanned island girl with dark hair and dark eyes, and she didn't need anything in the world beyond the twenty-two-mile-long island where she'd been born. Their relationship had started soon after Stilwell's arrival and their first lunch meeting. Stilwell had been coming out of a divorce at the time, and she'd just broken up with another island native.

She was also eight years younger than Stilwell, and that at first gave him pause. He was worried they would not be on the same page when it came to things like music and movies and politics. But soon that didn't seem to matter. Tash loved the outdoors — boating, fishing, and camping — and so did he. That was where they connected and where they could leave the world behind. They had initially decided to keep the relationship under wraps, until they saw how it went, but now they were no longer as protective of the secret.

"You want me to run you down to the pier in the cart?" Stilwell asked.

"No, it's downhill," Tash said. "An easy walk."

"Okay. Be good."

"And you be safe."

They kissed goodbye and Stilwell watched her walk down Eucalyptus toward the harbor. He thought about where they were in the relationship and where they were going. It had started out as a casual, no-demands sort of thing. They both were on the rebound from their previous relationships and moving cautiously. But as the months went by, their connection deepened, and then Tash started staying over most nights of the week. Stilwell stopped going to the mainland on his days off. He put the condo he'd bought after his divorce up for sale. Tash kept her apartment but mostly because a storage unit for her furniture would cost almost as much as her rent. Keeping the place also offered a refuge if things with Stilwell didn't work out. But they both knew that was the next move — if she gave up her place, they were in it for the long haul.

Stilwell felt his cell phone vibrate in his pocket. It was Mercy.

"Sergeant, we have a situation with a visitor from overtown."

"What's going on?"

"Looks like an alcohol poisoning at the Crescent Hotel. Paramedics on scene and they're calling a medevac."

Stilwell checked his phone screen. It was only 7:10 a.m., but the busy times were starting.

"Okay, Mercy, I'm on my way."

8

STILWELL WAS IN early at the sub on Tuesday so he could get a jump on the crime and arrest reports that had accumulated over the holiday weekend. He had to prepare case summaries that would be submitted to Monika Juarez on the mainland for decisions on whether charges would be filed. There had been twenty-six arrests over the three-day weekend. The vast majority were drunk-and-disorderly cases, though three of these had escalated to assaults when the sheriff's deputies showed up. There was also a scattering of arrests for property crimes and driving while impaired. Under California law, driving while intoxicated — with a blood-alcohol concentration over 0.08 percent — carried the same penalties whether you were in an automobile or a golf cart.

The sub's jail was holding four men, three of them on assault and one for grand theft — he had walked out of a bar on Saturday night, hopped into a golf cart that belonged to somebody else, and driven away. The cart was located the next day up at the Hermit Gulch Lookout with the man who had taken it passed out in the driver's seat.

Stilwell knew that Monika Juarez would reject most of the cases. Some would be filed but dismissed before they reached court. Juarez's job was to weed out the inconsequential cases that were not worth the time and money to adjudicate. The county jail system was already crowded and under federal oversight. Prosecutors had to be selective about whom they tried to put in prison.

From an island twenty-two miles from the coast, Stilwell viewed the system as not yet broken but getting close to it. His opinion was that when you installed a revolving door at the entrance to the jailhouse, you were inviting the system's downfall.

Knowing what awaited the weekend's cases at the next stop, Stilwell put most of his efforts into writing up the summary of charges against Merris Spivak. He'd been arrested Saturday night for assaulting a law enforcement officer. He had broken a bottle over Deputy Tom Dunne's head in a bar on Crescent. Dunne was backing up Deputy Eduardo Esquivel, who had entered the bar after a call regarding a fight between two patrons over whose song was next up on the karaoke stage. Spivak came up behind Dunne and bashed him on the head with an empty wine bottle he had grabbed off another patron's table. Dunne got a concussion, nine stitches, and a night in a medical clinic before being transferred to a mainland hospital. And Stilwell was down one deputy for the rest of the busy holiday weekend.

The assault on Dunne was captured by the bar's security camera, and the video would be the key evidence against Spivak. Stilwell attached the link to his report, then decided to watch it again. It had made him so angry the first time he had watched it that he realized he should add some of the details to the summary report to ensure that Juarez didn't defer charges.

The video link provided by the bar started thirty seconds prior to the assault on Dunne. It clearly showed that the attack was unprovoked. Spivak came quickly into the frame behind Dunne and hit him with the bottle with an overhead swing. Dunne went down, knocked out cold by the impact. Esquivel had his hands full and didn't see his backup deputy go down. Spivak, apparently not knowing he was on camera, turned, went back to the bar, took a seat on a stool, and acted like he'd had no part in the melee. That part of the video was bizarre. Stilwell watched it two more times, and, while it continued to make him angry, the oddness of Spivak's actions began to poke through the emotion. Stilwell got up from his desk and left his office. He walked through the day-room to the jail.

There were two four-bunk holding cells in the sub's jail. They were side by side and divided by a concrete-block wall. Guests in one cell could not see into the other. Stilwell had put Spivak in cell one by himself, and the other three detainees were in two. Stilwell had separated Spivak because his assault on a law enforce-ment officer was more serious than the others' alleged crimes. Stilwell walked to the bars that fronted cell one and saw Spivak asleep on one of the lower bunks. He had been in the cell for two days.

"Spivak," he said. "Wake up."

Spivak didn't move. Stilwell put his right foot between the bars and kicked the frame of the bunk, and Spivak jerked awake.

"What the fuck?" he said.

"Spivak, I've got a question for you," Stilwell said.

"Am I getting out of here?"

"No. I have a question for you."

"Are you taking me to county?"

"I'm keeping you right here until the judge comes out. That's usually Fridays. But if he's backed up on the mainland, it might not be till next Monday."

"Ah, fuck. You can't do that."

"Actually, I can, and I am. Did you know Deputy Dunne?"

Spivak was silent for a moment. Stilwell stepped back to the wall opposite the holding cell and turned on the lights. Though being in the bottom bunk kept Spivak in partial shadow, Stilwell could see his eyes when he came back to the bars. Spivak had a shaved head that was pointed like a bullet, a host of tattoos peeking out of his jumpsuit collar and sleeves, and a crescent-shaped scar below his left eye.

"Did you know him?" Stilwell asked again.

"Who the fuck is Deputy Dunne?" Spivak said.

"The deputy you clocked with the wine bottle and put in the hospital. Did you know him? Did you have any previous encounter with him?"

Spivak again went silent, which made Stilwell think he was hiding something.

"Talk to me, Spivak," Stilwell said. "You knew him, didn't you?"

"Aren't you supposed to read me my rights or something before asking me shit?" Spivak said.

"You already got 'em when we booked you."

"Then I ain't talking to you. I want my lawyer."

"You called your lawyer already, Spivak. That was your phone call. You decide you want to talk to me, I'll see what I can do about another call."

Stilwell left him thinking about that and went back to his office. On his computer, he ran Spivak's name through the crime index. He was forty-four years old and had a history of arrests in Los Angeles County for assault and other violent crimes, most of them in the Long Beach area. This furthered Stilwell's belief that there was a connection between Spivak and Dunne. He pulled up what he could on the prior arrests and did not see Dunne's name in any of the reports. The year before, Spivak had spent three hundred days in the Pitchess Detention Center after pleading guilty to a charge of aggravated assault. Pitchess was part of the county jail system; a sentence of less than a year was served in the county system, while a sentence of more than a year meant a transfer to state prison.

Stilwell picked up his phone, found Dunne among his contacts, and called him. It went to message.

"Tom, it's Stil. Just checking on you to see how you're doing. Give me a call when you get this. All right, man, talk to you."

He disconnected and thought about Dunne. He had been transferred to the Catalina sub seven months earlier. Stilwell had been told he was coming from the jail division but wasn't sure where he'd worked in the massive multifacility system. He was also not told what transgression had resulted in Dunne's transfer.

Stilwell went back to work and an hour later emailed the whole package of cases to Juarez. He didn't expect to hear from her until late in the day. She had a calendar to cover at the Long Beach courthouse and that would be her priority. Catalina was not high on any mainlander's to-do list.

Stilwell next started to review the crime reports that had come in over the long weekend and that he'd been too busy doing extra patrol or booking bodies to look at. There were sixteen, all crimes that did not involve arrests and that he, as the island's lone detective, would need to follow up on.

Catalina was shaped like a lopsided eight — or an infinity symbol, as many inhabitants of the island preferred to view it. Avalon was built on a natural harbor on the south side of the island and was far and away its biggest population center. Two Harbors was a small town at the isthmus between the two halves of the eight. A slow twenty-mile drive or a faster boat ride from Avalon, it was a place where residents wanted as little as possible to do with tourism and civilization, including law enforcement. The rest of the island was largely undeveloped except for small nomadic settlements of people who were all running from something or somebody.

Three of the crime reports had come from Two Harbors: a stolen outboard motor, a vandalized golf cart, and a crab-trap poaching. These were not major crimes, although the poaching was the third such occurrence in a month, and Stilwell put these aside to review later. He made irregular visits to Two Harbors to follow cases or simply to show the flag, but he usually waited until several reports had accumulated. He planned to get out there by the end of the week.

The remaining cases were a mixed bag of vandalism, petty thefts, and fraud involving visitors who had made online reservations that turned out to be phony for hotels, fishing charters, or island services. Their deposits had disappeared into the digital ether, and there had been no hotel, tour, or fishing boat awaiting them. Most of the reports were walk-ins and were handled by Mercy, who consoled the victims and then called around to see if she could find a hotel room or at least a seat on a ferry going back to the mainland.

Stilwell shuffled through the reports until one grabbed his attention. It was a felony theft report filed by the general manager of the Black Marlin Club. The BMC was a private club that was over a century old. It had an invite-only membership of moneyed families from the mainland who brought their yachts in from Newport Beach, Santa Barbara, Marina del Rey, and other wealthy enclaves along the California coast. The club was named after what had once been the sport fisherman's prize catch, and its members were much like the black marlin: sleek, fast, and rare in California waters. They were also dangerous — the members, that is — in terms of their reach into the corridors of power and wealth. Stilwell had been cautioned when he was transferred to Catalina to give Black Marlin members a very wide berth.

The report from general manager Charles Crane was on the theft of a small black-jade sculpture of a marlin rising from the ocean's surface. The sculpture had been on display on a pedestal in the entry hall of the clubhouse for nearly a hundred years. The pedestal stood next to a glass case containing other historical items from the club's past.

Deputy Tom Dunne had taken the theft report on Saturday just hours before he was attacked. According to Dunne's crime summary, it was unknown when the sculpture had been stolen, because the pedestal was in the front hallway, which was not routinely used by members or employees. Members usually arrived by boat and entered or left the premises through doorways connecting to the docks at the side and rear of the building. Employees were not allowed to use the front entrance and used a side door.

The sculpture was reported missing on Saturday when a housekeeper charged with dusting it once a week found the pedestal empty. Crane described the sculpture as ten inches tall and weighing three or four pounds. He gave its value as priceless because of its age, the quality of the jade, and its connection to one of the club's founders. What Stilwell zeroed in on was not the stolen object or its value but the suspect Crane had identified.

He'd told Dunne that the week before the sculpture was noticed missing, he had fired an employee named Leigh-Anne Moss for inappropriate behavior. The report said that Moss was a part-time waitress in the club's private restaurant and bar and that she had broken the rule forbidding socializing with members. Crane told Dunne that he suspected that Moss took the jade marlin on her way out of the club following the acrimonious meeting that had resulted in her dismissal.

From Moss's employment application, Crane gave the deputy her age and address. He also offered a description. He said that Leigh-Anne Moss had dark, shoulder-length hair with a purple streak along the left side.

9

STILWELL PULLED LEIGH-ANNE Moss's DMV records up on his computer. He studied the photo that was on her driver's license. There was no purple streak in her hair, but the license had been issued two years earlier. Because of the decomposition of the body recovered from the harbor, it was impossible for Stilwell to make a visual identification. Still, his gut told him he was looking at the woman from the water. He picked up the desk phone and called the general number for the sheriff's homicide squad. He asked the clerk who answered to connect him with Frank Sampedro. He waited a half minute before the call was connected.

"Detective Ahearn, how can I help?"

Stilwell almost hung up but decided he should not delay sharing the new information.

"I asked for Sampedro."

"He's not avail — wait, Stillborn, is that you?"

"Have you made an ID on the woman from the water?"

"It's not your case, man, why do you care?"

"Because if you haven't ID'd her, I've got a solid lead for you."

"Stillborn, I told you to stand down on this. Am I going to have to go to — "

"It came across my desk in an unrelated case, Ahearn. Do you want what I've got or do you want to keep fighting your little war? I can wait till Sampedro calls me back. You decide."

There was silence until Ahearn came back in a falsely cheery voice.

"Okay, give it to me. Let's see what you came up with."

"Check out Leigh-Anne Moss. I think she's your victim."

He spelled the first and last names and then gave Ahearn the birth date and address from the DMV records, which matched what was on her work application for the BMC.

"Her name came up Saturday in a report about a theft from the Black Marlin Club," Stilwell said. "She was named as a suspect and described as having a dyed purple streak in her hair."

"I got news for you, bright guy. Our vic was dead by Saturday."

"I didn't say she made the theft Saturday. I said the report came in Saturday. She was fired the week before that, and that's when the theft could have occurred. So the timing could still match up."

"What did she supposedly steal?"

"A small sculpture of a marlin. It was made of black jade, was ten inches high, and weighed about four pounds. I'll send you the report."

"Black jade for a black marlin."

"Has there been an autopsy yet?"

"You know I'm not going to talk to you about the case, Still-born. Why even ask?"

"Happened on my turf, Ahearn. If you're doing this right, I should be kept in the loop. I can also—"

"No, you should just fuck off."

Ahearn disconnected.

Stilwell sat quiet and unmoving until the anger passed.

He finally broke free of thoughts about Ahearn, called the coroner's office, and asked for an investigator named Monty West.

He and West had worked together on many homicides before Stilwell's transfer out to the island.

"Still the man," West said—his usual greeting.

"Monty, long time," Stilwell said.

"Sure is. What's happening, my brother?"

"Same old, same old, except now I'm out on an island doing it. How are you?"

"As long as the bodies keep dropping, I keep hopping."

"Speaking of, I'm wondering if you could check your computer for a case."

"You got a case?"

"Technically, no. But it happened on my turf and I'm just checking to see if there's been COD established."

"Lucky man. I'm at my desk and can put it into the box as we speak. Name?"

"No name. Actually, a Jane Doe. She was a sinker out here in the Avalon harbor. Coroner would have gotten the body Friday night."

"Right, I heard about that one. Stand by, let me find it."

Stilwell heard West's keyboard clacking, then silence as West read whatever had come up on the screen.

"No cause of death yet," West finally said. "Autopsy's later on today—scheduled at three."

"Got it. Any ID yet?"

"Uh, looks like a no on ID. Preliminary report is that skin slippage made prints unavailable. Waiting on detectives to make an ID through other means."

"Don't hold your breath."

"Yeah, this says it's A-Hole that's got it. I bet he's working his ass off."

Stilwell noted the sarcasm. Ahearn's reputation was known far and wide. "You have photos there?" he asked.

"Yeah, the preliminary examination was done this morning," West said. "What are you looking for?"

"I saw her in the water, so her hair was kind of all over the place. I'm thinking about the purple streak I saw. Is that in the pictures?"

"Yup, I got it here."

"Can you shoot that to me?"

"I can as long as you never say where you got it."

"It will never come up. Can you text it?"

"I can."

"Thanks, Monty. I owe you one."

"I might come out there to collect it. You can show me where all the aliens I've been reading about are hiding."

"Don't believe everything you read."

They disconnected and Stilwell waited for the text to come through. It took his phone a minute to download the file, and then he saw a photo of the woman from the water, her face almost unrecognizable as human and unmatchable to the DMV photo. But someone at the coroner's office had brushed her hair back from her face. Stilwell could see the purple streak in her hair. It started at the front scalp line on the left side of a middle part and looped down the length of her hair. Stilwell felt sure that he was looking at a death photo of Leigh-Anne Moss.

He also noted an abrasion on the right side of the forehead that disappeared under the thickness of the hair. There was no blood evident. Stilwell knew that the abrasion could have been a post-mortem injury sustained as the body was dragged by underwater currents. Or it could have been from the blow that killed her.

He put the photo into an email and sent it to himself. He then reviewed everything he knew about Moss. Neither he nor the general manager at the Black Marlin had an address on Catalina for her. The address on her driver's license and application to the BMC was a street in the Belmont Shore neighborhood in Long Beach. Stilwell knew the area well, having owned a condominium there. He wondered if he had ever passed Leigh-Anne on the street, on the beach, or in Joe Jost's or another restaurant. He wondered if the nexus of what ultimately put her in the water with an anchor chain wrapped around her body was over there on the mainland or here on the island.

He shut down the computer and left the office. Mercy was at her desk in the bullpen.

"Mercy, any news on Tom Dunne?" he asked.

"I haven't heard a thing," she said.

"I left him a message, but if he checks in with you, tell him I need to speak to him as soon as possible. It's not about what happened to him. It's about something else."

"Will do."

"And when you have time, can you do a social media roundup and see if you can find a woman named Leigh-Anne Moss? You know, Facebook, Instagram, wherever you usually look." He spelled the first name for her.

"Is she the one that was in the water?" Mercy asked.

"Maybe," Stilwell said. "It's not confirmed."

Stilwell got a fresh radio out of the charging unit on the wall.

"You going out?" Mercy asked.

"Yes, over to the Black Marlin," Stilwell said.

"What's happening there?"

"Just following up on the theft report Dunne took Saturday before he got knocked out at the bar. That's what I want to talk to him about."

"I hope he remembers. He's probably still a little fuzzy."

"Maybe. You know anybody who's a member there?"

"At the Black Marlin? No, they're all overtowners. They've never allowed locals to join."

"I thought the mayor was a member. Acts like it, at least."

"I think that's ceremonial. He can go over there and drink their liquor and eat their food, but they'll never give him a permanent membership. As soon as he stops being mayor, he's out of there. It's always been that way."

"Interesting. I'll be back in a bit."

"And I'll be here."

10

THE BLACK MARLIN Club was located in a two-story clap-board structure that sat on a private pier off St. Catherine Way on the north side of the harbor. The building had housed the club for more than a hundred years and had been deemed a historic land-mark by the county. Stilwell walked there from the sub. The front door was locked, and, remembering what had been noted in the crime report, Stilwell walked around to a side door. He pushed a button on a call box. Soon, a voice responded.

"How can I help you?"

"Detective Sergeant Stilwell with the sheriff's department. I'm here to follow up on a crime report taken over the weekend."

"Yes, of course. Please stand by and someone will let you in shortly."

"Thank you."

Shortly turned out to be a long few minutes. While he waited, Stilwell took out his phone and sent a text to Henry Gaston's cell. It said **24 hours.** He knew that Gaston would know what the cryp-tic message meant. There had been no reply by the time the door of the BMC opened and a man in a shirt and tie smiled at Stilwell.

"Sergeant Stilwell?" he said. "Charles Crane, general manager. Please come in."

He offered his hand, which Stilwell shook.

Crane carried an air of authority that went beyond being one of the few men on the island who wore a tie to work. He walked fast and talked fast as he led the way into the club.

"Let's go to my office," he said. "We can talk privately there. Have you ever been to the club before, Sergeant?"

"No, I haven't," Stilwell said. "Before we talk, can you show me the hallway where the theft of the statue occurred?"

"Oh, of course. Right here."

They walked through a sitting room with dark paneled walls and old leather chairs. It smelled faintly of cigars and money. From there they moved into a foyer where the front door was located. Crane turned left into a wide hallway also paneled in dark wood. Down the left side were multiple framed photos, most in sepia or black-and-white, of men over the past century standing next to their catches of marlins. Mounted above the line of frames was a marlin that Stilwell estimated was at least eight feet long, its black spine twisting, frozen in a fight lost a long time ago. A plaque below it said

983-POUND BLACK MARLIN
CAUGHT SEPTEMBER 14, 1931, ON THE *MARY MAC*
BY HORACE GRANT, MEMBER BMC

"Impressive, isn't it?" Crane said.

"Sure is. If you're into fishing," Stilwell said.

Museum-style glass cases lined the right side of the hallway. There were three of them and they were mostly filled with fishing lures that had been used over the years to go after the club's eponymous fish. There were unusual shells and pieces of coral, shark's teeth, and other knickknacks. Crane pointed to an empty pedestal that stood at the end of the line of cases.

"The sculpture was right here," Crane said. "For nearly a century. Donated by one of the first presidents of the club, Noah Rossmore."

Stilwell studied the marble pedestal.

"It wasn't secured?" he asked.

"This is a gentlemen's club, Sergeant," Crane said. "We don't lock things up and we don't expect them to be taken."

Stilwell nodded.

"So it could have just been lifted up without anyone having to touch the pedestal?" he asked. "No earthquake wax or anything that would make it difficult to come loose?"

"Nothing," Crane said.

Stilwell started asking questions he already knew the answers to, but it was good practice to ask them again because sometimes new information came to the surface.

"How was it discovered missing?"

"It was actually one of our cleaning people who realized it was gone. Mrs. Landry. One of her jobs is to keep this hallway and its contents in pristine condition. She was dusting and saw the empty pedestal. She alerted me and I immediately called your department."

"Got it. Is this a busy part of the club?"

"Well, this is our entry hallway, but most members come by boat and enter off the docks behind or on the starboard side of the building. Consequently, this hallway is used very infrequently."

"Which makes it difficult to pinpoint when the statue was taken."

"Yes, it does."

"You suggested to Deputy Dunne that Leigh-Anne Moss took it, yes?"

"The deputy who responded to my call asked if I had any suspicions about who might have taken the piece, and I did say that a week earlier I'd let Ms. Moss go and she was not happy about it. But I didn't directly accuse her of anything. I hope she doesn't think that."

"I haven't talked to her yet. Let's go to your office so we can talk about it."

"By all means. Happy to."

Crane's office was upstairs at the back of the building. His desk was in front of a window that looked out across the harbor, and it reminded Stilwell of the view from the harbormaster's tower.

"This is nice," Stilwell said.

"Allows me to see the arrivals of members and their guests," Crane said.

Rather than sitting in front of Crane's desk, Stilwell walked to the window and looked down. Behind the club, the pier extended into a wraparound deck with a hinged gangway connecting to a floating dock. There, members could tie up their skiffs when they arrived from their moored yachts. At the moment, a small sailboat and three other skiffs and workboats were tied to cleats on the floating dock. On the north side of the building, the dock was under an extended corrugated steel roof that allowed members covered access to the club's side door, protection from rain or blistering sun.

"I bet you had a busy weekend here," Stilwell said.

His eyes were scanning the harbor. He saw the lines of orange mooring balls. The harbor had largely emptied at the end of the weekend.

"Yes, we had a lot of members come out," Crane said. "It was very busy."

"So you have a full restaurant and bar in here, right?" Stilwell asked.

"Yes. We serve lunch every day and dinner Thursday to Sunday."

"What about rooms? Can members stay here or do they have to stay on their boats?"

"We have four rooms available to members and guests on a first-come-first-serve basis. But as you can imagine, our members have substantial vessels, and most elect to stay on them."

"Yes, I get that."

Stilwell had a view of the spot where the body had been found thirty feet down.

"You had a clear view of the body recovery on Friday," he said.

"I did," Crane said. "Terrible. Have you found out what happened? I heard it was a girl."

"A woman. They haven't identified her. But it's not my case. The theft of your statue is."

"Well, it's not *my* statue. It's the club's."

Stilwell stepped away from the window and took a seat in front of Crane's desk.

"Tell me about Leigh-Anne," he said. "Why'd you fire her?"

"I hate that word," Crane said. "*Fire, terminate* — they sound so harsh. But I did let her go. She had become . . . a problem."

"How so?"

"We have strict rules about socializing between the staff and the members. She knew the rules but elected to break them. Repeatedly."

"Repeatedly in what way?"

"She was overly flirtatious with several members and that was brought to my attention. I warned her once about it and then felt the need to act when I continued to get reports of this behavior."

"What does 'overly flirtatious' behavior mean?"

"To use an archaic phrase, she was a gold digger, Sergeant. She attempted several times to lure members to meet her outside the club. She was clearly looking for someone to marry or possibly extort."

"That's a pretty strong accusation. Did any of these meetings ever happen?"

"I don't know. I just know the invitations were made and we acted to protect our members."

"You said her flirtatiousness was brought to your attention. By who?"

"Well, my bar manager, for one, and I have to say, some members complained as well."

"Who were the members?"

"I'm afraid that's confidential, Sergeant. And I fail to see how it's germane to the question of whether Ms. Moss took the jade marlin."

"Tell me about when you fired her."

"Well, we don't have a human resources department here. With a small staff, I am HR, and I simply called her up here to the office, told her that she had been warned repeatedly, that she'd ignored those warnings, and that it was time for her to find another place of employment."

"And this was when, exactly?"

"Saturday morning, the seventeenth."

"What time would you say?"

"The Marlin Room opens for lunch at eleven, which means she would have been here by ten to help set up the room. I left word in the kitchen that she should come see me upon her arrival. So I would say our conversation occurred shortly after ten o'clock that morning."

"And how did she take it?"

"Not well, as you can imagine. She was angry and she stormed out of here."

"And on her way out, she grabbed the sculpture."

"Well, we can't say for sure that she took it. But a week later, a staff member noticed it was missing."

"Mrs. Landry."

"Correct. And she notified me."

"Is Mrs. Landry here today?"

"No, she's primarily here on weekends, when we have many members visiting. But I could call her in if you need to speak to her."

"I think we can hold off on that for the moment. But for the report, what's Mrs. Landry's first name?"

"Judith."

"And how long has she worked here?"

"I'd have to look that up—much longer than me, I can tell you that."

"Then how long have you been here?"

"This is my eighteenth year in the employ of the club, but it has been eight years since I was named general manager. I was second-in-command before I was promoted."

"Let's go back to Leigh-Anne for a moment. Were there a lot of members here when you fired her and she stormed out? Did they see or hear any of this?"

"Actually, the club was quite empty. We don't serve breakfast, and lunch starts at eleven. It doesn't get busy till noon or later. I chose that time to make the change because I knew the club would be quiet."

"Sounds like you knew she was going to get angry."

"I *suspected* she might be angry and try to create a . . ."

"A scene?"

"A distraction."

"You called it a gentlemen's club earlier. Are there no female members?"

"My mistake. We do have female members."

"How many?"

"Two members are female, but you have to remember that the club's bylaws cap membership at one hundred, and it's generational. It gets passed on. We have members who are the great-grandsons of our founders. New members are admitted only if an existing member resigns or there is no heir to come forward upon a member's death. So the transition has been slow. In my time, there have been only three openings, and two of those went to female applicants."

"Can I get a list of the members?"

"Uh, this is a private club, Sergeant, and it's my job to protect the privacy of our members."

"Is that a no?"

"I think you would need to come back with a search warrant for something like that. It would put me in a difficult position if I were to just hand over the membership list. I'm sure you understand."

"I do. I'll come back with a warrant if I need the list. Do you have the paperwork that Leigh-Anne Moss filled out when she applied for work here?"

"Yes, and I showed it to the deputy on Saturday."

Crane opened a desk drawer and took out a single-page document that was sitting atop a stack. He handed it across the desk to Stilwell, who studied it for a long moment.

"Did you ever call either of these references she lists?" he finally asked.

"No, I didn't," Crane said. "I should have. But applicants don't usually give you the names of people who are not going to speak glowingly about them."

"True. Can I get a copy of this?"

"Of course."

Stilwell handed the document back to Crane. Without getting

up, Crane rolled his desk chair over to a copy machine to his right. He fed in the document and soon had a copy to hand back to Stilwell.

"What else can I do for you, Sergeant?" he asked.

"By any chance, do you have a photo of the missing sculpture?" Stilwell responded.

"Yes. The deputy asked me that Saturday and I didn't have one readily available, but in our archives I found a photo of the presentation of the sculpture to the club in 1916. I have it here."

Crane opened another drawer and took out a file. From it he pulled a yellowed photo of two men standing next to each other, one passing the black marlin sculpture to the other. A typewritten caption was taped to the back of the photo.

Presented this day, April 4, 1916, from Noah Rossmore to BMC president Padgett Smith

"Can you make a copy of this too?" Stilwell asked.

"Gladly," Crane said.

Stilwell handed the photo back and waited as Crane rolled over to the copier.

"What else?" Crane asked after handing the photocopy to Stilwell.

There was a note of impatience in his voice. Stilwell knew he had outstayed his welcome. He didn't care.

"The résumé shows that Moss gave an address on the mainland," he said. "Do you know if she had a place here on the island?"

"I don't," Crane said. "She worked weekends here, which is when we are busiest. A lot of our employees do. Many live on the mainland and go back and forth, or they stay with friends over here. I don't know what Leigh-Anne's situation was."

"Did she ever stay in one of the four rooms you've got here?"

"No, of course not. Those are for members' use only."

"I thought that would be the case but I had to ask. What about security cameras? Are there any in the building?"

"No, there aren't. Again, we're an old club and we protect the privacy of our members. There were no cameras when the club was founded. There are no cameras now."

Stilwell nodded.

"One last thing," he said. "You said earlier that your bar manager was one of the people who complained about Moss breaking the rules about socializing with members. What's his name?"

"My bar manager is Buddy Callahan," Crane said. "He's been here almost thirty years."

"I need to talk to him. Is he here now?"

"I believe he is. But I would prefer that you speak to him when he's not serving our members."

"Mr. Crane, this is a criminal investigation. You started it when you reported the theft of a priceless object. The investigation goes where it goes when it goes. I need to see your bar manager right now."

"Very well, Sergeant."

Crane picked up the phone on the desk and punched in three numbers. He instructed whoever answered to send Buddy Callahan up to the office immediately, then hung up.

"He's on his way," Crane said.

"Thank you," Stilwell said. "And I want to speak to him alone."

"I feel like I should monitor the conversation. In case something he says needs clarification."

"It's procedure. I have to talk to him without anybody, including his boss, listening. Is there a —"

"Not a problem. You can have the office. I need to check on

something downstairs anyway. I must warn you, though, that Buddy is opinionated and very protective of the club and its members."

"Meaning what?"

Crane stood up.

"Meaning he shoots from the hip and speaks his mind," he said. "I'll go bring him in."

He moved around the desk and headed out of the office.

11

BUDDY CALLAHAN WORE a white shirt with a black bow tie and matching waistcoat, ready for a night of work in the BMC bar. Stilwell had moved around the desk to Crane's seat, preferring the position of authority. Callahan entered the office and stopped when he saw Stilwell where he was used to seeing Crane.

"Close the door, Buddy, and come take a seat," Stilwell said.

Callahan did as he was told. He appeared to Stilwell to have lived a hard sixty years and had the gin blossoms and bloated belly to prove it. After he sat down, Stilwell gave him a moment to say, *What's this all about?* But he sat there quietly, apparently having been given a heads-up about the subject matter by Crane. Stilwell filled in the rest.

"I'm Detective Sergeant Stilwell with the sheriff's department," he began. "I'm investigating the theft of a valuable object from the club here. Are you familiar with what I'm talking about?"

"Yeah, I heard all about it," Callahan said. "That statue been there the whole time I been here."

"Which I'm told is almost thirty years."

"Twenty-eight, to be exact. Longer than anybody else except some of the members."

"I'm guessing Buddy isn't your real name. I need your formal name for — "

"No, it's Buddy. Says it on my birth certificate. My mother, she was a big Buddy Guy fan. You probably never heard of him."

" 'Damn Right, I've Got the Blues.' I know Buddy Guy."

"There you go. And get this — my full name is Buddy Guy Callahan."

"That's cool." Stilwell smiled and moved on with the interview. "So, Leigh-Anne Moss, what can you tell me about her?"

"She was on the make, that one. I told Crane she was bad news from the start."

" 'On the make,' 'bad news' … what are we talking about here?"

"From day one she was trying to get her hooks into the members. She was looking for a sugar daddy."

"She worked for you?"

"She worked weekends. She'd do the lunch shift and then move into the bar at night. That was when she worked for me, and I saw her game right away. She couldn't put a drink down on a table without grabbing a shoulder or touching an arm. It was obvious. I told her to knock it off. She didn't listen."

"So you told Mr. Crane?"

"I wasn't the only one. Some of the members didn't like it. They complained."

"Does that mean some of the members *did* like it?"

"I can't say."

"Or won't say?"

"I didn't last twenty-eight years in this place by shooting my mouth off about members, and anyway, it's got nothing to do with what you're investigating."

Stilwell nodded.

"How about you, Buddy? Did Leigh-Anne ever grab your shoulder or touch your arm?"

"I didn't have the right bank account for that."

"Did that upset you?"

Callahan laughed loudly. A little too loudly. Stilwell thought he might have struck a nerve.

"No, it didn't upset me," the bar manager said. "I've seen a lot like her over the years and I managed to keep my dick in my pants, if that's what you're getting at."

"You married, Buddy?" Stilwell asked.

"Not anymore. Tried it and it didn't take. But I don't fish off the company dock."

"Mr. Crane thinks Leigh-Anne stole the statue on her way out. Did you see her on her last day?"

"Sure. I was the one told her the boss wanted to see her."

"When was that?"

"As soon as she came in. She was late for setup, as usual, so maybe ten fifteen or thereabouts."

"So you were here that early. I thought you ran the bar."

"I do. But Saturdays during the season are busy, especially when we start getting into the season. Bar's open whenever the restaurant is."

"What exactly are your duties as bar manager?"

"Glorified bartender. I'm in charge of inventory and maintenance, but I'm behind the bar too — five nights a week."

"I bet a woman like Leigh-Anne, the way you say she operated, she was pulling down a lot in tips. Did people get jealous? People like you?"

Callahan laughed again, his face getting red and his nose turning a deeper shade of purple.

"Aren't you people supposed to do your homework?" he said. "There are no gratuities at this club. Members aren't allowed to tip. For anything. There's a twelve percent add-on to every chit. It goes into a pool that's split evenly with everybody on staff at the end of the month. That girl complained about the money—the exact opposite of what you're getting at, Detective."

He said the last word with a double shot of sarcasm. Stilwell let it roll off him as he came back with a question.

"Why would she complain when everyone got an equal share?"

"Because it's prorated by the number of shifts you work. She was getting only four, sometimes three, shifts a week. The full-timers were getting more, and that meant more at the end of the month."

Stilwell nodded that he understood and pivoted, hoping a change of direction would keep Callahan uncomfortable.

"So what did you say to her that day after Crane fired her?"

"Nothing. I never saw her leave. She probably didn't want anybody to see her. That's why she went out the front."

"How do you know she went out the front?"

"Because if she'd gone out through the kitchen or the restaurant, we would've seen her."

" 'We'?"

"We all knew she was getting fired. No other reason to get sent up to the boss."

"Who were the members who didn't like her? Who complained about her?"

"Complaints would have gone to Mr. Crane. You have to ask him."

"Where was Leigh-Anne Moss living on the island?"

"No idea."

"Was she friends with anybody on staff? Anyone she might have roomed with?"

Callahan shook his head like he was dealing with a child. "You don't understand. No one liked her here. No one could figure out why she'd even been hired, except she was a looker. But nobody was going to let her bunk with them. That wasn't happening. I should get back downstairs. I've got deliveries coming in. It was a big weekend."

Callahan stood up to go.

"Sit down, Mr. Callahan," Stilwell said. "We're not finished."

Callahan slowly sat back down, anger crossing his face. He didn't like being told what to do. Stilwell had finished the interview, but he wasn't going to let Callahan dictate anything. He dropped back into a more cordial tone that he hoped would keep Callahan talking.

"Thank you for your cooperation," he said. "Last few questions and then you can get to your inventory. What do you think Leigh-Anne did with the statue of the black marlin?"

"How the fuck would I know?" Callahan said. "It's probably in a pawnshop in Long Beach. But I tell you what, she didn't steal that thing to sell it. She stole it as a fuck-you to this place."

Stilwell nodded as though Callahan had made an important point.

"Last question," he said. "Where do you think Leigh-Anne is right now?"

He studied Callahan's eyes for any sign of hesitation or dissembling as he answered.

"Same thing," Callahan said. "How the fuck would I know?"

Stilwell said nothing for a long moment, hoping the angry man in front of him would say more. But Callahan held his gaze and said nothing else.

"Okay, Mr. Callahan, we're finished here," Stilwell said. "You're free to go."

"About time," Callahan said.

He stood up and stepped over to the window to take a look at the harbor. Then he turned and gave Stilwell a dead-eyed stare before heading to the door.

Stilwell waited, and a few minutes later Crane returned to the office.

"How'd we do with Buddy, Sergeant?" he asked.

Stilwell got up to return the seat of authority to its rightful owner.

"He was helpful," he said.

He pulled a business card from his pocket and put it down on the desk.

"I think I've got enough information for now," Stilwell said. "If you think of anything else that would be helpful, you've got my numbers there. I'll show myself out."

"I can walk you down," Crane offered.

"Don't bother. Thank you for your cooperation."

"Thank you, Sergeant. I hope you recover our statue. It belongs here."

Stilwell thought of something and stopped at the office door. He turned back to Crane.

"You know, you said that when you terminated Leigh-Anne, you timed it so there wouldn't be a lot of members in the club. In case she made some kind of scene."

"Yes, that's right."

"So why didn't you walk her to the door? You know, to make sure she didn't act out or do anything else she shouldn't?"

"I obviously should have, but I had a call from a member and I had to take it."

"Was it that important that you'd let her walk out without being watched?"

"Sergeant, every call from a member is important here."

"Got it. Thanks."

Stilwell walked down the hallway where the four guest rooms were located, two on either side. The door to one of the rooms was open. Stilwell looked in and saw a woman in a maid's uniform making a bed. The room looked sparely furnished and basic. He could see why members would prefer the staterooms on their yachts.

Stilwell went down the stairs and checked out the dining room. People wearing red waistcoats, white shirts, and black bow ties were setting up tables with silverware and glasses, getting ready for lunch. At the far end of the room was the bar. It was all dark wood and green glass banker's lamps above shelves of bottles containing clear or amber-colored liquors. As he stood there, he saw Callahan enter from a door Stilwell presumed was the kitchen and move behind the bar. He was followed by a young man carrying something heavy, his arms straight but his hands below the bar top. He turned, raised his arms, and poured a full tub of ice into a bin behind the bar. As he did so, his grip on the tub slipped; he overcorrected, and a cascade of ice slid across the top of the bar and onto the floor in front of it.

"Goddamn it!" Callahan yelled. "You stupid asswipe, clean that up! We're about to open."

The kid looked mortified, like it wasn't the first time he had taken a verbal lashing from his boss. He turned and scurried back to the kitchen. Callahan glanced into the dining room and saw that Stilwell had seen his response to the ice spill. He nodded proudly, as if saying, from one manager of people to another, *This is how we do it.*

Stilwell turned and left the club.

12

BEFORE RETURNING TO the sub, Stilwell walked over to the hardware and marine-supply store on Marilla. The longtime manager was Ned Browning, and Stilwell knew him from following up on reported thefts from the store. Browning was in the back room, conducting an inventory of boat cushions.

"Sergeant Stil, how's it going?"

"Not bad, Ned. You?"

"The body in the water. Bad stuff. Terrible."

"Yeah."

"So you want to see my records on recent anchor sales?"

Stilwell was surprised.

"Why would you say that?" he asked.

"Because Denzel Abbott was in here this morning," Browning said. "He was ordering new air lines and filters. He told me all about the girl wrapped in an anchor chain."

"Do me a favor and keep that to yourself."

"Not a problem."

"So, have you sold any anchors of late?"

"That would make your day, huh?"

"It would."

"Well, sorry. I don't move a lot of anchors. Most boats come out here equipped."

"I kind of thought it would be a long shot."

"Just so you know, somebody already asked me about anchors today."

"Who was that?"

"A sheriff's detective from overtown called, a guy named Ahearn. I told him just what I told you. We don't sell a lot of anchors. We have 'em. We just don't move 'em."

Stilwell was surprised that Ahearn had taken such initiative so early in the investigation.

"Did he ask you about anything else?" he asked.

"Uh, no," Browning said. "Just the anchor."

"Okay, then. Did Ahearn ask you to call him if anybody comes in to buy a twelve-pound Hold Fast plow anchor?"

"No, he didn't ask that."

"Then you can call me if that happens."

"You got it."

Stilwell headed out, but as he was walking back through the store to the door, he thought of something and turned around. Browning was still where he had left him.

"Ned, you sell handsaws here?" he asked.

"Sure," Browning said. "What kind you need?"

"Like for cutting through PVC, fiberglass. Like that?"

"Aisle four."

Stilwell went back and found the saw section. It took him only a few seconds to see a package that included a saw with a handle like the one he had seized. The package came with two extra blades. He looped the package off the hanging peg and returned to the back room to talk to Browning a third time.

"Do you know who Oscar Terranova is, Ned?" he asked.

"Sure, I know him," Browning said. "Everybody knows him."

"Does he have an account here?"

"An account? No, we don't have accounts. Customers want something, they have to buy it. No credit. That's a deal with the devil, having to chase people to pay their bills."

"Is there any way of checking to see if he bought a package like this recently?"

"If he paid cash, no. If he used a credit card, we could go through the charges, but it would take a while."

"Would you search by customer name or product?"

"Product would be easier. Our inventory is digital. We could pull up sales of that individual product. Credit card is more involved."

"Good. I'd be interested in anybody who bought one of these in, like, the past sixty days."

"Okay."

"How long will that take?"

"Uh, give me a couple days. Is this about that buffalo beheading? Is that what they used?" He pointed at the saw.

Stilwell was never surprised by how fast word got around. Avalon was a small town, and everybody seemed to know everybody's business long before it ended up in the *Call*. "Look, Ned—"

"I know, I know. Keep it to myself."

"Please."

"No worries. I'll call you when I've looked."

"Thank you."

Outside the store, Stilwell checked his watch. The autopsy on the body of the woman from the water was still a few hours away. He pulled his phone and called Tash.

"Do you think I can grab a screen over there and go through the harbor cameras for earlier this month?" he asked.

"Shouldn't be a problem," she said. "I can set you up. It's pretty quiet around here."

"You want me to bring lunch?"

"That'd be nice. Blue Rose?"

"Sure. What do you want?"

"Chicken mole, please."

"Okay, I'll be over."

After he disconnected, Stilwell called Maggie's Blue Rose and put in an order for pickup. While it was being put together he walked back to the sub to check in with Mercy. Deputy Ilsa Ramirez was in the dayroom bent over some paperwork.

"Sergeant," she said. "I just took a missing person report on a guy Mercy said you asked about the other day."

"Who?" Stilwell asked.

"Henry Gaston? He works as a mechanic in the cart barn for one of the tour companies."

A dull thud hit Stilwell in the chest and he was silent for a moment as he digested the news.

"Who reported him missing?" he finally asked.

"His wife," Ramirez said. "She says he hasn't been home since Saturday morning."

"What happened Saturday morning?"

"Nothing unusual. She said he went into work because one of the tour carts broke down and they couldn't replace it because all the tours and carts were booked for the weekend. He said he'd be gone a couple hours while he fixed it, but he never came home after that."

"Did you take this by phone or in person?"

"In person. I went to their house up on Tremont."

"Did you ask if any of his clothes were missing?"

"Uh, no. I didn't think to—"

"He might be on the run. Go back up there and look around the house. Ask about his things. See if he packed a bag."

"But why would he do that and not tell his wife?"

"I don't know if he would, but on Friday I gave him until Wednesday — tomorrow — to come in and talk about the buffalo mutilation. He could've gotten scared and rabbited. Or he could actually be missing — as in forcibly missing."

"Oh, wow."

"Yeah. So you do that and I'll go check out the cart barn."

"Roger that."

She got up and left the bullpen. Stilwell turned and saw Mercy at her desk.

"Mercy, anything on the socials about Leigh-Anne Moss?" he asked.

"I found her on Instagram," Mercy said. "Her profile hasn't been updated in a while. Do you want me to send it to you?"

"I don't have Instagram. Can you print it out?"

"I think so. Might take me a bit."

"Fine. I'm going over to the desal district to check the cart barn."

Once he was in the Gator and heading to where Gaston worked, he called Tash.

"Tash, something came up and I can't make it for a while," he said. "But I did order the food. Can you go pick it up?"

"Uh, I can't leave right now," Tash said. "I'll see if Heidi can go over there."

Heidi Allen was a secretary in the harbormaster's office. She was also the mayor's aunt, which caused Tash some concern. She worried that the mayor had placed Heidi there so he'd have eyes on the internal operation of one of Avalon's most important and visible public services.

"Sorry about this," Stilwell said. "I'll come by to look at the cams as soon as I get free of this other thing."

"What's happening?" Tash asked.

"A missing person. I'll tell you about it later."

"Okay. I'll keep your lunch warm."

He was already up high and cresting the mountain on Wrigley Road. The air was crisp and clear, and the view across the bay was marred only by the hazy layer of smog that hung over the mainland like a warning. Stilwell often drove up here to contemplate his surroundings and think about what he had left behind in the dirty air over there. It always seemed to reinforce the idea that sometimes you don't know what you're looking for until you've found it.

He had found good things on Catalina. He had found Tash and he had found meaning in his work. He had initially objected to his transfer but now knew that he never wanted to go back. That he was home.

At the cart barn, the garage door was down and there was no sign of activity. Stilwell got out of the Gator and went up to the pedestrian door to the right of the garage. It was locked, so he knocked. He waited and then knocked again. There was a camera over the door. He looked up at it and guessed that there was someone inside watching him. He stared unblinking at the lens for a few moments before turning.

As he walked back to the cart, he heard the door open behind him. He turned to see Oscar Terranova standing in the doorway, leaning against the frame.

"You scared away my mechanic, Stilwell," he said. "Now I have to find a new one."

"*I* scared him away?" Stilwell said. "Or was it you?"

Terranova didn't answer. Stilwell walked up the drive and over to him. He stood close enough to make Terranova drop his relaxed position and take half a step back.

"I don't care where you stashed him or what you did with him," Stilwell said. "It's not going to stop anything. This doesn't end here."

"We'll just have to see," Terranova said.

"Yeah, we will. You take care, Baby Head. If I were you, I'd get myself a good lawyer — one of those slick guys from the mainland. You're going to need one."

"Yeah, but you're not me, right? So why don't you run along and fuck off."

Stilwell nodded, noting that it was the second time so far in the day that he'd been told to fuck off. He took that as a good sign on multiple levels.

13

STILWELL'S ENCHILADA FROM Maggie's Blue Rose
had long been cold by the time he got to the harbormaster's tower
on the pier. Tash popped it in the office microwave, and he took
it on a paper plate to a desk where she had set up a screen with a
feed from the cameras that were trained on the harbor from eight
different angles.

"Have at it," Tash said. "Anything in particular you're looking
for?"

"Just want to check the weekend before last," Stilwell said.
"See what boats were coming and going."

"Shit. I forgot to put that list together for you. I'm so sorry. I
just was so busy in here till today."

"It's okay. The video will show me and then I might have some
specific questions."

"You sure?"

"I'm sure."

"Well, let me know if there's anything else I can do to help."

"Actually, here's a question: How many moorings does the
Black Marlin Club have?"

"They have the eight balls right behind the club. The red ones are all theirs. Plus they have their own dock and they can put two to four boats there, depending on length. They usually keep the embarcadero open for drop-offs and pickups."

" 'Embarcadero'?"

"The covered slip on the side of the club. The people who use the mooring buoys come in on skiffs to the side slip and there's an entrance to the club's restaurant right there."

"Got it. I saw that this morning when I was over there. So do their members register with you when they come in and out of the harbor?"

"They're supposed to. It's best practice so we know who's here, but it doesn't always work that way. They have some members who think they're above the rules."

"Rich guys — got it. Do you keep a list of members?"

"Not really, but I could go through the logbooks and get you names of the boats that use their moorings. I'll have some of the owners' names. Those would be the most active members. You could get the registration information from the state if we don't have it."

"If you have time, that would be very helpful."

"Do you think they had something to do with the woman Denzel found? I thought the mainlanders were taking that case."

"They are."

"But you're working on it anyway?"

Tash didn't seem concerned, just curious about what he was up to.

"The club reported a significant theft over the weekend," Stilwell said. "A valuable sculpture was taken, and the manager over there thinks it was grabbed on the weekend I want to look at."

"But that's not really what you're investigating, right?"

"Uh…"

Stilwell paused. She knew him well, but this was a situation where it was too early to discuss case theory or the risk he was taking by investigating a case he had repeatedly been told to stay away from.

"Never mind," Tash said. "I know you can't say what you're doing. I'll leave you to it. It's so slow around here post–holiday weekend that I actually have some time to work on that list for you."

"Thanks, Tash."

She discreetly touched his hand as she turned away. Heidi Allen was at a desk nearby, and the shy move was a vestige of the time they'd kept their relationship secret.

Stilwell went to work. The screen showed live feeds from the eight camera locations. By moving the cursor to any square, he could click and enlarge the image to full-screen. He could also drop the squares showing camera angles he was not interested in. He cut his search down to four cameras, three of which had a range that included at least part of the Black Marlin Club's wrap-around dock and eight mooring balls.

A search window allowed Stilwell to enter a specific date and go back to the weekend Leigh-Anne Moss had been fired from the club. He started the playback of the four camera angles at eight a.m. on that Saturday.

He set the playback at quadruple speed but then did the math and realized it would still take him several hours to review the entire weekend. He bumped it up to twelve times normal speed. The review process would still be lengthy, and he knew he might have to do it piecemeal when he had time. He watched as a variety of boats and ferries charged in and out of the harbor. Whenever a boat docked at the Black Marlin or moored at one of its buoys, he slowed the playback to real time to carefully study the activity on the boat and dock.

Stilwell saw nothing suspicious during the daylight hours on the Saturday that Charles Crane said he had fired Moss. Stilwell kept the playback on high speed through the dark hours and watched the reflection of the moon move quickly across the harbor waters.

Then he stopped the playback because he thought he saw an unusual movement on the water. He clicked on the camera angle that gave the fullest view of the Black Marlin Club and rewound the video. He watched again in real time and saw a small workboat come out from the covered dock on the north side of the building. A figure at the back of the boat was controlling the tiller connected to the outboard engine. The boat moved across the water to the first line of moorings and disappeared between a large ocean yacht and a two-masted sailboat.

Stilwell noted the time at the bottom of the screen. It was 3:13 Sunday morning. He closed out that camera feed and went back to the full screen showing the four camera views he had started with. He checked each for a better angle on the space between the two vessels where the workboat had disappeared but found none.

He went back to the first angle and expanded it again. He hit the playback at quadruple speed and watched and waited for the workboat to show. Twenty-five minutes on the time counter went by before it emerged from between the two larger boats and headed back to the club. Stilwell zoomed in on the workboat, but the image lost clarity, and the figure holding the outboard's tiller remained unidentifiable.

Stilwell called to Tash and asked her to come look at something.

"What's up?" she said.

Stilwell pointed to the screen. "These two boats," he said. "How do I identify them?"

"Well, the ketch is easy," Tash said. "That's the *Emerald Sea*. The other one I'll have to look up in the registry. This is the weekend before last?"

"Yes, three thirteen Sunday morning, the eighteenth."

"Give me a few minutes and I'll get it for you."

"How do you know it's the *Emerald Sea*?"

"Because it's here a lot. The owner likes to leave it and comes back and forth by ferry."

"So it sits out there empty when he's gone?"

"A lot of the time, yes."

Stilwell got up and looked out the tower window in the direction of the Black Marlin Club. The *Emerald Sea* was gone.

"When did it leave the harbor?" he asked.

"Yesterday."

"You called it a ketch. What exactly does that mean?"

"A two-masted sailboat is a ketch."

"I'm not much of a sailboat guy. Who owns it? And where does it come from?"

"It's out of MDR, and the owner is Mason Colbrink. He's supposedly a big-time overtown lawyer."

Stilwell nodded. He knew she was referring to Marina del Rey in Los Angeles.

"He must do corporate law," he said. "I've never heard of him."

"He's supposedly retired," Tash said. "But I don't think you get a membership to the Black Marlin and a forty-foot ketch like that by doing criminal defense."

"Probably not. How do you know when he's here on the boat?"

"Because Mr. Colbrink always checks in with us. The harbor doesn't allow storage mooring. It's for active boating only. He's pushing it by leaving his ketch here for weeks at a time, so he always wants us to know when he's here and using it. He thinks that makes it okay."

"Got it. Do you keep that on the registry? His comings and goings?"

"We do to a point. Mr. Colbrink is sort of cagey about that."

Stilwell sat back down in front of the screen and pointed to the *Emerald Sea*.

"Can you tell me whether Colbrink was here on the weekend of the seventeenth?" he asked.

"I'll check on that and get you the name and owner of the other boat," Tash said. "This is fun."

"What is?"

"Being part of an investigation."

Stilwell watched her go back to her desk. He felt uncomfortable involving her in any part of his work. The last thing he needed was his girlfriend thinking this work was fun and wanting to join in. The reality was that you never knew when a phone call, door knock, or keystroke could bring mortal danger. Just the year before, there had been a story out of Los Angeles about a so-called amateur sleuth who ended up shot to death in her home office's closet.

14

WHILE TASH WENT to work at her desk, Stilwell returned
to the playback, continuing it at twenty-four times normal speed
and keeping his eyes on the two boats that the skiff had disappeared between. He was well into daylight Sunday and hadn't seen
any movement of the vessels by the time Tash came back.

"Okay, as far as I can tell, Mr. Colbrink was not here that weekend," she said. "He was here over Memorial Day weekend and took
the boat back to MDR or some other destination on Monday."

"Okay," Stilwell said. "What about the other boat?"

"That's the *Aventura* out of Mission Bay. It's registered to a corporation of the same name so it can be rented for charters. The
captain's name is Bernie Contrares."

"Mission Bay?"

"Between San Diego and La Jolla."

"Does it come up here a lot?"

"A few times a year at least."

"You know the captain?"

"A bit, from working out moorings. Bernie's an old navy guy.
He's always nice."

"Was the boat occupied that weekend?"

"I show it arriving Friday and leaving the following Monday morning, the nineteenth. I assume there were people aboard."

"You have something I can write all of this down on?"

"Here."

She gave him a slip of notebook paper where she had already written everything down. Stilwell saw that the information on the *Aventura* also included the owning corporation's address in La Jolla. Under her notes on the *Emerald Sea,* Tash had put down an address and phone number for Mason Colbrink in Malibu.

"This is great, Tash. Thanks."

"I'm also making a list of the Black Marlin members we deal with on the moorings. Everybody who's come in this year."

"That'll be helpful. Thank you, but then you can stop there."

"What do you mean? I said it was fun. I want to help."

"I know, and you are helping, but I want to be careful about it."

"Meaning what?"

"Meaning it's not all fun and games. I don't want you to go down a path that, you know, could become dangerous."

"I'm just sharing records and video."

"Okay, that's great, and let's leave it there."

"Well, you're the one who asked me."

"I know. I did. And now I'm saying we should stay in our lanes. You mean the world to me and I don't want — "

She bent down over his shoulder and kissed him on the cheek, apparently not caring that Heidi was nearby, then went back to the control desk. Stilwell watched her go, then glanced over at Heidi. She was oblivious, or at least acting like she was. He went back to the screen and continued the high-speed playback, hoping to see something that might explain what the midnight mission of the man on the workboat had been about.

He started skipping ahead, searching hour to hour and checking to see if there was any movement from either the *Emerald Sea* or the *Aventura*. An hour later, with a headache blooming behind his eyes, Stilwell slowed the playback and watched as a skiff delivered supplies and a crew of three to the *Aventura*. Shortly afterward, the big yacht left the harbor, confirming the time details that Tash had written in her notes. As it slowly made its way out of the harbor, crew members in matching white shorts and polos moved about its decks, prepping the craft for the journey ahead.

The cameras now had an unobstructed view of the *Emerald Sea*. Stilwell had no sooner returned to a faster playback when he saw movement and hit the pause button. The time code put it at 11:16 a.m. on the Monday after the weekend of Leigh-Anne Moss's firing. He played it at regular speed and watched as a male figure in what looked like the same workboat as before came from the covered embarcadero at the club and went directly to the *Emerald Sea*. The man wore a floppy fishing hat and sunglasses along with a baggy green windbreaker. When Stilwell zoomed in, the resolution of the video blurred badly and made identifying the man impossible. Stilwell watched as the man in the floppy hat tied the workboat to the stern of the ketch and then climbed aboard.

The man unbuttoned a canvas cover over the boat's cockpit and helm, then stepped down into it. He bent over and busied his hands with something on the floor of the cockpit that was out of Stilwell's view. He then stood, grabbed a gaffing pole out of a holder on the deck, and moved forward to the bow, where he used the gaff to pull a line off the mooring buoy.

With the boat free-floating, the man went back to the cockpit and positioned himself behind the large wheel and throttle. Under engine power, the *Emerald Sea* started making its way toward the mouth of the harbor at idle speed.

Stilwell quickly switched angles, moving to a camera that was located on top of the harbormaster's tower and offered the closest and clearest view of the harbor's opening to the Santa Monica

Bay. As the *Emerald Sea* moved across the screen, Stilwell saw the sun glinting off the bow and realized that a shiny steel anchor was attached at the boat's prow. He stared intently at the boat and the workboat in tow behind it. As it passed directly in front of the tower, the man at the helm stood tall in the cockpit, and the mainsail boom completely blocked his face. The boat then turned into the mouth of the harbor and headed out into the bay.

"Shit," Stilwell said.

Tash came over from her desk. "What?" she asked.

Stilwell pointed to the screen.

"The *Emerald Sea* just left, and the guy behind the wheel blocked his face with the boom," he said. "It felt like he was making sure the camera didn't get a clear shot of him."

"Let me see," Tash said.

Stilwell reversed the playback and let her watch.

"Definitely," she said. "He's standing on the cockpit bench so he'll be hidden behind the boom. You're not supposed to do that, because if you hit a wave wrong, the boom could knock you off the boat."

"You think it could be Colbrink?"

"I can't tell. But the thing is, Mr. Colbrink never sails without a crew. He always has one or two people with him when he crosses back to MDR."

Stilwell nodded.

"So would there be any record of this boat leaving?" he asked.

"Let me check the registry," Tash said. "Get up."

Stilwell jumped up from his seat and Tash sat down. She closed out the camera app and opened the harbor registry. Stilwell watched as she scrolled through a log listing various dates, times, boat names, and crew contacts.

"It doesn't say—wait, here it is," she said. "It left at eleven thirty but then it says it came back only an hour later. It was just counted as a day trip."

"And no explanation for it being so short a trip?" Stilwell asked.

"Nothing here."

"Who was in the tower that day?"

Tash usually had Mondays off unless it was a holiday.

"It was Eugene's shift," she said.

Stilwell knew that was Eugene Hester, who early on competed with Stilwell for Tash Dano's interest and affections. Having lost the competition, Hester wasn't one of Stilwell's biggest fans.

"Can you call him and ask if he remembers this?" Stilwell asked.

"Sure," Tash said. "But didn't you just tell me to stand down?"

"Okay, okay, you got me. I'll allow this, and then you stand down."

"Whatever you say. I'll call him."

"Ask why the boat came back so quickly."

Tash pulled her cell phone and made the call. Stilwell heard only her side of the conversation and didn't really like how she softened her voice when talking to Hester. He wondered if she was keeping her options open or if he was just getting a glimpse into how women had to navigate the world of men. She ended the call as soon as she got the information she needed.

"He said it was just a test run following repairs that had been done," she said. "Mr. Colbrink called it in to the tower, said he was just taking it out to the bay to open the engine up and blow out the carburetor."

"But we can't be sure that was Colbrink," Stilwell said.

"It could have been the mechanic or one of the crew Mr. Colbrink hires to move the boat. He still could have called it in to the tower."

"It didn't look like any work had been done on the boat. He just came out from the club, unbuttoned the helm, and took off."

"You want me to call Eugene back?"

"No, I'm just thinking out loud. Can you put the cameras back up so I can watch the boat come back? Maybe we get lucky and see a face."

Tash brought the cameras back up and then got up from the chair so Stilwell could sit down and work the angles. Soon he was looking at the *Emerald Sea* returning to the harbor. Disappointment hit Stilwell on two fronts. The first was that he could clearly see that the shining steel anchor was still attached to the prow of the boat. The second was that the man at the helm was once again using the boom to hide his face, this time standing tall on the other side of the helm as the boat made its way in.

Stilwell cursed under his breath. He tracked the boat through the cameras back to the same red mooring ball. The man hooked the buoy and moored the boat, then returned on the workboat back to the embarcadero at the Black Marlin Club.

Stilwell checked his watch. The afternoon had slipped by and it was after five. He pulled his phone, hoping to catch Monty West before the end of his shift at the coroner's office.

"Blunt-force trauma," West said by way of greeting.

"What?" Stilwell asked.

"I figured you'd be calling me about the Jane Doe."

"Cause of death is blunt-force trauma?"

"That's what it says on the preliminary. Damage to the skull and cerebral cortex. Contrecoup swelling, edema, the whole works."

"So she was dead before she hit the water."

"That would be the case, yes. But this is all preliminary. The report will be out tomorrow."

"Did anybody from the sheriff's office attend?"

"Let me check."

Stilwell heard a keyboard clicking.

"Sampedro from the SO was here," West said.

"Okay," Stilwell said. "Anything new on ID?"

"Still a Jane Doe."

"Anything that can help with identification?"

"They took X-rays. Dental work and two pins in the left arm from surgery to repair a break. Based on the hardware, the pins were set within the past ten years."

Stilwell was heartened. Both could lead to identification if the victim's medical records could be located.

"What else?" he asked. "Sampedro ordered a rape kit, I hope."

"Let's see..." West said. "It does say the victim was fully clothed. But, yes, here it is. No indications of sexual assault, but foreign DNA was collected for analysis. They did a rape kit."

"Collected from where?"

"The vagina."

Stilwell thought about what that could mean. If she was fully clothed when she was put into the water and there were no bruises or other injuries from a sexual assault, it was possible she had had consensual sex prior to her death.

"What about TOD?"

"Factoring in decomp and water temp, time of death is a range of days, not hours. Six to eight days."

"That's from today or from day of recovery?"

"Six to eight days before recovery of the body."

"Okay."

Stilwell did the math and put the day Leigh-Anne Moss was fired from the BMC at the front of that range.

"Anything else flagged in the report?" he asked.

"Nope," West said. "That's it."

"Okay, thanks, Monty. I owe you one."

"That's what you said last time. So you actually owe me two. Question is, when you going to pay up?"

"Soon, Monty. Soon."

Stilwell disconnected and considered things for a few moments. His sub-rosa investigation was leading to a kill theory — that is, an emerging picture of what happened and why. He knew he was very short on details, but his instincts told him that Leigh-Anne Moss was the woman in the water and that she had been killed by a blow to the head with the sculpture of the leaping black marlin. Her body had then been secreted aboard the *Emerald Sea* and taken out of the harbor and into the bay to be weighted and submerged.

Stilwell knew that not one part of his kill theory was provable at the moment, not even the identification. But he was undaunted. He would continue his efforts, if only to show up Ahearn and make Corum realize he had transferred the wrong man out of homicide. He would push the boundaries, even though he knew that the next moves he needed to make would take him off the island and back to the mainland, where he would be unprotected and anything could happen.

15

STILWELL CALLED TASH from the ferry dock, where he had secured passage on the next boat to the Port of Los Angeles.

"I won't be home tonight," he said. "I'm heading across to do a couple interviews and should be back sometime tomorrow."

There was a hesitancy in her voice when she asked, "Where are you going to stay?"

"Not sure yet," Stilwell said. "I'll try Gary Saunders, see if he can put me up, or I'll just get a motel."

"What interviews?"

"I think I have a line on the victim, and her overtown address is in Belmont Shore. I have to knock on that door, see if there's anybody there. Then I want to talk to the guy you gave me, Mason Colbrink, up in Malibu."

"You can't do those by phone?"

"Uh, no, always better to talk to a possible witness face-to-face. Why, is there a problem with me going? I'm about to get on the Express."

"No, I just…you know, I don't like you going across. Only bad things happen over there."

It was a line Tash had heard her parents repeat while she was growing up on the island. They had used it to quell her adolescent curiosity and keep her close. Now she used it to keep Stilwell close.

"I'll be fine," he said. "And bad things happen on both sides of the bay, Tash. You know that."

"I guess," she said. "Just be careful over there."

"Always."

He disconnected and thought about the brief conversation. He wondered if Tash's concern was really about something else — namely, that his ex-wife lived in Belmont Shore in the condo that was for sale.

He had his go-bag, which he always kept at the substation, a small duffel bag containing a change of clothes. The last passenger to board the Express, he headed up the steps to the pilothouse, where he knocked on the door and let the captain know he was on board. Deputies, in uniform or not, were allowed to ride the ferries for free as long as they didn't take a seat on a sold-out vessel.

Stilwell then moved to the stern, where he'd see the sun setting over the island and the dolphins that seemed to always follow in the wake of the ferries crossing the bay. The ferry was only half full, so he took a seat in one of the rows that was sheltered from the wind and sea spray. As the boat left the pier, he sent a text to Gary Saunders offering to trade pickled eggs and pool at Joe Jost's for the use of the guest room at his house in Long Beach. More than securing a place to stay, he wanted to spend time with Saunders so he could ask about the woman his crew had pulled up from the bottom of the harbor.

The trip across was slightly longer than an hour, and during that time the sky darkened and the temperature dropped. Stilwell pulled a windbreaker out of his duffel and put it on as he disembarked. He walked to the long-term parking lot, where many residents of Catalina kept cars for their visits to the mainland. His

1974 Bronco was caked in smog dust and grime. It had been at least two weeks since he'd come across and used it, but the old engine cranked to life with one turn of the key. He headed to the address in Belmont Shore that was on Leigh-Anne Moss's driver's license and her Black Marlin Club employment application. He could have gone to the sheriff's station in Compton to check out a plain-wrap from the carpool, but he wanted to fly under the radar on this trip and not risk word getting to Ahearn and Sampedro that he was on the mainland and working.

Leigh-Anne Moss's apartment was in a small, six-unit building at the corner of Roycroft and Division. It had no security gate, which allowed Stilwell direct access to the door of apartment 2. He knocked once, and the door was soon opened by a man with deeply tanned skin and sun-bleached hair. Stilwell was already holding up his ID card.

"Sheriff's department," Stilwell said. "I'm looking for the home of Leigh-Anne Moss. Does she live here?"

"Uh, no, not really," the man said. "I mean, this was her place, but we're not together anymore. I let her crash here sometimes, but she mostly stays over on Catalina. What's this about?"

"I need to find her and she's not on Catalina. I just came from there."

"Well, I don't know what to tell you, dude."

"Your name is . . ."

"Peter Galloway."

"This is the address Leigh-Anne Moss put on her driver's license. Is she in there?"

"No, man, she's not. I haven't seen her in a couple months."

"Mind if I come in and ask you a few questions, Peter?"

"Uh, I guess."

Galloway stepped back; Stilwell entered and looked around as if searching for Leigh-Anne Moss even though he knew in his gut that she was dead. The apartment was sparsely furnished but messy with the detritus of bachelorhood. Empty beer bottles and pizza boxes, a pink glass bong that Galloway picked up off a coffee table and hid with his body as he walked it to a cabinet in the kitchen. The bong wasn't illegal, nor was what he probably smoked with it. Concealing it was likely a force-of-habit reaction. It told Stilwell that the man tended to hide things from authority figures — parents, bosses, cops.

"Um, so, yeah, what's this about?" Galloway said. "What do you want to ask?"

"It's a criminal investigation involving Ms. Moss," Stilwell said.

"Why am I not surprised. What did she do?"

"Mind if I sit down?"

"Have a seat. Sorry about the mess."

"Not a problem. Thanks."

Stilwell sat in a chair across from the couch. It was all mismatched furniture that gave the impression of a college apartment, but Galloway was ten years past college age.

Galloway took the couch and picked up a half-full bottle of beer from a coffee table that was crowded with empties and crumpled pages from scripts.

"I'll ask you again," Stilwell said, "do you have any idea where Leigh-Anne Moss is?"

"No idea," Galloway said.

"Do you know where she stays when she's out on Catalina?"

"Not really. I guess she stays with whatever rich guy she's banging at the time."

Stilwell didn't respond to that at first. Galloway's tone gave him pause. He now had a direction to go with his questions.

"That seems kind of harsh," he said.

"Sometimes the truth is harsh," Galloway said.

"What do you do for a living, Peter?"

"I go to auditions, mostly. I'm an actor. But since the strikes, there's been like zero production out here. I'm thinking about moving to Atlanta, to tell you the truth."

"And leaving Leigh-Anne behind?"

"There's nothing between us, so there's nothing to leave behind. We broke up a long time ago."

"But this is the address she put on an employment application."

"Well, I had nothing to do with that."

"Do you know what she does on the island? For work, I mean."

"Same thing she always does. Bartender, waitress — she'd strip too, but I hear there's no places like that out there. Not officially, at least."

"What's that mean? 'Not officially'?"

"Let's just say L-A is available for private parties of any kind. Here, there, wherever she happens to be."

That tone again. Galloway could barely hide his contempt.

"She goes by L-A?" Stilwell asked. "Her initials?"

"Sometimes," Galloway said. "Like a stage name, I guess you'd call it."

"Is that how you met? At a club or a bar? Or on a stage?"

"We met when we worked for the same catering company up in Hollywood."

"When was that?"

"About five years ago. We met and after a while we moved in together."

"Long commute to Hollywood from down here."

"We moved down here after we left that job."

"Left or got fired?"

"I wasn't fired. I got a part in a movie and quit. She got fired for doing her thing like she always does."

"Coming on to the clients?"

"Man, you have all the answers. Why bother with the questions?"

"Because it's my job. So it sounds like she had this ... pattern of getting jobs that put her close to people with wealth."

Stilwell stopped there, hoping Galloway would continue. He didn't.

"What I'm getting at is, it sounds like she used her jobs to get to people — men — who could help her," Stilwell said. "Is that what you would say?"

"I think I already did," Galloway said. "What did she do, rip off one of those old fuckers? You ask me, he got what he deserved."

"So you knew that she ... was this way, had been this way as far back as the caterer. But you stayed together and moved down here?"

"Man, we broke up so many times ... but then we always got back together. Except the last time, I guess."

"You said that was a long time ago, but you also said it's been a couple months since you've seen her. Which is it?"

"I actually didn't see her. I talked to her. I still let her stay here when she has no place else to go. She's got a key."

"Is this a one-bedroom?"

"Yes."

He drew the word out in a long frustrated tone.

"She sleep on the couch?" Stilwell asked. "Or with you?"

"None of your fucking business," Galloway snapped.

"Okay, then tell me this. Was that the last time she stayed here, two months ago? That would be, what, March?"

"It was April. But I wasn't here. I had a gig in Georgia. She called up, said she needed to crash, and I said, have at it."

"What kind of gig? Acting?"

"You could call it that. I get booked as Deadpool at Comic Cons around the country. It's good money between the real jobs. I've got the same height, weight, and build as Ryan Reynolds."

Stilwell nodded. He knew Reynolds was a movie star. He and Tash had seen one of his films at the Casino. But he feigned confusion to draw Galloway out. The actor read him and started shuffling through the script pages scattered on the coffee table. Finally, he held up an eight-by-ten photo of a man in a red-and-black costume that covered him from head to toe. He had what looked like two ninja swords strapped to his back.

"That's me," Galloway said. "As Deadpool."

Stilwell nodded again and smiled.

"So, Deadpool is a character?" he said as if just understanding. "How often do you do this?"

"About once a month. I work the circuit. It promotes the movies. It's good money."

His saying the money was good twice made Stilwell think it probably wasn't.

"What about this month?" he asked. "Did you have a Deadpool gig?"

"That was a Comic Cruise. Left out of Tampa."

"When was that?"

"Like two weeks ago. It was a three-day cruise. Why are you asking about me?"

Galloway had just given Stilwell what appeared to be an alibi for the weekend Leigh-Anne Moss had been fired and — Stilwell thought — murdered. He assumed that the Comic Cruise had been held over a weekend, and two weeks ago would mean two weekends ago. It would be easy enough to check the dates of the cruise and confirm that he'd been on the ship.

"It's my job to ask questions," he said. "Let's get back to Leigh-Anne. Where is she from?"

"Originally Detroit," Galloway said. "Like everybody else, she came out here to find fame and fortune. But it didn't exactly turn out that way."

"Does she have family back there?"

"Well, she has a father back there who started raping her when she was thirteen. And a mother who let it happen. There's an older brother somewhere but they lost touch after he left home. And that's about it as far as she ever told me."

"You were her family — while it lasted."

"I guess so."

"But that's over. Correct?"

"Yes, correct. That's what I've been telling you."

"Well, what I'm trying to figure out is who she's with now. If I know that, then I can leave you alone and go knock on that door. You understand?"

"I understand but I can't help you. I have no idea who she's with. I only know she's not with me."

"And that hurts, doesn't it?"

Galloway shook his head and jumped up from the couch.

"That's it!" he yelled. "You need to go. Now. I'm not answering any more questions."

He pointed at the apartment's front door. Stilwell didn't move.

"Peter, sit down," he said. "Please. This is a criminal investigation. You have to understand that you either talk to me here or I take you to the Hall of Justice, where we talk in a room with no windows."

He waited and Galloway finally sat back down.

"Thank you," Stilwell said. "Tell me what you know about Leigh-Anne's job out on Catalina."

"I don't know anything about it," Galloway said, "except that she works at a private club."

"How'd she get the job?"

"I don't know. She met some guy at a party and he told her about it."

"A party here or on the island?"

"Here, I think. I wasn't there."

"Was this guy a member of the private club on Catalina?"

"I don't know. You'd have to ask her. It wasn't like I wanted to know all the details. All I know is she got a job over there."

"And she never talked about it with you?"

"She just said it was this fancy club full of rich guys and that it was supposed to be a fishing club — men only — but these guys just go out there to get away from their wives and fuck around. That's why she wanted the job."

"She was looking for a hookup."

"Wow, you must be some kind of a detective or something."

Stilwell ignored the sullen sarcasm. "Did you ever get on an Express and go see her over there?"

"No, I've never been there. I told you, man, we aren't together anymore. Why would I go?"

"Because you still want to be together?"

Galloway shook his head as though he were trying to shake off a bad dream. He looked away and didn't answer. But in his silence was the answer.

"Peter, I have to ask you one more thing," Stilwell said. "And then I'll leave you alone."

Galloway turned back to him.

"Jesus," he said. "What?"

"You must still have photos of her," Stilwell said. "I need to see them."

"Why do you need to see photos?"

"Because all we've got is a driver's license. It would help to have some candid shots."

"For what, like a wanted poster or something? What the hell did she do?"

"I can't tell you about an active investigation, Peter. Do you have photos?"

Galloway reached into a pocket and pulled out his phone. He tapped in a password, then opened the photo app. He scrolled through his photos for almost thirty seconds before he stopped.

"This is all I've got," he said. "But they're old."

He handed the phone across the coffee table to Stilwell. The shot on the screen was a close-up of Leigh-Anne, smiling, no purple streak in her hair. It was dated May 5, 2022. Stilwell thumbed through three more shots, all taken within seconds of the first photo, all showing the same unposed smile.

Callahan the bar manager had been right. She was a looker. Stilwell saw what all men, young and old, saw. But what mattered to him was something else. He saw a woman with light in her eyes, a true smile on her lips. A future that shouldn't have been taken from her.

16

THE PICKLED EGGS were served on a bed of salted pretzel sticks and came in a plastic basket that balanced nicely on the rail of the pool table where Stilwell and Gary Saunders played straight-up eight ball while discussing floaters and sinkers from years gone by. Joe Jost's was crowded and loud. The venerable bar was celebrating one hundred years of existence with ongoing beer specials to fuel the celebrants.

Stilwell and Saunders went way back. Saunders had mentored Stilwell when the younger man had been assigned to the sheriff's dive team. Saunders had never left the unit and now ran it. There had been times when Stilwell regretted transferring out. The dive team was a bubble in the department with a very specific task. As grim as the assignments were at times, it was a safe harbor from the politics and bureaucracy that seemed to crop up everywhere else in the agency.

Saunders won the first two games easily. This was new. They used to be more evenly matched, but Saunders was no longer married and Stilwell got the idea that he spent a good deal of his time off in bars with pool tables. Eventually, Stilwell casually steered the conversation to the body recovery in Avalon Harbor, asking questions as if he had only a passing interest in the case. He started with a question he already knew the answer to.

"How long you think she was under?" he asked.

"Oh, boy, I'd say four to six days, based on the wax," Saunders said, using the shorthand for *adipocere,* the soapy substance that forms on a body during decomposition in water.

"Yeah, I was thinking the same," Stilwell said. "Was there anything else in the bag that was useful?"

"No, not really. Except the bag itself, I guess."

"Why? It was just a trash bag, wasn't it?"

"No, it was a sail bag."

"What's that?"

"They said it was for a jib—the front sail of a boat."

"Like on a ketch? The front sail of a ketch?"

"I don't speak sailboat, dude. I'm a ski-boat guy. But if a ketch has a front sail, then yeah. It was for storing a jib sail."

"Who identified it as that?"

"I think it was the coroner's investigator who was on the boat with us. He's more of a sailboat guy."

Stilwell was silent while he lined up a shot on the seven ball. He missed badly and scratched the cue ball. His mind was not on pool. It was now racing with this new piece of information. It meant that the woman in the water had likely been dropped into the sea from a sailboat. He thought about the *Emerald Sea* and the midnight visit by someone from the Black Marlin Club and then the strange outing made out and back into the harbor the next day—all of that within the time frame consistent with the decomposition of the body.

With the cue ball in hand, Saunders easily lined up the eight ball and finished the game.

"You need to come over here and practice more often," he said. "You owe me another five."

"Not going to happen — the practice, I mean," Stilwell said. "I like the island. I like staying over there."

"At least you're away from all the bullshit."

"Not so sure about that."

Stilwell knew that Saunders was referring to his falling-out with the homicide unit. If it were not for Ahearn handling the Avalon case, it would be a distant memory for Stilwell. But now the bullshit had followed him to the island.

Saunders took four quarters off the rail and put them into the table's coin slide, then started racking the balls for another game. Stilwell's phone buzzed and he saw that it was Tom Dunne finally calling him back.

"Hey, I have to get this," Stilwell said. "Outside."

"I just racked," Saunders complained. "We don't play, we don't hold the table."

"I'm sure one of the fine ladies at the bar would love to take your money."

"Yeah, right."

Stilwell answered the call and told Dunne to hold on, then headed through the bar to the exit, stopping only to speak to a woman who was half Saunders's age.

He pointed toward the pool table. "That guy's looking for someone to teach him how to shoot pool," he said.

He did not stop to see if she took the bait. He pushed through the front door and found a quiet spot on the sidewalk to talk.

"Tom, still there? How are you feeling?"

"Uh, getting there. I still have some double vision and a head-ache. But today was better than yesterday, that's for sure."

"Good. Are you up for a couple questions about Saturday?"

"Sure. But I don't really remember anything. The last thing I remember is walking into that bar to back up Eddie E. After that, everything is a blur."

"That's okay. Do you remember anything from earlier in the shift?"

"Uh, I think so. I don't know. People have only been asking about me getting hit, not what happened before."

"Well, I did some follow-up on a report you took at the Black Marlin Club. Do you remember that?"

"The...theft of a sculpture? Is that what you mean?"

"Exactly. I was just wondering if there was anything you heard or saw that didn't make it into your report."

"Uh, not really. I mean...I don't think so."

"The report you filed is pretty basic. I thought maybe you were planning to add more after shift, but you ended up in the clinic that night."

"I really don't remember, Sarge. I don't know what happened to my notebook. I can look through that and see if there's something I didn't put in the report."

Stilwell made a note to himself to see if the notebook was at the substation or at the clinic where Dunne was first treated.

"I'll see if I can find it," Stilwell said. "The other thing is Merris Spivak. Do you know him?"

"He's the mook who hit me, right?" Dunne said. "I didn't even see him. I was blindsided."

"But you don't recognize the name?"

"No, should I?"

"I don't know. The whole thing was captured on camera and to me it looks a bit off."

"How do you mean?"

"Like maybe he knew you."

"Can I see it?"

"I can have Mercy send you a link. Give it a watch and let me know."

"Will do."

"Spivak did three hundred days in county lockup a couple years back. I know you came out here from jail division. Where'd you work?"

"I started at Biscailuz like everybody does, and then I was at Pitchess until I got the transfer to Avalon."

"Spivak was at Pitchess. Maybe he recognized you from there."

"Maybe. There were a lot of people there. Obviously."

"You know personnel records are private under the union agreement, so I don't always know what's behind transfers to Catalina. Anything I should know about you and Pitchess? Anything that might have to do with Spivak?"

"Uh, no, I don't think so. I mean... I don't know that name. I'll look at the video but I doubt I'll recognize the guy. There were too many people in those dorms out there."

It was clear to Stilwell that Dunne didn't want to talk about whatever it was that had gotten him transferred to a substation where he would operate below the mainland's radar. He decided to let it go for now.

"Yeah, you're probably right," Stilwell said. "So look at the video, and if it jogs anything loose, let me know."

"Will do, Sarge," Dunne said.

"Okay, rest up. We need you back."

"As soon as I can, Sarge."

"Just call me Stil."

"Copy... Stil."

Stilwell disconnected and went back into the bar. Saunders was still playing pool. The woman Stilwell had pointed to the table earlier was there along with another woman who had joined in a three-handed game.

"Just in time," Saunders said. "We can play teams."

"Actually, I have to go," Stilwell said. "And it looks like you already have a three-way going."

"Oh, come on. Stay. This is Brenda, and this is...Darlene. Girls, meet Stilwell. People call him Stil."

Stilwell uncomfortably raised his hand in a hello.

"Nice to meet you, ladies, but I really have to go," he said.

He waved Saunders over for a private moment. "I'll get the tab at the bar," he said. "Text me if I need to grab a hotel room."

"No, the guest room's yours," Saunders insisted.

"Not if you get lucky. I don't want to come in right in the middle of that."

"It's not a problem. Where you going, anyway?"

"I want to follow up on that sail bag. Need to go see a guy about it up in Malibu."

"Wait, what? It's not even your case."

"Yeah, but I get the feeling that if I don't follow up on it, nobody will."

"Oh, man. You dumb son of a bitch. You're going to step in it again."

"Maybe, but I have to do it."

"Same old Stil. Can't leave things alone. You should have stayed on the dive team, but no, you had to go solve murders."

"What can I say?"

"Happy hunting, brother."

"And good luck to you."

Stilwell nodded toward the two women, who were whispering to each other at the other end of the pool table.

"Well, my prospects just doubled," Saunders said. "We'll see what happens."

As he walked out of Jost's, Stilwell thought about the warning Saunders had just given him. His concerns were well founded, and Stilwell had to consider what he was doing and the motivation behind it. Most cops he knew grew tired ten or fifteen years into the job. Even hard-chargers became go-along-to-get-along guys.

They seemed to forget why they'd put on the badge: To be fair. To right the wrongs against the innocent. To prevent those wrongs from occurring in the first place. Stilwell never wanted to forget. Leigh-Anne Moss's motivations might not have been completely innocent, but she didn't deserve to end up in a black sail bag at the bottom of the harbor. Stilwell was sure that once Ahearn learned her story, he would pass judgment and leave her down there as he moved on to the next one, hoping for a victim he could like.

Stilwell was sure about one other thing: Ahearn be damned, he was not going to stop his forward motion or his investigation.

17

MASON COLBRINK LIVED in the bluffs above Carbon Beach in an eight-figure house that overlooked the Pacific and the far-off lights of Catalina. The house had somehow escaped the fires that had come over the hills from the Palisades in January and burned through Malibu to the ocean. Stilwell arrived at the gate at 9:15 p.m. He knew someone like Colbrink would view this as very late for a visit, but Stilwell had found over the years that calling on witnesses and suspects when they were not expecting it produced the best results, whether you were looking for candid or incriminating information. No appointments, no prep time.

The voice that came from the box at the gate sounded wary about the unexpected intrusion, but Stilwell used the magic words "Sheriff's department. We need to speak to Mason Colbrink," and the gate was opened without another word from the box. Stilwell drove up a curving road to the top of the hill. The front door of the mansion was already open and a man stood in the light coming from within. Stilwell parked in the circle and killed the engine, hoping the Bronco would not leak oil onto the blond-brick motor court.

Stilwell got out and approached the door and the man waiting for him.

"Mr. Colbrink?"

"Yes, that's right. What year?"

"Excuse me?"

"The Bronco."

"Oh — '74."

"And they don't give you a sheriff's car or something?"

"Well, I just came over from Catalina and it saved time to drive my own wheels."

"What's happening on Catalina?"

"That's what I'm here to talk about. Can I come in, sir?"

"You have ID?"

Stilwell showed him his sheriff's card.

"Yes, come in. I think you have to."

Stilwell knew from DMV records that Colbrink was fifty-six years old and had never been convicted of any crime, not even a traffic violation. He now saw that he was tall and thin with salon-cut-and-dyed brown hair, black-rimmed glasses, and a Malibu tan. He also had an aura that left no doubt about his wealth and standing. He led the way into what real estate agents called the great room. It was larger than most houses, with a two-story-high ceiling and matching stone fireplaces at either end. Each had its own grouping of furnishings around it. It was the kind of space where two separate parties could go on at the same time and neither would intrude on the other. Colbrink pointed to a couch in the first grouping and Stilwell sat down.

"I guess we should start with your name and what this is all about," he said.

"Yes, sir. My name is Stilwell. I'm a detective sergeant with the L.A. County Sheriff's Department. I handle all cases that originate on Catalina."

"I just heard there was a death out there in the harbor — a possible murder."

"Yes, that is being managed by the homicide unit. I'm actually here about something else. We received a report of a very valuable art object being stolen from the Black Marlin Club, of which I'm told you are a member."

"Was it one of the plein air paintings my father donated?"

"Uh, no. This was a small statue. A sculpture of a black marlin that was stolen from a display pedestal in the main hallway. It was described as priceless, and so we're taking the theft pretty seriously."

"I know the sculpture. I also know black jade and I would hardly say that it's a priceless piece of art. Whoever took it made a mistake. The paintings on the walls in the club's library are far more valuable."

Stilwell just nodded. He understood that Colbrink wanted to control the meeting by using his wealth of knowledge. He looked around the room as if noticing it for the first time.

"You have a beautiful place," he said. "Do you live here alone?"

"No, I don't," Colbrink said.

He offered no further explanation.

"Well, getting back to the black marlin that was stolen," Stilwell said, "as I mentioned, we're taking it seriously, no matter the actual value. We believe the theft occurred two weekends ago. The BMC has no exterior or interior cameras, but we were able to review other cameras located around the harbor and we saw that your ketch, the *Emerald Sea,* was in the harbor that weekend. I'd like to know if you were in the club on Saturday or Sunday and if you saw anything that was suspicious, a person who didn't belong or anything else that seemed out of —"

"I can stop you right there," Colbrink said. "My boat was there but I was not. I was here. And I can provide witnesses to corroborate that — several of them. Saturday the seventeenth was my wife's birthday and we had a number of people here to celebrate."

Stilwell forced a smile and held up a hand to stop Colbrink's explanation.

"Please don't misunderstand me," Stilwell said. "You're not a suspect, Mr. Colbrink. Not at all. I saw that your boat was in the harbor and thought you might have been there at the club or on the boat and that there was a chance you saw something."

"Well, I was not," Colbrink said.

"We actually have a suspect. Leigh-Anne Moss? She worked in the restaurant during lunch and in the bar at night. Do you by any chance know her?"

"I know many of the staff but not all of them by name."

"She's twenty-eight, has a purple streak in her hair. She was dismissed by Mr. Crane the same weekend as the theft. It's his theory that she took the statue from the pedestal after leaving his office."

"I remember the girl with a purple streak in her hair. I had no interaction with her other than giving her my drink order in the bar. I was, in fact, told that she was bad news."

That phrase again, Stilwell thought. "In what way was she bad news?"

"I heard that she was 'loose and looking,' if you know what I mean."

"Who told you this?"

"I don't really remember. It was just talk among the members in the card room. People like to gossip while playing poker. It distracts their opponents."

"So, other than telling her what you wanted to drink, you didn't have any interaction with Leigh-Anne Moss?"

"I already told you, I did not. Now, if that's all you came to find out, I'll ask you to leave." Colbrink started to get up.

"That's not actually what I came to ask you."

"Then what, Sergeant?"

"I'm sorry, sir. I'll try to be brief. Did anyone use your boat that weekend while you were here on the mainland?"

"No. I have a crew that sails with me, but there were no plans for that weekend. I was just out there over this past weekend, as you probably already know, and we sailed the *Emerald* home."

"To Marina del Rey?"

"Yes, I keep it at the CYC."

"CYC?"

"The California Yacht Club. Ask your next question."

"When you're not sailing the *Emerald Sea* back and forth, you use the Express?"

"Most of the time. Sometimes I take a helicopter. I can provide receipts if that's what you're getting at, but this is silly. Why would I take the damn statue?"

"I don't think you did, sir. As I said, you're not a suspect. I'm here because I think you can help me."

"How, Sergeant Stillwater? I don't understand where you're coming from."

"It's Stilwell."

"Whatever. What exactly do you want from me, Sergeant Stilwell?"

"When I was reviewing video from the harbor cameras, there was some unusual activity with your boat on the days we're looking at. I'd like —"

"What are you talking about? What unusual activity?"

"In the middle of the night, someone took a skiff from the club to your boat, stayed there for a short time, then went back to the club. Would you know who that was and what it was about?"

"*My* boat? Are you sure?"

"Not a hundred percent, no. There was another boat moored next to it, but it appeared that the *Emerald Sea* was where the skiff landed."

"What boat was moored there?"

"It was called the *Aventura*."

"I don't know it."

"Did you know that on Monday the nineteenth, someone took the *Emerald Sea* out of the harbor and then returned it a short time later?"

"I did not."

"Did you authorize anyone to take the boat out, maybe just to run the engines?"

"I did not. And the engines run fine. But what does this have to do with the sculpture? Connect the dots, Sergeant."

Stilwell looked at Colbrink for a long moment before answering. He needed his cooperation and the only way to get it was to reveal the true nature of his investigation. That was a risk. He wasn't sure if he could trust the man, and that could cost him if Ahearn caught up to his moves.

He leaned forward on the couch, elbows on his knees, hands clasped together in a pose that put him closer to Colbrink and hopefully signaled the need for confidentiality.

"What I need is to get on your boat," he said.

"Why?" Colbrink demanded, sounding more confused than combative now.

"Leigh-Anne Moss is missing. I came across the bay today to go to the apartment she lives at when she's not on the island. But she hasn't been there. Add that to the body we pulled from the bottom of the harbor Friday, and I think you see the dots connecting, Mr. Colbrink. Decomposition was extensive. As of now, there is no ID. It's a female, but that's as far as we've come in making an identification."

"I appreciate your candor but it doesn't answer my question. Why do you want to get on my boat?"

Again Stilwell hesitated. But he saw no other way to keep the momentum of his investigation going.

"The body in the harbor was in a sail bag," he said. "A bag for a jib sail. It was weighted with a twelve-pound stainless-steel plow anchor. I want to get on your boat to see if either of those items are missing."

"And you want to do this without a warrant?"

"I want your permission to search your boat. If you give me that, I won't need a warrant."

Colbrink stared hard at Stilwell as he made a decision.

"And when do you want to do this?"

"I'd like to do it tonight," Stilwell said. "I know it's late, but a murder case is like a shark — if it stops, it dies."

Colbrink nodded that he understood.

"Okay, then," he said. "Let's go."

"You don't have to come," Stilwell said. "I just need your written permission and —"

"Of course I'm coming. I'm not going to let anybody tromp around on that boat without eyes on them. I'll drive, you follow."

"That's okay, sir. If you're going, I'll ride with you."

Stilwell figured it was a half hour to Marina del Rey at this time of night. He knew that riding together meant a drive back to Malibu to pick up the Bronco, but he didn't want to miss the opportunity to continue the conversation with a Black Marlin Club insider.

"No, you drive," Colbrink said. "I want to ride in that Bronco. If I like it, I'll make you an offer you won't be able to refuse."

"That's unlikely, sir."

"We'll see. Let's go."

Colbrink stood up, ending the discussion.

18

THE CALIFORNIA YACHT Club was a vast complex of docks where the wealthiest of the wealthy kept their water toys. It was one of several private marinas that shared the inlet that was Marina del Rey. There were thousands of boats of all sizes and shapes. Without Colbrink, Stilwell would have had difficulty accessing the CYC dock grid and then locating the *Emerald Sea*. Colbrink's insistence on coming along saved time and confusion.

It had taken them forty minutes to get there from Malibu, due to nighttime roadwork on the Pacific Coast Highway. During the drive Colbrink talked about his life and work, seemingly no longer bothered by Stilwell's intrusion on his evening.

Colbrink had been an attorney who handled high-end mergers of businesses with nine-figure valuations. He'd retired early and now put his own money into mergers, and he'd built a life that included mansions and sailing yachts on both sides of the country. Like his father before him, he was an active member of the Black Marlin Club, for which he felt a sentimental love. He lamented the damage that a murder tied to the club might do to its reputation.

"I know it's an anachronism, but my father was a member and

his father before him," he said. "And I don't even fish — I sail. But I love the place and would hate to see its name splashed across the headlines in connection to a tawdry murder."

"Well, we're a long way from that," Stilwell said.

For the rest of the drive, he thought about Colbrink dismissing the murder of a woman who had been wrapped in a bag and weighted down with an anchor as tawdry. It was clear that on his hilltop in Malibu, he was sequestered from many harsh and violent realities.

The guard at the CYC gate waved the Bronco through once he identified Colbrink in the passenger seat. They parked in the empty lot and headed down a gangway to the grid of docks lined with lights at every slip.

"How long will this take?" Colbrink asked. "You want to check the sail bags and the anchor. What else?"

"Depends," Stilwell said. "When you were over there this past weekend, did you stay on the boat?"

"I did, yes."

"By yourself?"

"Uh, no. I had someone with me."

"Your wife."

"No."

Stilwell paused and waited.

"I married a woman who doesn't like to sail...or do other things," Colbrink said. "And that's all I will say about that."

Stilwell was willing to let it go for the moment. But he would come back to it.

"I understand," he said. "What about your crew?"

"It's basically a crew of one. My guy can bring others if needed."

"Does he live near the marina?"

"No, he lives on the island — Two Harbors. He doesn't stay on the boat. He comes over from the isthmus when I need him."

"Who is that? If he's in Two Harbors, I might know him."

"Duncan Forbes."

The name didn't resonate with Stilwell.

"So he came with you to bring the boat back here after the weekend?"

"He did. Monday morning."

"Did you have the boat cleaned after you brought it back?"

"Duncan did that, yes."

"He do a good job?"

"I haven't been back to see the boat, but, yes, he usually does. He's been working for me for almost seven years. I don't keep anyone that long if they're not doing the job."

"Then I think any sort of forensic evidence will be gone or compromised. So let's just check the bag and anchor and go from there. I'll get you back as quickly as possible."

"Thank you."

The *Emerald Sea* was backed into a slip at the end of a pier closest to the rock-lined inlet that led to the bay. As he got his first up-close look, Stilwell could tell it was a wood-hulled antique.

"How old is it?" he asked.

"It's a 1960 Mayflower I had shipped in pieces from Wisconsin and then restored," Colbrink said. "Took almost four years from start to finish. It's a duplicate of my father's boat, which went down in a storm."

There were boarding stairs on the dock. Colbrink climbed aboard first, and Stilwell followed. Colbrink opened the hatch in the helm and carefully descended a set of steep stairs into the dark interior of the boat.

"Let me get some lights going," he said.

He disappeared from Stilwell's sight, and a few seconds later, lights came on inside the cabin and then from the top of both masts, illuminating the entire deck of the vessel. Colbrink climbed back up out of the cabin.

"Everything you're interested in is up on deck," he said. "Let's check the sails first."

He moved to the bow of the boat, where he unlocked and slipped back a hatch that was on rails on the forward deck.

"We keep extra mainsails here, along with the jib and the chute."

"The 'shoot'?"

"Chute, like in *parachute*. The spinnaker is what it's really called. It looks like a parachute when it fills up with air."

"Got it."

Stilwell stepped over and looked down into the storage compartment. There were two white drawstring bags along with one red and one black one. Colbrink pointed into the space.

"Nothing's missing as far as I can see," he said. "We've got two mains in white, the spinnaker in the red bag, and the jib in the black. Color-coded so we know which is which. Sometimes you change sails on the fly."

Stilwell looked down into the hatch, but the contents were in shadow. He saw the colors of the bags but little detail.

"Can I pull out the jib?"

"Be my guest."

He crouched, grabbed the black bag's drawstring, and yanked it up onto the deck, where the lighting was better. Still crouched, he pulled out his phone and turned on its light. He ran the beam over the bag and noticed a gridwork of creases.

"This looks like a new bag," he said. "Still has creases from being folded. Did you recently get this?"

"No," Colbrink said. "Had that sail and the bag for years."

Stilwell loosened the drawstring and opened the bag to reveal the folded jib sail inside. The sail was white but worn by use in the sun and wind. It was clear to him that the bag was newer than the sail. He felt a slight whisper go down his spine as he realized that he wasn't spinning his wheels. He had made a significant jump in the case. The woman in the water had been stuffed into a sail bag from this boat.

"The bag has been switched out," he said, more to himself than to Colbrink.

"Okay," Colbrink said. "What's that mean?"

Stilwell turned his head and looked toward the front of the boat. A stainless-steel anchor was secured on rubber rollers on the prow.

"It means I want to look at your anchors," Stilwell said. "You've got that one at the front. Any others on the boat?"

"Yes, we carry a stern anchor and a spare," Colbrink said. "You've got to be able to securely anchor the boat. The winds off the barrier islands are formidable."

"Different sizes of anchors?"

"No, all the same. That way they're interchangeable."

"Can you show me the others?"

"This way."

Stilwell kept his phone light on as they made their way back to the stern. Colbrink stepped down into the helm, where the boat's wheel was located. Behind the wheel was a bench with a white pad on it. Colbrink lifted the pad, revealing another storage hatch underneath. This one had no locking device. He reached down to open it.

"Hold it a second, Mr. Colbrink," Stilwell said.

Colbrink straightened up.

"What is it?" he asked.

Stilwell was pulling a pair of disposable gloves from the pocket of his windbreaker.

"The sail bags would not have held prints," he said. "But the lid of that compartment may. Let me open it."

Colbrink stepped back and Stilwell opened the hatch, revealing two anchors with chains and coiled rope attached.

"Nothing missing," Colbrink announced.

Stilwell aimed his light into the hatch. The two anchors appeared to be a match to the one that had been used to weigh down the body in the harbor. He wanted to pull them out for further examination but thought better of it. Even though the boat had recently been cleaned, there could be fingerprint evidence on the anchors.

"Do you know the weight and brand of these?" he asked.

"Twelve pounds each," Colbrink said. "Made by a company called Hold Fast."

Stilwell nodded and bent down farther, using his light to study the two anchors for any indication that one was new.

"Does that mean anything to you?" Colbrink asked.

Stilwell ignored the question.

"Mr. Colbrink," he said. "I'm going to give you my card so we can be in contact. I ask that you stay off the boat and keep others off it until I can get a forensics tech out here."

"I thought you said any evidence would be gone by now," Colbrink said.

"I changed my mind. Especially with these anchors being in the compartment. You opened the front hatch with a key. Did you bring that with you?"

"No. It hangs on a hook in the cabin by the chart table."

"So it's always on the boat."

"That's right."

"And the cabin hatch is not locked?"

"Not usually. The CYC has armed security on the premises twenty-four seven. I never lock the boat. That way I can have Duncan come out and make sure the bilge-pump battery hasn't lost its charge."

"Not sure what that means."

"Old boats like this leak, Sergeant. The bilge pump clears the water out so that the boat stays afloat. If the bilge pump goes down, the boat could go down. It's important to keep the battery charged."

"Got it."

Stilwell stared down at the anchors and thought about the timeline. It had been ten days since the unusual activities associated with the *Emerald Sea* had occurred in Avalon Harbor. If he assumed that those activities involved moving a body onto the ketch and then out of the harbor to the place where it was bagged, wrapped in an anchor chain, and dumped overboard, then there had been plenty of time to replace the anchor and jib bag with duplicates.

"What are you thinking, Sergeant?" Colbrink asked.

Stilwell was thinking that he wished it were his case so he could make the moves he knew needed to be made. But he didn't say that to Colbrink.

"I'm thinking that I'd like to look around inside the cabin," he said instead.

And he was thinking that he needed to talk to Colbrink's crew member and cleanup man, Duncan Forbes.

19

TWO HARBORS WAS little more than a fishing village at the island's isthmus. There was a scattering of small independent hotels, restaurants, and markets that catered to the hillside homes, campgrounds, and fishing guides. Duncan Forbes might have moved there in an attempt to fall off law enforcement radar. No driver's license was needed on the island to operate a boat or golf cart. No marine license was needed if you were crew for someone with the proper licensing. And there was no need for bank accounts and other electronic tails if you were a day player paid in cash for your work on the water.

But with a name like Duncan Forbes, he could not completely escape the grid. There were only two people named Duncan Forbes in the sheriff's crime-index computer. One was seventy-four years old and lived in Sacramento. He had a criminal record that included convictions for domestic abuse, DUIs, and assaulting a police officer. The other Duncan Forbes was thirty-three years old and wanted on a minor warrant for jumping probation for a marijuana arrest before California legalized recreational use of the drug in 2016. In law enforcement parlance, it was a chickenshit warrant, but it was still on the books and it was all Stilwell needed to talk to Mason Colbrink's part-time crew member.

After getting back to the island Wednesday morning, Stilwell dispatched Deputies Lampley and Ramirez on the sheriff's Zodiac to Two Harbors to locate Forbes, arrest him on the outstanding warrant, and bring him back to Avalon. They could have taken one of the sheriff's two SUVs that were kept on the island for use outside Avalon, but the drive to the isthmus took twice as long as the trip by boat and Stilwell didn't want to waste time.

While Lampley and Ramirez were following his order, Stilwell cleared out the sub's one interview room, which was rarely used for its stated purpose and had become more of a storage unit for office supplies as well as a community lost and found. There were paddleboards, fishing poles, life vests, laptops, and suitcases left behind on the ferry docks. Cardboard boxes contained sunglasses, cell phones, and wallets that had been turned in over the past year or so. Stilwell had a strategy for his interview with Forbes and wanted the room to be clean and clear when they sat down face-to-face.

Once the room was prepped, Stilwell radioed Lampley to get his ETA. Lampley replied that they had Forbes in custody but had not left Two Harbors yet. They were heading to the Zodiac now, which put them close to thirty minutes out.

"Any trouble with him?" Stilwell asked.

"Only trouble we had was finding him," Lampley said. "People out here didn't want to give him up. But we got him. He says we have the wrong man."

When the deputies questioned why they had to go all the way to Two Harbors on a chickenshit warrant, Stilwell had told them the real reason, but he hoped they hadn't shared that with Forbes.

"You mean he says he's not the guy on the warrant?" Stilwell asked.

"Yeah, the warrant," Lampley said.

"Tell him I'll explain it all when he gets to Avalon."

"Roger that."

The delay gave Stilwell time to leave the sub and go to the harbormaster's tower. As he headed out, he told Mercy he'd be on the radio.

After he was buzzed through the door to the tower, he saw both Tash Dano and her boss, Dennis Lafferty, in the control room. Stilwell had only come by to see Tash and tell her he was back, but Lafferty's presence made the moment awkward. Lafferty knew that Stilwell and Tash were a couple, but he wasn't keen on seeing it displayed in the workplace. Stilwell kept a professional demeanor.

"Just checking in," he said. "Wanted to see what the weekend looks like."

"The season is underway," Lafferty called from the control desk. "Another full house."

Stilwell nodded. "Okay, we'll be ready," he said. "Anything else happening that I should know about?"

"Not here," Tash said.

"They figure out who that was in the water last week?" Lafferty asked.

"Not as far as I know," Stilwell said. "Overtown sheriffs are handling it."

He gave Tash a surreptitious wink. She suppressed a smile.

"Figures," Lafferty said. "Happens here, and they investigate from over there. No wonder shit never gets solved."

"Not my call," Stilwell said. "Anyway, let me know if you need me." He said it looking at Tash.

"Will do," Lafferty said.

"Dennis, I'm going to hit the restroom," Tash said.

"Go with God," Lafferty said.

On the stairs down to the lower level, where the restrooms and Lafferty's office were located, Tash squeezed Stilwell's arm and whispered, "Welcome back. How did it go over there?"

"Not bad. Got some stuff done. How's everything here?"

"Same old, same old. Waiting for the weekend crush."

When they got to the exit, she gripped his arm tighter and then swiveled him into a hard kiss. Stilwell went with it.

When she broke it off, she said, "Just remember, you belong out here."

"I know," he said. "Your place or mine tonight?"

"Yours. I'll be by."

"Okay, bring more of that."

She smiled and he smiled back as he pushed open the door. He watched her duck into the restroom, and then, a grin still on his face, he turned to find Lionel McKey waiting for him.

"No comment," he said before the reporter could speak.

"No comment on what?" McKey asked.

"Whatever you're about to ask me."

He started walking down the pier. McKey followed.

"You don't even know what I'm going to ask you."

"Okay, go ahead."

"Anything new on the body in the water?"

"Before I answer that, how did you know I was here?"

"I was just hanging out and I saw you go in."

"Really?"

"Yeah, really. So . . . the body in the water?"

"No comment. Not my investigation."

"That's not true from what I hear."

"Yeah, what do you hear?"

"That you went through all the harbor videos the other day. Probably why you were in there just now."

The question told Stilwell that McKey had a source. Only

Dennis Lafferty, Heidi Allen, and Tash Dano knew about him going through the cams, and Stilwell didn't think Tash was the leak.

"I was just getting a rundown on moorings for this weekend," Stilwell said. "But I do have a question for you, Lionel."

"Okay, ask me," McKey said.

"How'd the mayor take the front page Saturday?"

"Ugh. Back at you with the 'No comment.'"

"Now you see how it works."

"But, speaking of the mayor, are you looking into the Big Wheel proposal?"

That came from left field. Stilwell was intrigued but didn't want to show it.

"Should I be looking into it?"

"Well . . . seems like there's some cozy cousins involved in that deal."

"What does 'cozy cousins' mean?"

"Just a newspaper term, I guess. But I've been doing some digging into who exactly is behind the Big Wheel and there's some smoke there."

"And you're hoping that I take the bait and look into whether there's any fire? Then you get the headline without actually doing the work."

"Well, there are some firewalls I can't get through but somebody with a badge can. You could always feed me off the record, you know."

Stilwell stopped and turned so he was face-to-face with McKey.

"I want to make something clear to you so it doesn't end up in the paper," he said. "I am not looking into the Big Wheel project. If you print that I am, then we're going to have a major problem. Understand?"

"I understand," McKey said. "I'm not trying to bait you. I'm just saying that...there's some smoke there, that's all. And maybe law enforcement on the island should take notice."

"But last I checked, being cozy cousins wasn't a crime. So you go about your business and I'll go about mine."

"Okay, okay. I was just making conversation."

They were near the entrance to the pier. Stilwell saw Lampley and Ramirez on the four-seat UTV driving on Crescent toward the sub. A man he assumed was Duncan Forbes was in the second row, his hands cuffed to the bar that ran behind the front seats.

"I gotta go now, Lionel," he said.

"Sure," McKey said. "But one last thing. Anything new on the mutilation case? I heard you went across last night. Was wondering if that had anything to do with—"

"No, it had nothing to do with anything. It was a personal matter that I had to take care of and I was back here on the first boat this morning. I have nothing new for you on the mutilation case. Still working it but no comment at this time. I'll talk to you later."

He left McKey there and headed to the sub to interrogate Duncan Forbes.

20

FORBES WAS ALREADY in the interview room when Stilwell got to the bullpen at the sub. Lampley had turned on the room's camera and was looking at Forbes on the computer screen at his desk.

"Are you recording?" Stilwell asked.

"Not yet," Lampley said. "Now?"

"Yeah, now. Where's Ramirez?"

"She went back out. Mercy had a call for her."

"What call?"

"Somebody ran out on their tab at the Bluewater and she went to take a report, maybe go catch the guy before he gets on the ferry."

"Then she might need backup."

"I doubt it. Anyway, I want to watch the master do the interrogation."

"Just be ready. If she needs you, I want you there."

"Copy."

Stilwell looked at Lampley's screen. Forbes was sitting at the table but his back was to the camera.

"You put him in the wrong seat. The camera should be on his

face, not mine. And he shouldn't be by the door. He should have to go past me to get to the door."

"Oh, shit, you're right. I wasn't sure where the camera was in there—we haven't used this room since I've been here. I'll go back in and—"

"No, I'll handle it. You make sure Ilsa doesn't need you. You can watch the video of this later. It's recorded."

"Copy that."

Stilwell went into his office, locked his sidearm in a drawer, and grabbed his laptop. He then went to the interview room, where he was greeted by a sign on the door that said NO FOOD STORAGE. He wished he had taken that off when he cleared out the room.

He entered, startling Forbes, who now had his head down on the table.

"About time," Forbes said. "I'm falling asleep in here."

"Sorry about the wait," Stilwell said. "Stand up for me, Duncan."

"Where are we going?"

"Just the other side of the table. Stand up."

Forbes slowly rose from his seat, confused by the need to switch. Stilwell saw that he was not a big man. Five eight, at most, with a lean build, long curly brown hair, and a dark complexion.

His hands were cuffed in front, which was another fuckup on Lampley's part. But Stilwell was not concerned. He had sized Forbes up and knew he would be able to handle any confrontation. He had at least four inches and twenty-five pounds on the younger man. He had also been through the department's physical-combat training.

Forbes moved around to the other side of the table and sat down.

"This is bullshit, man," he said. "There's no warrant on me. That's old shit."

Stilwell took the seat across from him.

"Actually, the warrant is still good," he said.

"No way. Pot is legal now, in case you haven't heard."

"You're right about that. But you jumped probation before that happened. The warrant isn't for the pot charge. It's for the probation violation. You understand? The warrant's still good and that's why you're sitting here."

"I understand that it's complete bullshit."

"Well, I can't say I disagree with you, but the bottom line is there's an arrest warrant that's got your name on it. I think there's a way we can take care of it and not have to send you over to the county jail. But you've got to work with me here, Duncan."

"Work with you how? What the fuck is this?"

"Give me your hands and I'll take the cuffs off. Then we can talk."

Forbes reached his hands across the table and Stilwell pulled out his keys and freed him.

"Okay, let's talk," he said. "First of all, I'm Detective Sergeant Stilwell and—"

"Talk about what, man?" Forbes said. "I was minding my own fucking business over there when they show up and haul my ass away."

"First things first. If you want to talk to me and get back over to Two Harbors tonight, you have to waive your rights."

"What the fuck? You can't be serious. This is a trap."

Stilwell didn't answer. He turned over a piece of paper that he had placed on the table after clearing out the room. He read the Miranda admonishment off it and then looked at Forbes.

"Do you understand your rights as they have been read to you?" he asked.

"What if I say no?" Forbes asked.

"Then you're on the Express to the mainland and county jail.

I'll alert the probation department and they'll handle it from there. You'll need to get yourself a lawyer."

"Oh, man, I can't do that. I don't have that kind of money."

"Did you listen to what I just read you? If you can't afford an attorney, one will be appointed to represent you."

"And how long is that shit going to take?"

"A few days, at least."

"And I'm sitting in county for some bullshit warrant? Nah, man, I ain't doing that shit."

"Look, all I can tell you is I can't talk to you or help you until you tell me that you understand your rights and that you waive them."

"Okay, whatever, I waive."

"Answer the question, Duncan. Do you understand your rights as I have read them to you?"

"Yes, yes, I understand. And I waive. Let's get whatever this is over with."

Stilwell pulled a pen from his pocket and told Forbes he had to sign the rights form he had just read from. Forbes grabbed the pen and scribbled a signature.

"Okay?" he said. "Can we do this now?"

"We can sure try," Stilwell said.

"Then ask your questions."

"Let's start with Leigh-Anne Moss. Tell me how you know her."

"Who?"

Forbes shook his head and spread his hands. Stilwell studied his reaction. He saw no tell that would indicate Forbes knew the name or was anything other than surprised by the question.

"Leigh-Anne Moss," Stilwell said again. "You know her."

Once again, he didn't pose it as a question.

"I got news for you, Deputy Doo-Dah," Forbes said. "I know no one named Leigh-Anne Moss. That was easy. Can I go now?"

"Not quite," Stilwell said. "You work on the *Emerald Sea,* right?"

"Sometimes, yeah. When I'm needed. It's a part-time gig."

"What do you do for this part-time gig?"

"I keep it clean and I help the guy who owns it sail it back and forth from MDR. That's it. What's it got to do with this bullshit warrant?"

Stilwell ignored the question. He opened his laptop and pulled up the DMV photo of Leigh-Anne Moss. He turned the screen to face Forbes.

"You recognize her?" he asked.

"Sorry, no," Forbes said. "Is that the girl? Leigh-Anne?"

"You sure you don't know her, Duncan? You lie to me, and I'm just going to book you into county. I'll let your probation officer deal with the warrant. Those guys, they have awesome caseloads. You'll be lucky if your PO gets to you in a month."

"Fine, it's a zero-bail county. They haven't changed that yet."

"It's nice that you know that, Duncan, but the warrant's got a no-bail hold. You'll be in there till your PO decides to show up. And he won't be in any hurry."

"They can't do that. It's zero-bail."

"They can do it for violations of probation and parole. And they'll do it with you."

Stilwell could see the panic start to enter Forbes's eyes.

"Look, I'm not lying, man," Forbes said. "I don't know her. If I did, I would tell you, but I've never seen that girl in my life!"

"Purple streak in her hair?" Stilwell suggested.

"No, man, I don't fuckin' know her."

"Well, we're going to come back to her. Meantime, let's talk about you. Two weekends ago, where were you?"

"I don't know. I was here. No, two weeks ago I was fishing. We were booked the weekend before Memorial Day."

"We're talking about Saturday, May seventeenth."

"Yeah, the seventeenth. I was fishing."

"Fishing where?"

"We had clients. We were out the whole weekend. Up around Anacapa. We anchored off Frenchy's Saturday night. I got pictures on my phone."

Anacapa was one of the Channel Islands that included Catalina. It was to the north, was uninhabited, and was one of the smaller islands in the chain, but Stilwell knew Frenchy's Cove was a popular shelter up there where overnighters anchored.

"Okay, where's your phone?" Stilwell asked.

"I don't know," Forbes said. "Those two deputies took it from me. And by the way, neither one of them knows shit about running that Zodiac. I'm lucky they didn't flip it out there. And I was cuffed. I coulda drowned, man."

"Never mind the boat, Duncan. You're here, you're safe. When you say 'We had clients,' who are you talking about?"

"I crew on a boat at Two Harbors. Like with the *Emerald Sea,* but there's more work out there. It's fishing, not sailing."

"What boat?"

"It's called *Sea Mistress*. The captain is a guy named Tracey Bonnette. He'll vouch for me. We were out the whole weekend."

Stilwell stood up. "I'll be right back," he said.

He stepped out of the room and closed the door. He went to Lampley's desk and saw a property bag containing an iPhone, wallet, keys, and a thin fold of money. He opened the bag, took out the phone, and headed back to the interview room. As he sat down, he slid the phone across the table to Forbes.

"Unlock it," he said.

"I'll show you," said Forbes.

"Just unlock it and give it back. I have the same phone. I'll find the photos."

Forbes tapped in a combination to open the phone. Stilwell caught the sequence — 112392 — and knew it was his birthday.

Forbes slid the phone back across the table, and Stilwell opened the Photos app. He tapped the All Photos button and was presented with a gridwork of pictures he could scroll back through by date. When he got to May 17, he opened one of the photos and saw the stern of a sport-fishing boat crowded with smiling men holding up their catch. Halibut, yellowtail, lingcod, and calico bass — they'd had a good day on the water.

Stilwell used his thumb to slide through the other photos from the outing. Forbes was not in any of them, but it was his phone and it was likely he had been the photographer. One of the photos had been taken from an up angle and captured the boat captain — Bonnette, he assumed — looking down from the helm on the bridge. He wore mirrored sunglasses. Stilwell used his fingers to expand the photo, and in the mirrored lenses he saw a reflection of the photographer. It was Forbes.

The last photo in the day's set showed a sunset from what Stilwell assumed was Frenchy's Cove on Anacapa. The time stamp said *May 17, 7:52 p.m.* He moved on to the photos taken on May 18, and there were shots of men holding up fish and cans of beer. He also came across a selfie taken by Forbes on the bridge, where he was steering the boat. The time stamp on that shot read *May 18, 10:13 a.m.*

Stilwell thought it was a near-perfect alibi, even though there were several hours between the sunset shot on Saturday and the first photos of fishing Sunday. It could possibly be argued that Forbes had made his way back to Avalon during those hours, taken the skiff from the Black Marlin Club to the *Emerald Sea* in the middle of the night, and gotten back to Anacapa in time for a morning of fishing. But Stilwell put the chances of that at slim to none. He believed Forbes was telling the truth.

21

NO LONGER A person of interest, Forbes was now a witness. Stilwell had to rethink and retool his approach. The interrogation had become an interview. He started by telling Forbes what the man wanted to hear.

"I'm going to go to bat for you, Duncan," he said. "I'll talk to probation and the DA's office about making this warrant go away. I'll tell them you've been very cooperative in this investigation."

"It's such bullshit," Forbes said. "They better fix it."

"Well, the more you help me, the better the chance of that happening."

"But I told you, I don't know anything about that girl."

"That's fine. But I want to talk to you about the *Emerald Sea*."

"What about it?"

"You sailed the boat back to Marina del Rey this past Monday, right?"

"Monday morning, yeah."

"How did that get set up?"

"The way it always does. The owner, Mr. Colbrink, just called me and said he wanted to take it back across. That was Sunday — he wanted to go Sunday. But I was working on the *Mistress* and told him I couldn't. He then said Monday morning and I said I could do that."

"Why did he want to leave in the middle of the holiday weekend?"

"He just said it was too crowded."

"So, on Monday, was it just you two on the boat?"

Forbes hesitated. He leaned back and scanned the confines of the room, his eyes eventually going to the camera mounted in the corner over Stilwell's left shoulder.

"Man, this could cost me my job with Mr. Colbrink."

"Everything in an investigation is kept confidential, Duncan."

"You mean until it isn't."

"Look, I told you. You want my help with the warrant, you gotta help me. I'm asking you, was it just you and Colbrink on the trip back to Marina del Rey?"

"No. He had a lady friend who went back with us."

"Who was that?"

"I don't know. I'm just the hired help. He didn't make any introductions. I heard him call her Bree, I think. Or Breezy. I think both, maybe."

"And she had stayed on the boat with him over the weekend?"

"Yeah, I guess so. I got there Monday, and so I only know about Monday."

"How old is Bree or Breezy?"

"At least forty."

Forbes had confirmed information Stilwell had gotten from Colbrink during the ride from the mansion in Malibu to the boat in Marina del Rey. But the confirmation served to raise Stilwell's confidence in Forbes's truthfulness.

"I want to show you something," Stilwell said.

He typed a few commands into the laptop and opened the video Tash had emailed him of the skiff moving from the

BMC to the *Emerald Sea,* then turned the screen so Forbes could see it.

"Who do you think that is?" he asked.

Forbes watched the video to the end of the clip before responding.

"I don't know, man," he said. "That's weird."

"Is it Mason Colbrink?" Stilwell asked.

"I doubt it. That time stamp right? This on the eighteenth?"

"Yes, the eighteenth."

"But you were just asking me about this past weekend."

"I'm asking you about both weekends. Look at the video. Could that be Mason Colbrink?"

"I doubt it."

"Why?"

"Because I don't think he was on the island then."

"Okay, well, whoever the guy is, what do you think he's doing?"

"No idea. Probably trying to steal shit."

Stilwell turned the computer back around and closed it. He hadn't considered that the man on the skiff might be taking things from the boats in the harbor. It was a reminder of how easily tunnel vision could hijack an investigation.

"Why do you say that?" he asked.

"Well, because there was some shit missing."

"From where?"

"The *Emerald Sea.*"

"Like what?"

"An anchor, for one."

"What else?"

"Somebody fucked around with the sails. Dumped one of them out of its bag and then I couldn't find the bag."

"Anything else?"

"Nah, I think that was all."

"Where was the anchor taken from?"

"It was a spare that was kept in a locker with the stern anchor."

"Did you notice the missing anchor and sail bag or did Colbrink?"

"On Monday when we got the boat back to MDR, I cleaned it up and opened up the lockers because of mold. I always let everything air out—Mr. Colbrink has a big thing about mold on the boat. So I opened the hatches and I saw stuff was missing or fucked with."

"What did you do about it?"

"Well, Mr. Colbrink has an account at the ship's store over there. I went over and got replacements."

"What's the name of the store?"

"Topsail Chandlery. Mr. Colbrink lets me sign on the account for supplies and stuff."

"Did you tell him about the anchor and the sail bag?"

"Not yet. I actually kind of forgot. I left my phone at Two Harbors that day, so I was going to call him when I got back, but then I forgot. Anyway, he doesn't really care about that stuff. He just wants the boat to be ready and clean for the next time he goes out, and he wants no sign that anybody else has been on it."

"Meaning what?"

"Like in case his wife checks the boat out. He doesn't want any lipstick on the glasses in the galley, extra toothbrushes in the head. Like that."

Stilwell nodded. Forbes was helping things fall into place in the investigation, but the information didn't move Stilwell any closer to figuring out who the man on the skiff was or who had used the anchor and sail bag from the *Emerald Sea* to submerge the body of a young woman.

"All right, Duncan," he said. "I want you to think hard. Was there anything else missing or unusual about the boat when you went through it to clean?"

Forbes slowly shook his head.

"No, man," he said. "I can't think of anything."

"Okay, let's back up for a second," Stilwell said. "Think about when you were cleaning the boat. Where did you start?"

"I always start inside—the forward cabins—and then I back my way out, you know? I do the deck and wipe all of the topside stainless last."

"Okay, start with the cabins. Nothing unusual or out of place?"

"Not that I remember."

"No toothbrush to get rid of?"

"Nah, not this time."

"Then what, the salon? Is that what you call it?"

Stilwell was using a well-worn and effective interview technique of taking a witness back through what was perceived as a mundane experience and drawing out details with questions that moved the story moment by moment.

"There was the usual," Forbes said. "Dishes in the sink. I cleaned it all, put everything on the rack. I took out the trash and then mopped."

"Where'd you get the mop?" Stilwell asked.

"There's a closet in the galley where the cleaning supplies are."

He snapped his fingers as he remembered something.

"That's right," he said. "The mop head was missing, and I never leave it that way."

"Explain that to me," Stilwell pressed.

"Last thing I do is either bleach the mop head or put on a new one so it's clean and good to go for next time. Mr. Colbrink likes everything super-clean. He's a germophobe. He's always got the hand sanitizer, and he wipes his phone constantly. Half the time, he's wearing a mask. Even on the boat. He was the one who told me to always keep a clean mop. If you start with a dirty mop, you're not gonna get a clean boat. He told me that the first day he hired me like six years ago."

Stilwell recalled that when they'd driven from Malibu to the marina the night before, Colbrink had put on a mask.

"So the mop head was missing," he said.

"Right," Forbes said. "I had to put a new one on, and that isn't how I leave things."

Stilwell was thinking about how this seemingly insignificant detail about the mop fit with his evolving theory of the crime.

"Is that important?" Forbes asked.

Stilwell came out of his reverie.

"Uh, it could be," he said. "Every detail counts. You remember anything else? Did you find the mop head that was missing in the trash or somewhere?"

"No, it was just gone."

"Okay. Were any other cleaning tools used?"

"Yeah, I had to open a new bottle of Three-Oh-Three," Forbes said.

"What's Three-Oh-Three?"

"It's the marine cleaner I put in the bucket for the mop. Somebody left an empty bottle in the supply cabinet, so I opened another."

Stilwell felt another charge go through his chest.

"What happened to the empty bottle?" he asked.

"It got tossed with the stuff from the fridge I cleaned out," Forbes said.

Stilwell's hope for a surface containing fingerprints was immediately dashed.

"You mean you took it to a dumpster or something at the marina?" he asked.

"Yeah, they have trash cans there," Forbes said. "At the end of the dock."

Stilwell nodded. He thought he had gotten from Forbes everything he could in a first-round interview.

"Okay, we're going to take a break," he said. "I'm going to call your PO and see what we can do about the warrant. You can stay here or I can put you in a cell where there's a bed if you want to lie down. I don't know how long it's going to take me to work this out."

"Man, can't you just let me split?" Forbes pleaded. "I mean, you know where I live. I'm not going to take off or anything."

Stilwell shook his head.

"Can't," he said. "You were officially taken into custody. I can't just let you walk out without clearing this up. So, here or the cell?"

"I guess I'll take the cell," Forbes said dejectedly.

"Good choice."

"It doesn't seem like it."

"Let's go."

Stilwell stood up, opened the door to the room, and led Forbes out and toward the jail. He put him in the cell next to the one where Merris Spivak was still detained. Cell two had been emptied of the three other men arrested over the holiday weekend, as one had made bail and Monika Juarez had declined to file charges on the other two—an unofficial sentence of time served. After locking Forbes in, Stilwell moved down the bars to cell one to check in on Spivak, who was lying on his back on a bunk. Without looking over at Stilwell, Spivak raised a middle finger to him.

"Still not talking, Spivak?" Stilwell asked.

"I don't talk to cops," Spivak said.

"You know we're going to find out."

"Find out what?"

"How you know Deputy Dunne."

"I don't know what you're talking about, boss."

"Yes, you do. It was Pitchess, wasn't it? I know you were both there at the same time. What did he do to you that would make you blindside him like that?"

"Didn't we have this conversation? I'm not telling you jack, Jack."

"Yeah, well, assaulting a law enforcement officer on camera — you won't be going back to Pitchess this time, Spivak. You're going upstate. See how that works for you."

Spivak gave another middle-finger salute, this time shaking his hand intensely as if that would make the move more insulting. Stilwell just nodded and headed back to the bullpen to call the state probation office.

22

THE CASE OFFICER who had put out the warrant on Duncan Forbes for violation of probation was long retired. It took Stilwell fifteen minutes and four different phone calls to locate the inheritor of the long dormant and inconsequential file. His name was Rodney Willingham and he worked out of a satellite office in the south county. Stilwell's first two calls were diverted to a message center that reported that Willingham's message box was full. He finally got through to him on the third call.

"Willingham."

"Uh, yeah, this is Detective Stilwell with the sheriff's department. I got a guy here on one of your warrants."

"Case number?"

"Fifteen-dash-seven—"

"Whoa, whoa, whoa—you're talking about 2015?"

"I am."

"You gotta hold on, then."

"How long?"

"Let me just get my computer going."

Stilwell heard the phone clunk down on a desk and waited. He heard typing and then Willingham picked up the phone and asked for the case number again. Stilwell gave it to him, heard typing, and then Willingham started reading from his screen.

"Forbes, Duncan. Violated May third, 2015."

"That's him."

"This is a chickenshit case. Just book him and I'll eventually make my way to him."

"That's what I want to talk to you about. I want you to drop the violation and lose the warrant."

"Now, why would I do that—what did you say your name was?"

"Stilwell. I need you to drop it because Forbes is an important witness in a case I'm working."

"Really, now. What case?"

Stilwell had hoped he wouldn't ask that. He had to have high stakes to convince Willingham to drop the warrant. Telling him it was a theft investigation wouldn't cut it. Stilwell needed more gravity than that, but he knew if he mentioned the murder, he would be creating one more witness to his crossing the lines of authority.

"It's a homicide," Stilwell said. "And I need Forbes clean when he testifies. I don't want him on the stand wearing Wayside blues. You understand, Rodney?"

Wayside was the former name of the Pitchess Detention Center, and Stilwell used it to signal to Willingham that he had been around the system for a long time and knew that the probation officer could do what he wanted him to do.

"I understand," Willingham said. "It says here he stopped coming in to piss and skipped out on his rehab sessions. This mofo's a regular douchebag."

"I know all of that. He told me. But this was on a bust for something that's not even illegal anymore. It's chickenshit. You said it; you know it. So can you do me a solid on it or not?"

"Oh, yeah, I can do you a solid. The question is, what are you going to do for me?"

Stilwell shook his head. It seemed that everybody wanted something from him.

"I don't know you, Rodney. What do you want?"

"Tell you what, I'm gonna keep this number — this your cell?"

"Yes, it's my cell."

"Then I'm gonna keep your number and call you next time I need a pickup, and I don't want you to shine me on like you all like to do over there at the sheriff's. I'll say I got a guy needs to be tossed back into county and you have to help me go get him. That's when you say, 'I'm on it, Rodney.'"

Willingham had no idea that Stilwell was posted on Catalina, twenty-two miles from the mainland and even farther from the sheriff's homicide bureau. Willingham was thinking a downtown deputy would owe him a favor.

"I can do that," Stilwell said. "Deal."

"All right, then, we good," Willingham said. "We good."

"So I can let Forbes walk?"

"You can set him free."

"Beautiful. Thank you."

"Have a good one. And remember, I'm going to call you."

"Anytime."

Stilwell disconnected the call. He unlocked his desk drawer and removed his sidearm. He holstered the weapon and got up to release Forbes. But the desk phone buzzed on his direct line and the read-out said SHERIFF'S HOMICIDE. He sat back down and took the call.

"Stillborn," he heard.

"A-Hole," he said. "What do you want?"

"What I want is to take your badge, and this time I think I've got it."

"You haven't got shit, Ahearn. Why don't you try to work on the case instead of on me?"

"I am working the case, and guess who I just talked to?"

"I don't know, Ahearn, but I'm sure you're dying to tell me."

"Your pal Peter Galloway, and he told me all about you knocking on his door last night. He almost didn't talk to me because he said he already told you everything he knew about the girl."

"Yeah, that's bullshit."

"No, you're bullshit. You fucking crossed the line, Stillborn, and I can prove it. I already went to Corum, and he's got everything he needs to bench your ass. And that will be only the first step."

"Ahearn, listen to me, I can help you. I have information, but you told me to fuck off. Now, if you want to close the case, let's share what we've—"

"We're not partners and you're not homicide. You're going to be a nobody as soon as Corum takes your badge. And you know what, I'm going to see if I can mount it on the wall here over my desk."

"You're pathetic, Ahearn. You'd put your shit with me over solving—"

He stopped. Ahearn had hung up on him. He sat still, trying to control the anger that was welling up in him. The phone buzzed again and he saw that it was another call from the homicide bureau. He answered with a full head of steam.

"I said, you're pathetic. You'd put our shit ahead of closing the case when I—"

"This is Denise from Captain Corum's office."

Stilwell realized his mistake.

"Oh, um, sorry, I thought it was some—"

"Captain Corum would like you to come in today for a meeting. What time can I schedule it?"

"Uh...can I talk to the captain?"

"He asked me to set this up."

"I'm not coming in, Denise. So please put him on the phone. I'll hold."

"Very well."

She put Stilwell on hold and he rehearsed what he would say to the captain if Corum took his call.

A solid five minutes went by before Denise came back on and said the captain would be with Stilwell shortly. She hit the hold button again and Stilwell wondered if Corum was really tied up or simply playing a power game and making Stilwell wait.

When Corum finally came on the line, he came with fire.

"Goddamn it, Stil. I put you out there so you would be below the radar, and what do you do? You take out your dick and piss all over the place."

"Captain, you've only heard one side of this thing. I can practically give Ahearn the case, but he's only interested in burning me, not closing a murder."

"That's where you're wrong. It's not your case to give, but you're off the island, running all over the county chasing it. You give me no choice here, Stil."

"Can I explain something before you decide whatever you're going to decide?"

"I don't know what good it will do, but go ahead, say your piece."

"Is Ahearn there? Sounds like I'm on speaker."

There was a pause before Corum confirmed the obvious.

"He's here but I told him to keep quiet," he said. "Now, do you want to explain or not?"

"Sure, and I'm glad he's there," Stilwell said. "So he can fucking listen and stay quiet."

"Fuck you, Stillborn," Ahearn said.

"Ahearn, enough," Corum said. "Stil, go ahead."

Stilwell took a deep breath, tried to clear the image of Ahearn's smug face out of his mind, and began.

"On Saturday we received a report of a theft of a supposedly priceless piece of art from the Black Marlin Club out here," he said.

"A painting?" Corum asked.

"No, a small sculpture of a black marlin. It was taken from a display in the main hallway of the club, where it had been for almost a hundred years. Do you know anything about this club, Captain?"

"I've heard of it, yes. People with money and power."

"Exactly. So, the report was taken by Deputy Dunne and it got lost for a couple days because Dunne was the deputy who got assaulted Saturday night and he's out with a concussion. The report didn't cross my desk till yesterday, and then I started working it."

"What's this have to do with you coming over here and interviewing witnesses in the murder case?"

"I'm going to get to that, Captain, if you let me tell the story."

"Go ahead, but I don't have all day here. You need to land the plane."

"I went to the BMC and talked to the general manager, who had made the initial report. His name is Crane and he said no one noticed the sculpture was missing till Saturday, when he made the report, but that it had likely been gone a week. Then he pointed the finger at an employee he had fired the week before, Leigh-Anne Moss. He said he suspected that she stole the statue on her way out of the club right after he fired her."

"Fired for what?"

"He said she was fraternizing with the members and that's a big no-no."

"Okay, go on."

"Well, I ran down Leigh-Anne Moss and learned that she had a dyed streak of purple in her hair. I'd seen the victim we pulled out of the harbor, so I put two and two together and called Ahern to give him the name. He invited me to fuck off, to use his words. So I did and kept going with my case. But everywhere I went, it rubbed up against the harbor case."

"That true? He gave you the name?" Corum said.

Stilwell knew he was speaking to Ahearn.

"He mentioned the name," Ahearn said. "But we made the ID through DMV on a thumbprint. I go to the address on her DMV, and the boyfriend tells me the sheriff's already been there. Still-born should have called me before he even got on the ferry."

"Did you not tell him to fuck off?" Corum asked. "And stop using that name. I find it offensive."

"I meant stay the fuck away from my case, and he didn't," Ahearn responded.

"Jesus Christ, what am I going to do with you two!" Corum erupted. "Stilwell, did you take it further than that?"

Stilwell paused to compose a truthful answer as well as open a path through this thicket that would allow him to keep his job.

"There are no cameras in the BMC, so there was no way of confirming who stole the sculpture from the display," he said. "But I went over to the harbormaster's tower and reviewed video from the harbor cams that had angles on the club. I saw something suspicious on the night after Moss was fired and the theft presumably occurred. This involved a boat that belonged to a member of the club. A man named Mason Colbrink. He lives in Malibu. I followed that up and just this morning confirmed that both an anchor and a sail bag had been taken from the boat and replaced with new ones."

"You have a suspect?" Corum said urgently.

"No. Colbrink and his one-man crew, a guy named Duncan Forbes who lives out here, both seem to have pretty solid alibis for that whole weekend," Stilwell said.

"So, then, what's your theory?" Corum pushed.

"I think Leigh-Anne Moss was killed inside the Black Marlin Club," Stilwell said. "Then her body was put on the boat in the middle of the night and the next day taken out of the harbor.

The body was put in the sail bag, weighted with the anchor, and dumped out in the bay. The underwater currents brought her back in once the body began to bloat."

Stilwell heard Ahearn make a derisive chortle. He didn't respond to it, but Corum did.

"All right, let's stop there," he said. "You did good work on this, Stil, but it's a homicide and it's not your case. There are special circumstances because you're over there and the case is over there and you know the lay of the land. I want you part of the investigation. How soon can you get back here to get in a room with these guys? You need to hash this out and decide next —"

"We don't need him," Ahearn interrupted. "Sampedro and I can handle the case."

"He's already jumped the case four moves ahead of you," Corum said. "This is a perfect setup. You'll have him on the island. He knows the people out there. He's inside the wire."

"We can handle it," Ahearn insisted.

"Are you forgetting who's in command of this unit?" Corum asked.

"No, sir," Ahearn replied meekly.

"This is not a suggestion," Corum said. "It's an order."

"Yes, sir," Ahearn said, his voice almost inaudible over the speaker.

Stilwell wished he could see Ahearn's face.

"We're talking about a murder here, gentlemen," Corum continued. "Put aside your petty differences, get your heads out of your asses, and get the job done. If you can't do it, I will find people who can. Am I clear?"

"Clear," Stilwell said.

"As glass," Ahearn said.

"Stil, how soon can you get over here?" Corum asked.

"I'll jump on the next Express," Stilwell said.

"Good," Corum said. "I'll have Ahearn and Sampedro meet you at the dock to drive you in."

"I've got a car in a lot over there."

"Let me send them. By the time you're back here, I expect you three to be working like a well-oiled machine. I hear anything suggesting otherwise, there will be consequences. That's it."

The call was disconnected. Stilwell sat at the desk unmoving for nearly a minute. He was apprehensive about the setup. He didn't expect Ahearn to change his attitude toward him, but he was pleased to be officially on the case. He thought of the woman with the purple streak in her hair and how someone had taken away her hopes and dreams of a better life. Stilwell knew he could put up with Ahearn and Sampedro as long as together they brought her killer to justice.

23

FRANK SAMPEDRO WAS waiting for Stilwell at the Express dock in Long Beach. He was leaning against a gray plain-wrap, his arms folded across his barrel chest. He was over six feet and stocky. His suits were always ill-fitting — baggy in the shoulders, too wide at the waist. He dyed his hair and mustache jet-black. As soon as he saw Stilwell approaching, he pushed himself off the car and went around to the driver's door without a greeting.

Ahearn hadn't made the trip, which pleased Stilwell because no cop likes to sit in the back seat of a car that has transported all manner of miscreants, but he wondered what that meant in regard to Corum's well-oiled machine. Even so, it was a relief to Stilwell that he would not have to spend the next hour driving up to the homicide unit in downtown Los Angeles listening to Ahearn's insults and threats.

Starting out, Sampedro kept quiet. But once they got up on the 110 and were heading downtown, he unexpectedly opened up.

"Look, just so you know, I got partnered with Rex after you left," he said. "So all I've ever heard was his side of things, you know what I mean?"

A crack in the partnership; Stilwell hadn't seen that before.

"I do," he said. "And I know just what he said about me and that case."

"Yeah, well, there you go," Sampedro replied. "But like the captain said, we got *this* case to solve, so I'm putting all of that other stuff to the side. Seems like you've done some good work on this so far. Let's keep it going."

"Does that mean you were also in Corum's office during the call today?"

"I was. He wanted us both in there."

It annoyed Stilwell that Corum had not told him anyone else was on the call until he had asked, but it worked out. Stilwell was on the case, which was where he wanted to be. He took Sampedro's olive branch as sincere and a good sign. It made him think that he could work on an equal level with him at least, if not with Ahearn.

After a few more minutes of silence, Sampedro brought up the case about which he knew only one side of the story.

"Just to clear the air, what I heard was that you thought there was a murder case against a guy, and Rex, who was lead on it, said there wasn't. Said it was self-defense. He took it to the DA's office and they signed off on it as self-defense. Then you tried to make an end run around them, and the shit hit the fan."

"That's putting it mildly. But to clear the air, as you say, I'll tell you exactly what happened. I flat out accused him of taking a dive on the case."

"That's a pretty strong statement."

"Yeah, well, it's the truth. You ever know a guy named Carl Dobbin? He was a deputy worked out of Lennox until they caught him on camera shaking down street dealers for cash and coke."

"I didn't know him. Never worked Lennox, but they had a lot of problems down there with that kind of stuff."

"They did, and IAB came in and cleaned it up. Dobbin was one of the guys that got washed out. That was seven, maybe eight, years ago."

"Okay, so what did he have to do with the case you and Rex locked horns on?"

"Everything. After he left the department, Dobbin was able to get a PI ticket because they let him retire with a clean record. Then two years ago, he ends up killing a guy in a divorce case he was working. He claimed self-defense, said that the guy he was following confronted him and pulled a gun, but Dobbin pulled his and got off the first shot. Because he was an ex-deputy, our whole team rolled out on the case. So I was there that night. Ahearn was lead but I worked the first night. I got next-of-kin duty on the dead man. I went to his sister's house to notify her that he was dead, and she told me she believed it was a setup. Her brother had told her he thought his soon-to-be ex was going to try to kill him so she'd get all the money."

"You believed her?"

"I believed the claim should have been investigated, but Ahearn didn't do it. He just took Dobbin at his word and presented the case to the DA as a self-defense. The DA signed off and that was it. Then, guess what: I get a call from the sister. She still has my card from when I made the notification. She's absolutely livid because Ahearn never talked to her and never even looked into her suspicions that it was an orchestrated hit."

"So, let me guess — you did."

"Yeah, I did some digging. The gun the dead guy supposedly pointed at Dobbin had been reported stolen ten years before. I pulled the records because Ahearn had never checked. It was stolen during a burglary in Lennox, and guess who took the initial report."

"Dobbin?"

"Yeah, Dobbin. The gun was listed on a supplemental report. The house had been ransacked, tons of stuff taken, and the owner wasn't initially sure what all he had lost. So, two days later, he comes into the substation in Lennox with a whole list of stuff he said was gone, and the gun was on that list."

"Your theory was that Dobbin piggybacked on the burglary, that he saw the gun when he was there to take the report and grabbed it?"

"Pretty much. Then he kept it in his sock in case he ever needed a throwdown. He eventually gets booted out, gets his private ticket, and this shooting goes down. The stolen gun ends up in the dead man's hand."

Stilwell let that sink in for a few moments before continuing.

"There was a lot at stake in the divorce," he said. "The dead guy was a former gangbanger and drug dealer who'd turned completely legit and invested in businesses all over South L.A. There was a lot of money on the table that he didn't want to split with the wife. So the wife hired Dobbin to supposedly get the goods on him to use as leverage. But what if Dobbin told her he could make it so there was no money split and she got it all?"

"You know what I call that? A lot of coincidence and conjecture."

"I'm not arguing with that, but it should have been investigated and it wasn't. Ahearn either took a dive or just looked the other way. I did some digging on that too, and it turns out Ahearn and Dobbin were in the same academy class. They went way back. So now you have another coincidence, and that is one too many not to be looking at this."

"You go to the captain with it?"

"Nope, and that was my mistake. I went straight to IAB when I should have started with Corum."

"And the bureau took a pass."

"They used the same words you did —*coincidence and conjecture*. That's what our vaunted Internal Affairs Bureau said. It went no further. Ahearn ended up with an 'unfounded complaint' in his jacket and I got sent to the Island of Misfit Toys. End of story."

"Till now."

"Till now. Ahearn has the ding in his jacket that he blames me for and he can't see past it to properly work the case. His ass must be burned that Corum is making us work together."

"He's not too happy, but he's a professional. It'll be fine."

"I'm glad one of us thinks so."

"What was your thinking back then? That Dobbin paid Ahearn off?"

"Or he just looked the other way for an academy pal. And once he did that, Dobbin owned him. But I don't really care which it was, and for the record, I didn't care too much about the dead ex–drug dealer either. But Dobbin is still out there and people who get away with stuff tend to think they can do it again."

Sampedro drove in silence for a few more moments before speaking.

"I appreciate the detail," he said.

"And I appreciate the position you're in," Stilwell said. "I want you to know, on this thing, I'm all about the woman in the water. That's it. I'm not interested in tangling with Ahearn about that old case. I want to close *this* case."

"Good to know."

Stilwell didn't mean all of what he had said, but he guessed that Sampedro would eventually summarize the conversation to Ahearn. That was what partners did. It would hopefully put Ahearn at ease so that the Leigh-Anne Moss investigation could proceed unfettered by the friction between them.

The homicide unit was in the old Hall of Justice building across Temple Street from the Criminal Courts Building. Stilwell knew it well from his previous assignment there. Sampedro parked in the county garage and called Ahearn to say that they were on their way up. Ahearn was waiting in one of the conference rooms. He had already wheeled in a whiteboard with *Leigh-Anne Moss* written in red at the top. There were a few dates and other notations beneath it and then a line drawn down the center of the board separating the headings *Catalina* and *County*. Ahearn clearly understood that there was work to do on both sides of the bay.

Ahearn said nothing when Stilwell and Sampedro entered. He was sitting at the oval table at the center of the room in the chair closest to the whiteboard — a signal that he was in charge of deciding what went on it. Stilwell noticed a stack of documents at the seat farthest from the board and understood that this was his spot. The stack appeared to be copies of documents produced by the Ahearn-Sampedro team during the first five days of the investigation, with the preliminary autopsy report on top. Stilwell took that as a good start to the fraught partnership and sat down in his designated chair.

"That's all the documentation on the case so far," Ahearn confirmed. "What I'd like to do with this meeting is establish clear lines of responsibility for all three of us and map out our next moves."

Stilwell could have easily said that this was already the directive from Captain Corum but he decided not to poke Ahearn. He nodded instead.

"Stilwell, you seem to have the inside track on this — at least according to the captain," Ahearn said. "So why don't you start. What should Frank and I be doing? What are you going to do?"

Stilwell noted that it might have been the first time in years that Ahearn had addressed him by his correct name. Another sign of cooperation.

"Well, since you have it divided between here and there, I

think there are a few things over here that we need to do right off the bat," he began. "The boat I mentioned on the call with the captain is called the *Emerald Sea*. It's a forty-foot ketch that is currently docked at the California Yacht Club in Marina del Rey. I've talked to the owner, Mason Colbrink, and he agreed to stay off it until we can get a forensics team in there to process it."

Ahearn got up and wrote the boat's name down in the *County* column. He stayed standing.

"What are we looking for?" he asked.

Stilwell knew he had to protect Monty West at the coroner's office.

"I haven't seen the autopsy," he said. "Was the victim cut? Any indication of blood loss?"

"Frank took the autopsy," Ahearn said.

"Cause of death is blunt-force trauma," Sampedro said. "She was bludgeoned with an unknown object prior to death. Head wounds are usually bleeders. Of course, with the body being in the water for several days, we lost all trace of that."

"There's a guy on Catalina who crews on the *Emerald Sea*," Stilwell said. "I talked to him this morning and he said that when he cleaned the boat after bringing it back to the marina on Monday, he found that somebody had taken the spare anchor and a sail bag. He also said a mop head was missing."

Ahearn turned to the board and wrote *crime scene* under the name of the boat.

"We'll get forensics out there," he said.

"But he cleaned the boat?" Sampedro asked.

"He did," Stilwell said. "Which means it was cleaned twice — once by whoever used the mop, then by him."

"We still have to let forensics do their thing," Ahearn said. "If there's blood, they'll find it."

"The crew guy also said he found an empty bottle of a boat

cleaner called Three-Oh-Three," Stilwell said. "But he threw it away. It was probably handled during the first cleaning."

"Dumpster-diving," Ahearn said. "That's Frank's area of expertise."

"Yeah, fuck that," Sampedro said.

"My guy said he put it and stuff from the boat's cooler into a trash can at the end of the dock," Stilwell said.

Ahearn wrote *303* on the board and then turned back to Stilwell.

"So, Stilwell, what's your kill theory?" he asked.

"You really want to hear it?" Stilwell asked.

"Of course we do," Ahearn said. "We're a team, remember?"

It was said with full snark, which Stilwell ignored.

"Like I said on the call with the captain, I think she was killed in the Black Marlin Club with the jade sculpture," he said. "Her body was hidden in there somewhere until the middle of the night, when it was moved to the *Emerald Sea*. The next day, it was taken out to the bay and dumped."

"In broad daylight?" Sampedro asked.

"It's twenty-plus miles from the coast," Stilwell said. "A lot of open water out there once you're out of the harbor."

"And you're saying the current just brought her back in?" Ahearn asked. "Like some kind of underwater ghost returning to haunt the scene of the crime?"

Ahearn had dropped the snark but put in a note of disbelief.

"I don't know about underwater ghosts, but I do think the tide brought her back," Stilwell said. "Avalon Harbor has a wide mouth and strong tidal currents."

"Well, I do like a wide mouth," Ahearn said. "Okay, what else?"

"Like, where's the jade statue?" Sampedro asked.

"Probably ended up in the bay with her," Stilwell said.

"That was stupid," Sampedro said. "If she was killed at the club, why wouldn't the killer just clean it up and put it back?"

"I was thinking about that," Stilwell said. "Maybe he panicked. It's possible none of this was planned. Or maybe the thing broke when he hit her. Then he couldn't put it back."

"It's all conjecture until we know more," Ahearn said. "We need something solid to move on right now."

"Her cell phone," Stilwell said. "She had to have had one and it also probably ended up in the bay when she was dumped. But we need to get her calls, texts, and contacts. And the GPS might give us the location where she went into the water."

Ahearn wrote *cell* on the board on the County side.

"We'll take that," he said. "What else?"

"Leigh-Anne's friends," Stilwell said. "Anybody she might have told who she was involved with on the island and in that club. Hopefully her phone or Galloway can lead us to her friend group over here. And I still need to find out where she stayed on Catalina. There could also be dating apps and social media to check. My office manager found her on Instagram but the account hadn't been updated recently."

Ahearn put it all on the board, including the first additions to the Catalina column: *friends* and *address*.

"And then Colbrink, the guy who owns the boat," Stilwell said. "He's got an alibi for the weekend in question. Was over here in Malibu for his wife's birthday. We need to confirm all of that, and then we need to talk to his mistress, someone named Bree or maybe Breezy, who was on the boat with him on Catalina this past weekend. Maybe she saw something amiss on the boat. We just need to cover all the bases, and she's one of them."

Ahearn dutifully wrote it on the board on the County side.

"That's going to keep us busy," he said. "You're looking a little light, Stilwell. Anything else for over there?"

"Yeah," Stilwell said. "I've got to get into the Black Marlin Club."

"You're talking about a search warrant?" Ahearn asked. "Good luck with that."

"We'll see," Stilwell said. "I know a judge who might go for it."

24

AFTER SAMPEDRO DROPPED him off, Stilwell caught the last Express back to Catalina. It was dark by the time of his arrival at the pier. He stopped by the sub to pick up the Gator and check on things. He had to use a key to enter because the p.m. watch deputy wasn't there; he was likely out on patrol or answering a call. Stilwell checked his office and the bulletin board for messages and found none. He took a two-way out of a charger and, after consulting the personnel schedule on a separate bulletin board, radioed the deputy on duty.

"PM One, come up."

A few seconds later Deputy Eduardo Esquivel responded.

"Here, boss."

"What's your twenty?"

"Up at the Zane Grey for an eviction."

The Zane Grey was a boutique hotel and one of the better places to stay on the island. Having once been the home of the famed Western writer and sport fisherman, it was a major draw to the island as well. Though Catalina served as the last resort for many facing financial troubles, the Zane Grey was an establishment that attracted the more well-heeled visitors. Its proprietors rarely called the sub about problems with nonpaying guests.

"What's the story?" Stilwell asked. "You want backup?"

"Affirmative," Esquivel responded. "This guy is not going to go quietly, I don't think."

"On my way, then."

"Roger that."

Stilwell thought about grabbing his vest out of his locker but decided it might only serve to provoke a confrontation if the situation at the Zane Grey was simply a misunderstanding. He left it behind and headed for the door but stopped when he heard a shout come from the jail. Spivak was being held in a cell until his court appearance on Friday. Stilwell went back into the jail section and found Spivak standing with both hands gripping the bars.

"Hey, are you people going to feed me tonight or what?"

"You didn't get food?"

"Been waiting all night, man."

Esquivel had apparently forgotten his feeding duties. Stilwell checked his watch and saw that it was 8:20.

"Why don't you sit down, Spivak," he said. "I'll go look for something."

He walked quickly back through the bullpen to the kitchenette that was off the rear hallway. He started opening cabinets, looking for something he could give Spivak to tide him over until he or Esquivel could pick something up from one of the takeouts. He found two packs of Lance ToastChee crackers on a shelf marked *Dunne—Do Not Touch*. He took them off the shelf and back to the jail. Spivak was still at the bars.

"I told you to sit down," Stilwell said.

"I don't have to sit down," Spivak said. "I can do whatever I want in here. You call that shit in your hand dinner?"

"It's a snack, Spivak. Somebody will bring you dinner in a bit. Go sit down and relax. It's not even eight thirty and you'll get a hot meal soon."

Stilwell tossed the packages of crackers through the bars to the bunk he had seen Spivak using before. One package bounced off the bed and onto the floor.

"Now, see," Spivak said. "That's how they get crumbled."

"Just stay calm," Stilwell said. "Somebody will be back with dinner."

"You know, it's probably against the rules for you to leave me alone in this place. There could be a fire and nobody to get me out."

"Or a flash flood or even a tsunami."

"It's not a joke."

"Then you better start praying, Spivak. Because I'm leaving."

"I could fucking hang myself in here and then your ass would be on the line, I bet."

"Interesting idea. There would be a big investigation, I'm sure. But in the end it would come down to a guy who tried to kill a deputy with a wine bottle killing himself in a cell, and nobody will really give a shit. But I'm sure I'd get my wrists slapped, if that would make it worth it to you."

Stilwell grabbed the keys to the John Deere as he left and locked the sub. Spivak happened to be correct. It was a violation of regulations to leave someone in custody unsupervised. If anything happened, Stilwell would get more than a slap on the wrist. The irony was that the PM watch was down to one deputy because Spivak had put the second deputy, Dunne, out of commission.

The Zane Grey was up on Chimes Tower Road and it offered its guests one of the best views of the harbor by day or night. Stilwell saw Esquivel's UTV parked near the entrance. He found the lobby empty and the front desk unstaffed, but he heard raised voices from the right wing of the hotel and headed that way.

He saw Esquivel and another man standing in the hallway in front of the open door to one of the rooms. He joined them.

"What's happening, Eddie?" he asked.

"Sergeant, this is Fred Nettles, the night manager," Esquivel said. "And this is Mr. Starkey, who says he won't leave the room."

"When we charged the first night's stay on his credit card, it went through," Nettles said. "The second night was rejected and he said he would handle it. He didn't. The third night was rejected and now he's been here five nights and only paid for one."

"I'm fixing the problem!" Starkey yelled.

Starkey was the smallest of all four men, and Stilwell knew there was not going to be a problem removing him from the premises if push came to shove.

"I've been in constant communication with my bank and the credit card company," Starkey said. "They're processing payment, but it's well after hours on the East Coast and this won't be resolved until morning."

"He's been saying that for three days," Nettles said.

"You gotta go, man," Esquivel said. "You can't stay. You get it fixed, then you can come back."

"Where am I going to go?" Starkey yelled. "There are no more boats tonight and I can't check in anywhere else."

Stilwell tapped Nettles on the shoulder and nodded for him to follow. They walked down the hallway and out of Starkey's earshot. Stilwell spoke quietly.

"He's got a point," he said. "We kick him out now and he can't leave the island, and he can't check in anywhere if his credit card doesn't work."

"What are you saying?" Nettles said. "That I have to eat another night with him?"

"I want to give him till the morning. He gets it fixed and he pays you, or we escort him to the pier and he's gone."

"That feels like a big win for him and a big loss for me."

"I understand. Do you know anything about him? Like what he does for a living or what he's doing here."

"He says he's a writer. We get a lot of them here. Not all of them are *deadbeats*." He intentionally turned his head back toward Starkey's room as he barked out the last word.

"You're just making it worse," Stilwell said. "We're not going to remove him. So decide if you want to argue with him all night and disturb your other guests or give him the morning deadline."

Nettles shook his head in frustration.

"Banks open at nine," he said. "I'll give him till ten if you promise to come take him if he doesn't pay."

"You got it," Stilwell said. "I'll go tell him."

He walked down the hallway to the open door where Esquivel stood. There was no sign of Starkey.

"Where'd he go?" he asked.

"He's in there making a call, I think," Esquivel said.

Stilwell walked into the room, down a short entryway, and past the bathroom door. Starkey was sitting on the bed, the room's phone to his ear. Stilwell made a signal that he wanted to talk to him.

"I'm on hold," Starkey said.

"With who?" Stilwell asked.

"My agent. I'm trying to see if he'll pay."

"Mr. Starkey, the hotel has agreed to let you stay one more night. You have till ten tomorrow morning to settle your bill or we will evict you from the hotel and take you to the Express. Do you understand?"

"What if I pay? Do I still have to leave?"

"That will be between you and the hotel. But right now I need to hear you say that you understand that if you don't pay by ten a.m., you are leaving the hotel."

Starkey hung up the phone.

"I get it," he said. "And it won't be a problem. I just want to be left alone to write."

"That's fine, sir, but you need to pay for the room," Stilwell said. "I'll be back at ten tomorrow. I hope you get it fixed. Good night, Mr. Starkey. You want me to close the door?"

"Please. I've had enough of that man out there."

Stilwell left and pulled the door closed. Nettles was gone, and only Esquivel was waiting.

"We'll handle this in the morning," Stilwell said. "You can roll."

"Roger that," Esquivel said.

"Meantime, get our prisoner some food. He's hungry."

"Who, Spivak? I fed him."

"When?"

"About six. I got him a hamburger from Luau Larry's."

"Asshole tried to get another meal off me."

"Fuck him. He's fed."

"You didn't know him before the other night, did you?"

"No, why?"

"Just curious why he jumped in and hit Dunne. On tape it looks like he was targeting Dunne, like he knew him from somewhere. Was wondering if he knew you."

"Not as far as I know. Did you ask Dunne?"

"Yeah, but he's still fuzzy. Anyway, make sure you leave a report on this for day watch. I want the deadline on Starkey enforced. I'm heading home. I need you to get back to the sub and babysit Spivak. If you get a serious call — not bullshit like this — call me and I'll come in."

"Will do."

Stilwell took the Gator up to his house. Tash Dano was sitting in one of the Adirondacks on the front porch, a glass of red wine in her hand.

"How'd it go over there?" she asked.

"About what I expected," Stilwell said. "I'm on the case."

"That's good, right?"

"I'll take it."

"But you have to work with A-Hole?"

"Ahearn, yeah."

"That's the first time I've heard you call him by his real name."

"Yeah, well, he started calling me by my real name, so, you know..."

He took the glass from her hand and took a sip.

"There's more in the bottle," she said. "And half a chicken sandwich from the Sandtrap, if you're hungry."

It was Stilwell's favorite restaurant on the island. He nodded.

"Sounds perfect," he said.

He took another slug of wine and handed the glass back to her. He leaned down and they kissed.

"I need to take a shower," he said apologetically.

"I can wait," she said.

He went in through the open door. She soon followed.

25

STILWELL ATE THE sandwich from the Sandtrap in the morning with fresh-brewed coffee. He ate quickly, filled a Yeti with more coffee, and left the house early — while Tash was still asleep — to get to the sub to start working on a search warrant for the Black Marlin Club. He knew the probable cause statement would need to be bulletproof in order to get by Judge Harrell, but that would be only the first test it would face. If a case was ever built against a defendant in the Leigh-Anne Moss murder, the search warrant would be his lawyer's first stop in an effort to derail it, and that didn't even take into consideration the appeals that would very likely come later. Prosecutions often succeeded or failed based on the underpinnings of probable cause. Stilwell knew it and wasn't going to let his warrant be the Achilles' heel of this case.

Mercy was already at her desk when he got there.

"Good morning," she said cheerily.

"Morning, Mercy," Stilwell said. "I'm going to set up in my office today to do some writing work. Try to keep people off me if you can."

"Not a problem."

"Anything going on that I should know about?"

"All quiet except back there in the jail. That man can get on my last nerve."

Stilwell had forgotten about Spivak. He put the Yeti on the desk in his office and went back to the jail. Once again, Spivak was standing right at the bars like he was waiting for him.

"The big boss," he said. "I thought you were bringing me dinner last night."

"I was until I found out you already had dinner," Stilwell said. "So, listen, Spivak, I'm not going to fuck around with you today. I need you to cooperate and that means you keep it down back here. If that's a problem for you, we have the means to keep you quiet."

"You going to gag me?"

"If we have to. We have a spit harness I'm authorized to use. When you're back here yelling, it's a threat to the people who work in this building. I'm authorized to do what I have to do to alleviate that threat. If you want to be cuffed to the bars with a harness wrapped around your face, that'll be your choice."

"You try that on me and you'll end up in the hospital next to your deputy."

"If I have to call in every deputy on the island, I'll do it. My people have jobs to do, Spivak. And I'm not going to let them work in an environment where they feel unsafe. Consider yourself warned."

"When am I getting my fucking hearing?"

"Tomorrow. I'll make sure you're first up."

Stilwell turned and left the jail section. In the bullpen he told Mercy to keep an eye on the camera feed from Spivak's cell. He then went into his office and closed the door, a clear sign he did not want to be disturbed.

For the next three hours Stilwell worked at his computer. First he outlined the accumulated facts and evidence: The victim in the harbor had been identified as Leigh-Anne Moss and she had been fired from the Black Marlin Club probably on the same day that she was murdered and the jade statue was stolen. He noted that the new anchor and sail bag on the *Emerald Sea* were similar to those used to submerge the body. He added descriptions of an unidentified person making a middle-of-the-night trip from the club to the *Emerald Sea* and the ketch's short trip out to the bay and back the following Monday — both of which were unauthorized by the boat's owner.

Next, Stilwell spun his wheels online looking for any kind of tidal or ocean currents report that would support his belief that Moss's body had been dumped from the *Emerald Sea* into the bay and then brought back into the harbor by such underwater movement. He gave up after forty minutes of searching but knew it was a weakness in his crime theory that could possibly raise a red flag with a judge or jury. He made a note to find an oceanography expert who could testify to the possibility that Leigh-Anne Moss's body had returned to the scene of the crime like, as Ahearn had said, a ghost.

Last, he set to work on a summary showing probable cause to search the BMC for forensic evidence of the murder, the missing sculpture, and all records of membership, personnel, and use of the club's guest rooms on the weekend in question. His goal was to make the statement complete and concise. It was a sales pitch to the judge, urging him to buy Stilwell's theory of the crime and demonstrating the need to take the investigation into the hallowed confines of the wealthy private club.

By the time he finished the first draft, he realized he was famished. He checked his phone and saw he'd been working for more than three hours straight. He sent the document to the printer and left his office to grab it from the tray before anyone else could see it.

He saw Ralph Lampley at a desk working at a computer, and it prompted him to remember the ten-o'clock deadline imposed on Starkey up at the Zane Grey.

"Ralph, did you get the report on the eviction at the Zane Grey?" he asked. "What happened up there?"

"I was going to tell you but Mercy said not to knock on your door," Lampley said.

"Tell me what?"

"The guy up there got his bank to wire money to the hotel, so everything turned out fine."

"How'd you find this out?"

"I called the manager. He said the bank wired enough for two weeks, so he's letting the guy — Starkey — stay, and now everybody's happy. The hotel got the money and Starkey can finish writing his book or script or whatever it is."

"Well, good, then. What are you writing up?"

"Just a bunch of bullshit. Somebody graffitied the Casino last night. They're painting it out today but they want a report for insurance."

Stilwell wondered if the vandal was a local. Catalina had no street gangs but that didn't stop gangsters from coming over on the ferries from time to time.

"What did the graffiti say?"

"Just two names, Sleepy and Mako."

"You might want to go up to the school and talk to the maintenance people. They've had some graffiti issues up there this year. Maybe see if they've had anything with those names. That way we find out if they're local or from off island."

"Copy that," Lampley said. "I'll go up after I finish this."

Stilwell walked over to Mercy's desk and she held up four pink message slips.

"These came in," she said.

The first was from Mayor Allen. There was no message, just a number, and Mercy had checked the CALL BACK box.

"You probably should have knocked on my door for this one," he said. "Any idea what he wanted?"

"It was actually one of his assistants who called," Mercy said. "She let slip that the council just approved a ten-thousand-dollar reward on the harbor case. The mayor wanted to tell you and give you the parameters."

Stilwell stared at the message, trying to decide if the reward was a good or bad thing. It would likely bring in multiple calls with information he would have to chase down — a lot of spinning of his wheels. But it could also bring in a solid lead. He had seen rewards work both ways when he was on the homicide unit.

The next message was from Ned Browning. It said *No go on the sales records,* and Stilwell understood this to mean that Browning had found no record of the purchase of a handsaw by Henry Gaston or Oscar Terranova. That would have been too easy, Stilwell thought.

Message three was from Lionel McKey, and Stilwell guessed he was calling for comment on the reward. Stilwell crumpled that slip up and tossed it into the trash can next to Mercy's desk.

The last message was from someone named Leslie, no last name or phone number given. Mercy had written *Wanted to know if the dead girl was Leigh-Anne Moss.*

"She had the name?" he asked. "What did you tell her?"

"You told me not to give out information on cases," Mercy said. "So I told her we didn't have an ID yet, and before I could ask anything else, she hung up."

"Damn."

"Well, I'm pretty sure she works at the Sandtrap if you want to talk to her."

"Why do you say that?"

"Because I could hear plates and voices in the background and someone saying, 'Leslie, pickup.' I think that's why she hung up so fast."

"Okay, a restaurant kitchen. Why do you say it's the Sandtrap?"

"Well, that part's a guess, but there's a girl who works up there named Leslie. She's waited on me before."

It was Mercy who had told Stilwell about the Sandtrap being the best place for lunch when he first came to the island. She went there often on her lunch break.

"That's really good, Mercy," he said.

Stilwell had eaten half a sandwich from the restaurant that morning but it looked like he would be going there for lunch now. He told Mercy to call him if anything came up and headed out of the sub.

Up at the golf course, he asked the hostess for a table at the Sandtrap and requested Leslie as his server. It was before noon, and the lunch rush hadn't started. In case this was a dead end, Stilwell had brought the printout of the search warrant with him to edit while he ate.

Soon, a woman in her twenties with her brown hair in a ponytail came to his table. The name tag clipped to her light blue golf shirt said LESLIE. He recognized her from his past stops at the restaurant but realized he had never registered her name. He was in his usual uniform—tan cargo pants, holstered weapon and badge on his belt, green polo shirt with a sheriff's badge embroidered on the left breast—but it didn't seem to register.

"What can I get you today?" she asked.

"I'll go with a BLT on wheat toast," Stilwell said.

"Anything to drink?"

"Iced tea."

"You got it."

"Are you the Leslie who called our office this morning about Leigh-Anne?"

She raised her eyes from her order pad and seemed to notice the embroidered badge on Stilwell's shirt for the first time.

"How did you know that?" she asked.

"The woman you talked to is a regular customer here," Stilwell said. "I know you're in the middle of work now, but I need to ask you about Leigh-Anne."

"Uh, okay. Was she the girl they found in the water?"

"I can't really answer that at the moment. But why did you call about her?"

"Because she owes me money and I sort of heard that there was going to be a reward for, you know, information that helps with the case."

"How did you hear about the reward? That was just approved."

"Oh, you hear a lot of things at the tables. City Hall people have breakfast here almost every day. I heard them talking about the reward this morning."

Stilwell nodded. "You said Leigh-Anne owed you money. For what?"

"She rented a room from me and stopped paying."

"When was this?"

"She started renting it in January but she stopped staying there a couple months ago and she didn't pay me for the month before she left."

Stilwell sat forward, fully focused on the piece of luck he had just been served.

"What's your full name, Leslie?"

"Leslie Sneed."

"So Leigh-Anne stayed with you while she was working at the Black Marlin Club?"

"Usually she was here on the weekends. Sometimes on Thursdays if she got a shift. And then she stopped staying and decided she didn't have to pay me for the last month."

Stilwell nodded sympathetically.

"Listen, I need to talk to you more about this, but this is not really the right place to do it," he said. "Can you come down to the sheriff's station with me?"

"You mean, like, now?"

"Yes, now."

"I...uh, I don't think the manager will let me leave. It's about to get busy here and I also need the tip money."

"I understand. When will the lunch rush be over?"

"Probably around two."

"Okay, let's do two. After I finish eating, I'll leave, but then I'll come back at two to give you a ride down to the station."

"So it *was* her."

"We'll talk about that."

"I knew she was going to get into trouble."

Stilwell felt the whisper on the back of his neck again. He was beginning to think that finding Leslie Sneed might significantly advance the case.

"Well, we'll talk about that too," he said.

She left to put in his food order. Stilwell took a pen out of his pocket and started to read and edit the search warrant. But he soon stopped. He couldn't concentrate because of his excitement over finding Leslie Sneed and because he knew she might provide information that would have to go into the request to search the Black Marlin Club.

He put the document aside and started thinking about how he would handle things at two.

26

AFTER FINISHING HIS BLT, Stilwell had an hour to kill while Leslie Sneed worked the lunch rush at the Sandtrap. He drove the Gator down to Crescent and posted up on the side of the road where he had a view of the Black Marlin Club's front door and the embarcadero dock on the side. He pulled out his phone and called the cell number Frank Sampedro had given him.

"Just checking in," he said. "You guys at the boat yet?"

"Well into it," Sampedro said. "And we got blood."

"Really? Where?"

"The bottom of the helm. It was cleaned up, but forensics found it in a hinge on one of the floor hatches. We got enough for DNA matching. We're just hoping it's not fish blood."

"It's gotta be the victim's. Colbrink told me he doesn't fish."

"Good to know."

"Anything else from the boat?"

"We're still working it. Forensics is down in the cabin now."

"What about the cleaner? The Three-Oh-Three."

"Nothing there. We checked the trash cans on the dock and even the dumpster where everything gets emptied. It all was picked up yesterday by county sanitation."

"That's too bad."

"Yeah, but we got the blood in the helm."

Getting fingerprints would have been better, Stilwell thought.

"Is Colbrink there?" he asked.

"He was," Sampedro said. "Rex took him downtown for a formal interview."

Stilwell didn't say anything to that. He was thinking about what he remembered of Ahearn's interview techniques. They were generally heavy-handed, and he hoped Ahearn wasn't going to offend a cooperating witness and lose the access they currently had to both Colbrink and what was likely a floating crime scene.

"When you talked to Colbrink, did he tell you about Yacht Lock?" Sampedro asked.

"No. What's Yacht Lock?" Stilwell replied.

"It's like LoJack for boats. A lot of these big boats get stolen and it's like a hidden GPS so the boat can be tracked. Colbrink said he has it on this thing because it's a custom-made one-of-a-kind boat. We're thinking we might be able to pinpoint where the boat stopped when it went out into the bay and the body was dumped."

Stilwell became fully alert.

"It's that precise?" he asked.

"Supposedly it's precise to a fifty-foot radius," Sampedro said. "That's a lot better than phone GPS."

"How do we get the location?"

"I called the company down in San Diego. They need a search warrant. I'll get going on it when I get back in."

"Good deal. We get the spot and we probably get the murder weapon."

"And maybe the phone."

Stilwell was silent for a moment. He knew that search warrants took forever with cell service providers, and their data revealed only numbers called or texted. The texts themselves were stored on the actual phone.

"I know what you're thinking," Sampedro said. "Salt water. I already talked to tech services. Fresh water, not a problem. But two weeks in salt water is going to make it a long shot."

"Well, I guess we have to find it first."

Stilwell was hopeful about Yacht Lock. It might cut a needle-in-a-haystack search down to a contained and viable target location.

"What's going on out there?" Sampedro asked.

"I've got the search warrant for the club almost ready to go," Stilwell said. "The judge comes over in the morning. And in an hour I'm interviewing a waitress who rented a room out here to Leigh-Anne Moss earlier this year. Until she apparently started staying with somebody else."

"Do we know who?"

"That's what I'm going to try to find out. I'll keep you posted."

"Let us know what you get."

"You too. And one last thing. If the judge signs off on the warrant tomorrow, I could use some help out here with the search. There will be a lot of ground to cover in the club. Are you guys going to come out, or should I use some of my people here? I don't think they have much investigative experience or have even served search warrants before. I could also use somebody from forensics in case we find biological evidence."

"I'll talk to Rex."

"I could really use the help. It's gotta be done right."

"Tell you what, I'll come out for sure and I'll bring the tech we've got working on the boat. That way we have some continuity. Just let me know when you've got the warrant signed, sealed, and delivered."

"Will do."

Stilwell disconnected. He liked the cooperation he seemed to be getting from Sampedro. But he knew it was fragile. Ahearn was the senior partner and could change the level of openness at any time.

He had seen no one come or go from either the front or the side of the BMC during his short vigil. He suspected that the next day, when the weekenders started coming in, things would get busy. He turned the cart around on Crescent and headed back up to the golf course. The Sandtrap was nearly empty when he entered, and there was no sign of Leslie Sneed, but another server told him that she was in the break room and pointed him through the kitchen. Stilwell went through a swinging door and found Sneed at a table near the back. She was counting tips.

"How'd you do today?" he asked.

"Not bad for a Thursday," she said. "But I need a big weekend."

Stilwell pulled out another chair at the table and sat down. There was no one else in the break room.

"I thought you said we had to go down to the station," Sneed said.

"We will," Stilwell said. "But I wanted to ask you a few questions first."

"Okay."

"You said Leigh-Anne stopped staying with you a couple months ago?"

"Yeah, just stopped coming or paying me."

"Did she come back for her things or leave anything behind?"

"I kept her shit. I changed the lock and told her she could have her stuff when she paid what she owed."

"So her stuff is still at your apartment?"

"That's right. I guess it's all mine now."

"What's there?"

"Just some clothes and some books. I think what she really

wanted was her phone charger, but I told her she could have that when she paid her back rent. She hung up on me and that was the last time I heard from her."

It seemed unlikely to Stilwell that a phone charger was what Moss wanted back.

"Do you remember when that was?" he asked.

"A couple Saturdays ago," Sneed said. "I remember I was here when she called. She had tried to sneak into the apartment 'cause she knew I worked mornings on Saturdays. She hadn't counted on the lock being changed."

"So she didn't get her things?"

"Uh-uh."

"And she had her own bedroom there?"

"It's not really a bedroom. More like an enclosed porch. My place is kinda small."

"Could we go over there first? I want to see what she left."

"I guess so. I need to be back by four thirty to set up for the dinner shift, though."

"I'll have you back in time for that. Can you leave now?"

"Yeah, I told my boss. He said it was okay as long as I was back to work dinner."

"Good. I've got a cart, so we can go."

Leslie Sneed lived in Eucalyptus Gardens, an apartment complex on Banning Drive. In his year on the island, Stilwell had slowly been learning the characteristics of Avalon neighborhoods. He knew that Eucalyptus Gardens was one of five low-income-housing projects where many people in the tourism and service industry lived.

Sneed's apartment was small and sparsely furnished, with a Taylor Swift poster taped to the wall over a hand-me-down couch that might have been older than its owner. Swift was holding a cat in the poster and there was an undeniable smell of litter box to the apartment.

The living room connected to a kitchenette that had a half-size refrigerator and a two-burner stove. There was an adjoining bedroom, a single bathroom, and a small porch off the living room that had been enclosed with louvered windows. There was no door to the porch, but a curtain had been hung across the entrance for privacy. Sneed pulled the curtain back and held out her hand to signal Stilwell in.

"Sorry about the cat litter," she said. "I have to close up when I go to work."

She walked onto the porch and started cranking open the windows. The litter box was in the corner, and a black cat was sleeping on a daybed on the other side of the porch.

"So this was Leigh-Anne's room?" Stilwell asked.

"Yep," Sneed said.

"Is the cat hers or yours?"

"He's mine. I just moved the litter box in here when she stopped coming."

There was no closet, but there was an old wooden cabinet against the wall next to the bed.

"Do I have your permission to open the cabinet and look through this room?" Stilwell asked.

"Have at it," Sneed said. "If you find drugs, they were hers, not mine. I've been sober since I moved out here."

"Don't worry, I'm not looking for drugs. Where'd you move out from?"

"I grew up in the San Fernando Valley."

"What part?"

"Panorama City."

Stilwell nodded. He didn't know much about Panorama City except that it had drive-through drug markets. Moving to an island to get away from it was probably a smart idea.

Stilwell pulled a set of disposable gloves from his pocket and snapped them on. He opened the cabinet's two doors. The left side had shelves, and the right side had a hanging bar for clothes. There were a few blouses and pairs of black chinos on hangers. He searched the pockets of the pants first but found them empty. He checked the labels on the blouses and saw nothing recognizably expensive.

"How long have you lived on the island?" he asked.

"Four years in July," Sneed said.

"And you've been in this apartment the whole time?"

"Not at first. You have to live on the island for ninety days to qualify to live here. So I sort of stayed on couches until I could get in. Sort of like what Leigh-Anne was doing."

As she talked, Stilwell noted the folded clothes on the cabinet shelves as well as a few cardboard boxes with the Amazon logo. One shelf held a small collection of books stacked on their sides.

"How did you connect with Leigh-Anne about renting out this room?" he asked.

"I had a friend who worked at the Black Marlin and he connected us," Sneed said.

"Who was he?"

"Just a guy who worked at the Trap but then got a job there for a while."

"He's not there anymore?"

"No, he went back to the mainland. A friend of his opened a bar in Studio City and he went to work there."

"What's his name? I might want to talk to him about Leigh-Anne."

"Todd Whitmore. I can't remember the name of the place he works at now."

Stilwell took one of the Amazon boxes off the shelf and opened it on the bed next to the sleeping cat. It contained various unopened hair products, including two tubes of Colors hair dye.

Both had purple screw-on caps and were labeled NIGHTSHADE. Stilwell thought of the purple wildflowers that grew on some of the island's hillsides.

"Nightshade," Sneed said. "She loved that color. Like the flower. I said to her once, 'Don't you know that nightshade is poisonous?' But she didn't care."

Stilwell closed the box and moved on to the next one.

"So you said she wanted to get her stuff but you wouldn't let her in," he said.

"That's right," Sneed said. "She owed me two fifty for the last month she did stay here — that was March — and then I told her it was another two fifty for the month she stopped staying but didn't tell me. I could have tried to find somebody else if I had known."

The second box was more personal-care products. After looking through it, Stilwell put it back on the shelf.

"Was there something in particular she said she wanted to get?"

"No, she just said she wanted her things."

"Did she say she'd pay you the money?"

"She said she would, that she had a boyfriend who would cough it up, but that never happened."

Stilwell remembered Peter Galloway and didn't think it was likely that he was the boyfriend who could cough up five hundred dollars.

He moved on to the stack of books. The first one he recognized because Tash had read it when they'd gone on a camping trip to Little Harbor on the back side of the island. It was called *If I'd Known Then.* Tash told him it was a collection of letters women in their twenties and thirties had written to their younger selves with words of advice they wished they had received back then. The edge of a business card used as a bookmark stuck out from the middle of the book. Stilwell flipped it open to find that it was a card from Charles Crane, the general manager of the Black Marlin Club.

The next book was called *Everything I Know About Love* by Dolly Alderton, and its bookmark was near the end of the book. It was a business card from a Los Angeles attorney named Daniel Easterbrook. The last book was called *Fruiting Bodies* by Kathryn Harlan. It too had a business-card bookmark, this one from a Century City oncologist named Leonard Koval.

Stilwell laid the business cards out on the bed and took individual photos of them before returning them to the pages where he found them. He wasn't sure why he was re-marking the pages when he knew Leigh-Anne Moss would never finish the books.

"Looks like she was a reader," he said, more to himself than to Sneed.

"I don't have a TV," Sneed said, "so she did a lot of reading."

"Did she keep any of her property anywhere else in the apartment?"

"No, just in here."

"Can we move the cat? I want to check the bed."

Sneed went to the bed and picked up the cat, who mildly protested at being woken, and held him while Stilwell checked under the pillows and then lifted the mattress off the box spring to look between them. He found nothing.

Stilwell next got down on his hands and knees and looked under the bed. He saw a shoebox and nothing else. He slid the box out and opened it. It contained a pair of black high-heeled pumps.

"Prada — nice," Sneed said.

Stilwell saw the brand mark on the insole.

"Yours or hers?" he asked.

"Hers, definitely," Sneed said. "Too small for me." She giggled.

"What?" Stilwell asked.

"It's just funny," she said. "I never saw her wear those and I can't think of a place on this island where you would. Except up at the Ada, maybe."

The Mount Ada was the island's only four-star hotel. It was once the Wrigley mansion and sat high up on the hill overlooking the harbor and Santa Monica Bay. It had a formal dining room, but Stilwell knew that Sneed was right — the island wasn't a place for high-end high-heeled shoes. So the question was, why did Leigh-Anne Moss have these shoes on the island? He doubted she would have brought them from the mainland. They had to have been a gift from someone here.

"She didn't wear these for work, right?" he asked.

"No, no way," Sneed said. "You can't work with those spikes. Not when you're on your feet all day."

"Probably a gift, then. Any idea who from?"

"None. She never even mentioned those to me. I'd never seen them before you pulled them out."

"You think they're the reason she wanted to get back into the apartment? Prada stuff is expensive, right?"

"Very. Those probably cost somebody a grand, at least. Probably one of the guys she was playing."

Stilwell looked up at her for a long moment.

"Let's go down to the station," he said. "I want to talk to you about that."

"Fine with me," Sneed said.

"I'm going to take these, see if we can figure out where they came from."

"Take 'em. They wouldn't fit me."

Stilwell closed the shoebox and got up off the floor.

27

STILWELL PUT THE shoebox in a large plastic evidence bag from the storage chest on the Gator. At the sub, he left it on Mercy's desk as he walked Leslie Sneed to the interview room. He pointed her to the witness chair.

"Have a seat and I'll be right with you," he said. "Can I get you anything? Coffee, a Coke?"

"A Diet Coke would be nice," Sneed said.

He left her there, closed the door, and went back to Mercy's desk.

"Mercy, there are numbers on the side of that shoebox. Can you take a shot at tracing them back to a purchase point?"

He knew it was the kind of request she loved because she didn't have to leave the office and it interrupted the thankless task of answering the phone and radio all day. He also knew she was a tenacious keyboard warrior. She owned the internet when it came to researching.

"It was probably bought on Amazon," Stilwell said. "But worth a try."

"Was this a gift to our victim?" she asked.

"Most likely. They're expensive. Why?"

"Because I doubt you can get Prada from Amazon's warehouses. You'd have to go through a third-party seller, and then there's always the possibility of counterfeits. You can buy them used through resale sites, but you're saying they were a gift, and no man's going to give a girl used heels. He'd probably get them at a store."

Stilwell nodded. It made sense.

"Well, see what you can find," he said. "How's our prisoner? One more day to go."

"He's been quiet since breakfast," Mercy said.

Stilwell went back to the jail and looked into the cell where Spivak was held. The prisoner was on the floor, shirtless, doing sit-ups with his feet hooked under the metal frame of the bed.

"Spivak, your first appearance is tomorrow morning," Stilwell said. "Your lawyer going to be here?"

Spivak stopped the exercise and just lay there, back on the floor, chest heaving from exertion.

"Fuck off," he said.

"Been hearing that a lot lately," Stilwell said. "You know what a TBI is, Spivak?"

Spivak said nothing. He got up off the floor and came to the bars — an attempt to intimidate Stilwell with his heavy breathing and pumped-up pecs. Stilwell saw the many tattoos covering his torso, all of them fading, all of them made with what looked like dull blue prison ink. He wondered if he had done time in Mexico or another country, since no prison record had come up on Stilwell's search of the National Crime Information Center database other than the three hundred days at Pitchess, which hardly seemed like enough time to complete the interlocking images that covered almost every inch of his upper body.

"A TBI's a traumatic brain injury," Stilwell said. "It's looking like Dunne might have a TBI, which will probably cost him his career. We'll be sure the judge knows that tomorrow."

He saw no reaction from Spivak other than a vessel pulsing in his left temple.

"Why'd you do it, Spivak?" he asked. "Somebody put you up to it, didn't they?"

That was a flier. Stilwell was convinced the attack on Dunne hadn't been random. Spivak smiled slightly.

"Like I said, fuck off," he said.

"Right," Stilwell said.

He left the jail, went to the break room, and grabbed two cans of Diet Coke from the refrigerator. On his way back to the interview room, he turned on the camera that would record the session with Sneed.

He put the two cans down on the table and sat across from her. On the way to the station from Sneed's apartment, Stilwell had confirmed her suspicion that Leigh-Anne Moss was dead and had been identified as the woman found at the bottom of the harbor. Sneed had remained quiet the rest of the way in.

"First of all, thanks for your time," he said. "You've already been very helpful."

"You think I could get some of the reward if I'm helping?" Sneed asked.

"Well, I'll be sure to tell them you've been a help. Usually those things pay out only if there's an arrest. Sometimes it's not till they get a conviction. But it was just announced, so I'm not sure how it will work."

Sneed nodded. "It's so weird," she said.

"What is?" Stilwell asked.

"Her being dead now. I kind of feel guilty because we ended up not being friends and I said some things I probably shouldn't have."

"You said them to her or somebody else?"

"To her. I mean, not directly to her face. But when she stopped taking my calls and I changed the lock, things got heated. I'm sure you heard the messages I left on her phone. And she left some mean ones for me."

"We haven't found her phone and we're working on a search warrant for her records. Do you still have any messages from her?"

"I kept the last one. Just in case."

"In case of what?"

"I don't know. Like in case something happened to me. She was pretty mad."

"Can I hear it?"

"I guess so."

She pulled her cell phone out of the back pocket of her khakis and played the message over the speaker. Stilwell knew he was recording it on the room's camera and sound system:

"Bitch, you don't want to fuck with me. You can't keep my stuff. Your ass will be sorry as fuck. And if you think changing the damn lock is going to stop me, you are dead wrong, honey. Don't fucking play games with me. You will lose."

Stilwell was silent for a few moments after listening to the victim's angry voice.

"She didn't mince words, did she?" he finally said.

"No," Sneed said. "That's why I kept it."

"What's the date and time on that message?"

Sneed looked down at her phone screen.

"May seventeenth at nine forty-one a.m.," she said. "I was working the breakfast shift."

"Did you purposely not take the call?"

"No, my manager doesn't let us have our phones on when we're working, so I missed the call and she left the message."

"Did you respond to it? Call her back?"

"Yeah, I called her back after the lunch shift but she didn't answer. I left a message. I told her again that as soon as she paid me the five hundred dollars she owed me, she'd get all her shit back. I didn't know about the shoes under the bed. That's probably what she really wanted. Her other stuff was basic crap."

Stilwell considered the timing of the calls. Moss had likely left the message before going into the Black Marlin Club on Saturday the seventeenth, and Sneed had probably called Moss back after she was dead.

"Now, when we were up at your apartment, you said something about the guys she was playing," he said. "Can you tell me more about that?"

Sneed opened her can of Diet Coke and took a sip before answering.

"I feel a little weird saying something bad about the dead," she said.

"Leslie, I need to know everything there is to know about Leigh-Anne," Stilwell said. "No matter what kind of person she was, she didn't deserve what happened to her. I'm trying to find who did it, and to do that, I need every piece of information about her I can get. I don't want it cleaned up and pretty. I'm looking for the truth, and I think you can help me."

Sneed nodded and looked down at the can she held on the table in front of her. She kept her eyes on it as she spoke.

"She . . . wasn't a good person. She talked about all of these guys. Guys who would give her stuff, you know, if she fucked them. But the thing is, she didn't like any of them, I don't think. She'd come back to the apartment and sort of brag about how she was just using them. Like how she had an old boyfriend on the mainland who had a place where she could stay and how he was hopelessly in love with her."

"But she didn't love him back."

"No. No way. She called him 'the schmuck.' She didn't love anybody, you ask me."

"What about over here on the island? Was she doing the same thing?"

"Oh, yeah, she talked about a couple guys she was seeing on and off."

"From where?"

"From the club, I'm sure. I mean, she didn't say so specifically, but she said she was through dealing with guys who didn't have any money."

"And we're talking about the Black Marlin, right?"

"Definitely. That's why she got the job there. She said it was like shooting fish in a barrel. All these old guys over there stepping out on their wives. She'd go with them if there was something in it for her."

"Did she ever mention any names?"

"No—she was smart enough not to do that. Girls like that know the rules of the game, I think."

It appeared that Leigh-Anne might have broken the rules or at least threatened to, Stilwell thought.

"Do you remember anything else she said about these men she was seeing?" he asked.

"She just said it was hard sometimes to keep everything separate," Sneed said.

"What did you take that to mean?"

"Well, like that she was going with different men and had to keep them all separate so one didn't know about the others."

"Did she ever mention that there was a problem with any of them?"

"Not really. I think the guy on the mainland knew what was going on over here and was jealous. She said something about that, but she also called him a puppy dog that she had on a leash."

"You're talking about the guy she called the schmuck?"

"I'm pretty sure it was the same guy."

Stilwell would pass that piece of intel on to Sampedro and Ahearn, since they were now handling the mainland aspects of the case.

He tried to get more information out of Sneed.

"But she never mentioned having any problems with anybody over here?" he asked. "Nobody from the club?"

"Not really," Sneed said. "With her, it was like a balancing act."

"Do you know if she dated anyone over here who was not from the club?"

"I don't know, but I don't think so. I remember she once called that club a target-rich environment."

"Her words? 'Target-rich environment'?"

"Yeah, that's what she said."

Stilwell was about to end the interview but thought of something else.

"Those heels from Prada, they were probably a gift," he said. "Do you remember if there were other gifts from these men?"

"She got some stuff," Sneed said. "Most of the time she just sold it for the money. That's how she paid me, until she didn't."

"How did she do that? Sell the stuff, I mean."

"Online. Fashionphile and the RealReal. A lot of sites resell good stuff like that."

Stilwell nodded. He knew he had to add some of this information to the probable cause statement in his search warrant application. It would support the need to get inside the club.

"Okay, I think that's good for now, Leslie," he said. "Thank you for your help. I'll get you back up to the Sandtrap or your apartment or wherever you want to go. Just give me a minute."

"And you'll put me in for the reward money?" Sneed asked.

"If we make an arrest, I think you will be very eligible for at least part of it."

"Okay, thanks."

Stilwell stood up and left the interview room, hoping to find one of the day-shift deputies in the sub who could run Sneed back up the hill.

Only Mercy was there.

"Everybody's out?" he asked.

He noticed that she was wearing disposable gloves and that the shoebox was out of the evidence bag and open on her desk. The pumps and the tissue paper they had been wrapped in were next to the box.

"Everybody's out," Mercy replied. "I found this at the bottom of the shoebox. Did you see it before?"

She held up a card with a drawing of a smiling kitten on the front. Stilwell had no gloves on, so he didn't touch it. "No, I didn't see it before," he said. "What's it say inside?"

Carefully holding the card at the edges, she opened it. There was a handwritten note: *For you, Nightshade — Dan.*

Stilwell pulled out his phone and looked at the photos he had taken of the business cards used as bookmarks. He focused on the card with the name Daniel Easterbrook — the attorney from L.A.

"We need to bag that separately and send it to the lab for fingerprinting and touch DNA," he said.

"I'll send it over on the Express tonight," Mercy said.

28

AFTER DROPPING LESLIE Sneed off at the Sandtrap, Stilwell went back down to Crescent and then up Wrigley Road to the Mount Ada hotel. He agreed with Sneed that in a golf-cart town, only the Mount Ada was formal enough for Prada pumps, and he decided to check it out. The small but upscale two-story bed-and-breakfast catered to the wealthiest visitors to the island. The rooms were easily a grand a night on weekends in season. The opulence of the setting was accentuated by the man behind the front desk, who wore something seldom seen on Catalina: a suit and tie. Stilwell introduced himself and then pulled up Leigh-Anne Moss's driver's license photo on his phone. The deskman had a nameplate on his jacket pocket that said GILBERT.

"I'm wondering if you recognize this woman," he said. "This photo doesn't show it, but she might have had a purple streak in her hair. It was in the front and went down the left side of her face."

Gilbert didn't hesitate.

"Sure, she's been here," he said.

"You mean she stayed here?" Stilwell asked.

"A few times, at least. I checked her in."

"Was she by herself or was someone with her?"

"I just recall checking her in. I don't know who she was with or who she might have met, sir."

"And you're sure it's the woman in the photo?"

"When you mentioned the purple streak, that made me remember her, yes."

"She paid with a credit card?"

"That would be required, yes."

"When was the last time she was here?"

"I would have to look that up."

"Can you do that for me? The name is Leigh-Anne Moss."

"Do I need to have a search warrant for that?"

"Not if you volunteer the information. I'm sure you want to help your local law enforcement, Gilbert."

"I just don't want to get in any trouble."

"If you can't do it for me, I'll need to see your boss. I don't know if that will cause you trouble or not."

Gilbert took one step to his left and started typing on a computer keyboard.

"That's L-e-i-g-h, dash, then Anne with an *e,*" Stilwell said. "M-o-s-s."

"Got it," Gilbert said.

Stilwell couldn't see the computer screen. Gilbert studied it for a moment before speaking.

"The last time she was here was May ninth and tenth," he finally said. "Before that, it was May second and third."

"Anything before that?" Stilwell asked.

"Yes, two other times—both weekends in April. Do you want the dates?"

"Yes, please."

Gilbert gave the details of two more stays, one for three nights and one for four. Stilwell calculated that Moss's stays at the

Ada coincided with when she stopped living at Leslie Sneed's apartment.

"Is there anything else you need?" Gilbert asked.

"What kind of room did she reserve?" Stilwell asked.

"She took the grand suite each time. It has the balcony with a wonderful harbor view."

"I bet it does. What credit card did she use to pay for the room?"

Gilbert checked his screen.

"A Visa."

"I'm going to need that number, Gilbert."

Gilbert read the number off the computer screen without question or protest. Stilwell asked him to write it down. He did so on a small pad with the hotel's name embossed on it.

"What was the name of the cardholder?" Stilwell asked.

"It was her name," Gilbert said. "She would have been required to show ID."

"Of course. Is the grand suite occupied right now?"

More typing followed the question.

"That room is reserved starting tomorrow," Gilbert said. "For the weekend."

"So it's empty now?" Stilwell said. "I'd like to take a look at it."

"Why would that be necessary?"

"Because this is a murder investigation, Gilbert, and I need to see the room."

"You mean she's dead? Leigh-Anne Moss is dead?"

"Yes. Murdered. So can you give me a key to the room, please?"

Gilbert turned around, reached into an old-fashioned rack of cubbyholes, and pulled out an actual key attached to a leather fob with 4 printed on it. He handed it to Stilwell.

"You can go up the stairs," he said.

"Thank you," Stilwell said.

Stilwell took the stairs up to a short hallway with doors on both sides. Suite 4 was at the end on the left. Inside was a small sitting room with a fireplace and an open door to a bedroom on the left. Stilwell imagined that it had at one time been the master bedroom of William Wrigley, the Chicago magnate who had once owned the island and built the mansion as a winter getaway. The Ada was named after his wife, and for a time, Wrigley brought his baseball team, the Chicago Cubs, out to Catalina for spring training. Stilwell knew that baseball greats such as Dizzy Dean, Hack Wilson, Roger Hornsby, and Grover Cleveland Alexander played on the field in Avalon Canyon. Nineteen Hall of Famers in all had trained on the island. Stilwell had learned all of this from Tash, who wasn't so much a baseball fan as a fan of the island's history.

Stilwell took a quick look around and then went through the double doors in the sitting room that led to the private balcony. He stepped out and took in the expansive view of the harbor and the iconic Casino below. He could see the Black Marlin Club and the line of mooring buoys in the water behind it. He imagined Leigh-Anne Moss standing in this same spot and looking down at the club. He could only guess what she would have been thinking.

Stilwell's instincts told him that Moss had booked the room for liaisons with somebody she had met at the club. He guessed that the credit card charges were paid by that person as well. The circles he was making around the case were growing tighter, and the Black Marlin was still at the center. He recalled Leslie Sneed telling him Leigh-Anne had said that targeting men at the club was like shooting fish in a barrel. He was beginning to believe that one of those fish was a shark.

When he returned to the front desk, he asked Gilbert if there were any security cameras that would have images from the dates when Leigh-Anne Moss stayed in the hotel.

"We have only one camera here in the lobby," Gilbert said.

"But it's on a fourteen-day loop. She hasn't been a guest here in the past two weeks."

Stilwell nodded. That would have been too easy.

"Can you check another name on the computer?" he asked. "See if he's stayed here?"

Gilbert looked very put out by the request but didn't refuse.

"What's the name?"

"Daniel Easterbrook."

Gilbert typed and then frowned.

"I show that he hasn't stayed here in at least a year," he said.

"What was the date of that stay?" Stilwell asked.

"He stayed for five days in May last year. The weekend of Cinco de Mayo."

Stilwell knew that was before Leigh-Anne Moss's time on the island. But the information did confirm that Easterbrook was familiar with the Mount Ada.

"Did he book the grand suite?" Stilwell asked.

"Actually, no," Gilbert said. "He took the Windsor room. I don't suppose you want to see that room too?"

"No, that won't be necessary."

"Good."

The desk clerk seemed relieved. Stilwell put the key down on the counter.

"Thank you for your help, Gilbert," he said.

29

STILWELL HAD AN unexpected guest waiting for him when he got back to the sub. Mercy reported that the missing Henry Gaston had walked in and told her he was in danger and needed to speak to Stilwell. She gave him a Diet Coke and put him in the interview room.

"He's nervous," she said. "He says he needs protection."

Stilwell nodded as he looked down at her computer screen, which displayed the image of Gaston sitting in the lately busy interview room. He was leaning forward, arms on the table, both hands clutching the can Mercy had given him.

"All right, I'm going in to talk to him," Stilwell said. "You get anything yet on the Prada shoes?"

"Actually, yes," Mercy said. "I identified them as satin cutout pumps that retail for fourteen hundred dollars new."

Stilwell could not comprehend how shoes with a few straps and four-inch heels could cost so much.

"I was also correct when I said you can't get these shoes directly through Amazon," Mercy continued. "They're available through retail outlets like Nordstrom and Neiman Marcus and Prada's own shops. There's one on Rodeo Drive in Beverly Hills. But here is a cool thing that may help you: They're chipped."

"What do you mean, 'chipped'?"

"There's a huge counterfeit market for designer stuff. Prada puts radio-frequency identification chips in its products to help detect counterfeits as well as for supply-chain tracking. So if you buy something you think is Prada, you can go into a Prada store, and they have a chip reader that will tell you not only if it's real but when it was manufactured and where it was sold."

"That's perfect."

"The chip readers are only at Prada, though — they don't have them at Nordstrom. I called the store in Beverly Hills and they said they could check the chip in these pumps, but you'll have to go over there."

"It's looking like I may have to go across for other things anyway. I could go to Beverly Hills. Great work, Mercy."

"Well, it doesn't mean they can tell you who bought them, but if you narrow it down to the point of purchase, you might get lucky."

"You never know. It's definitely worth a shot." He pointed at her screen. "Are you recording?"

"I was waiting for you to get back. I'll start the recording now."

Stilwell went to get another Diet Coke. He now had two mainland leads — the Prada pumps and Daniel Easterbrook — that he could pass on to Sampedro and Ahearn, but he was reluctant to give them up. He knew he would risk the ire of his two temporary partners as well as Captain Corum if he didn't, but he had momentum and didn't want to lose it while waiting for moves to be made by people he didn't have confidence in. He knew he was once more crossing a line but would do it without hesitation.

Stilwell got a rights waiver out of the wall-mounted caddy next to the interview room. The moment he opened the door and stepped in, Gaston jumped up and started talking in staccato bursts like a machine gun.

"You gotta help me, man," he said. "They're going to take me out. And for what? A fucking side of beef? They're going to take me out for a stupid buffalo?"

Stilwell put up his free hand and made a calming motion. "Okay, slow down, Henry," he said. "Let's just sit and talk about this rationally. Okay?"

"I can't sit down, man. I'm fucking scared. They're looking for me. I saw them."

"Sit. Please. Then we'll talk."

Stilwell put the Diet Coke on the table and sat down. He picked up the can on Gaston's side and shook it. It was empty.

"I don't know if I should give you another one of these. You're riding a little too much caffeine."

"I need it. I'm still thirsty."

"Okay, take it. But drink it slow. Okay?"

"Okay, okay."

Gaston finally sat down. Stilwell noticed that his blue jumpsuit was dirty and greasy and was possibly the same thing he had been wearing when Stilwell last saw him at the Island Mystery Tours cart barn. Gaston opened the second can and took a large gulp.

"Okay, Henry, I was told you want to talk to me. Is that true?"

"I'm here, aren't I? I'll tell you everything, but you've got to take care of me."

Stilwell slid the single-page document across the table to Gaston.

"All right, that's a rights waiver. You need to sign it if you're going to talk to me. But first I'm going to read it to you."

He slid the page back and read it slowly and loudly, then said, "Do you understand your rights as I have read them to you?"

"What do you mean?"

"That you have a right to an attorney. And that what you tell me today can be used against you in a court of law. Do you understand all of that, Henry?"

"But you're going to make me a deal."

"Well, before we can talk about that, you have to sign that you understand your rights."

"Okay, I'll sign. Give me a pen."

"You have to answer first. Do you understand your rights as I have read them to you?"

"Yes, I understand. Jesus, why is it so complicated?"

"It's actually not. So, you understand and you're willing to waive your rights so we can talk?"

"Yes, I told you."

Stilwell pulled the pen out of his shirt pocket and handed it across the table.

Gaston signed the document and slapped the pen down on top of it. Stilwell put the pen back in his pocket and pulled the document to his side of the table.

"Okay, Henry, let's start with where you've been for the past few days. Did you know your wife reported you as a missing person?"

"I couldn't tell her where I was. They'd be able to get it out of her."

"So where were you?"

"I was camping up near Eagle's Nest."

Stilwell had been up there. It was on the west side of the island. He'd gone out there on a Catalina Island Conservancy ecotour as part of his learning process when he was first transferred from the mainland.

"What made you come back?" he asked.

"Because I can't stay out there forever. I got a wife and I gotta figure things out."

"What are you looking for from me, Henry?"

Gaston held his hands up, wrists together like they were cuffed.

"I want to stay out of jail, man. I only did what I was told. It was that or lose my job, and now I'm fucked. He wants me dead."

"Who wants you dead?"

"Baby Head. I know too much. I heard he brought somebody over to do it."

"Who?"

"I don't know, man."

"Well, who told you that?"

"I don't want to get anybody else in trouble. I just know. Once you came to the barn and took the saw handle, the shit hit the fan. I knew then he was looking at me funny. Like I was no longer on the team, you know? I was somebody he had to deal with."

"Killing you is sort of extreme, don't you think?"

"You don't know these people like I know them. They do whatever they want, and I'm fucked."

"All right, Henry. This is what I can do. If you tell me what happened up there with the buffalo, I'll go to bat for you. I can't promise you a deal that keeps you out of jail, but I will protect you here. Tomorrow morning when the DA is here for court, we'll sit with her and she'll evaluate what you have and make a deal or not. You understand how that will work?"

"That's bullshit. I need something solid. I need you to get me off the island and to someplace safe. My wife too."

Stilwell shook his head.

"It doesn't work that way. I can put you in a cell here overnight. Monika Juarez, the deputy DA who handles court here, will be coming in tonight for court tomorrow. I'll meet with her either tonight or first thing in the morning and we'll try to work something out. But before we get to that, you need to tell me what you can give her to make a deal."

"Fuck me."

"Yeah, that's about right. But you need to choose which way

you want to go. Should I leave you here to think about it? I can bring in a phone if you want to call your wife to talk it over."

"No, man, I talked to her. She's scared to death they'll go after her to get to me."

"That seems unlikely. We're talking about a dead buffalo."

"No, man, I know more. I heard things. This is big, man. This is the Big Wheel. Him and the mayor had their meetings out at the barn, and I was there."

"The mayor? What are you talking about? What meetings?"

"I'm not saying till I have a deal."

"Henry, we're talking in circles here. There is no deal; we're not even going to talk about a deal until you tell me what you can provide. It's called a proffer. I take it to the DA and then she makes the call on what she's willing to do. Understand?"

"Fuck me."

"Yeah, you said that. Now you have to decide if you want my help or not."

Gaston raised his hands and wearily rubbed his face. He was all over the place but Stilwell was intrigued about what he was hinting at — the things he had overheard, his mention of the mayor. And then the tip Stilwell had received from Lionel McKey about the Big Wheel project. Stilwell felt as though he was fishing in dark water and something down there was nibbling at the bait. He could feel it. He had to be patient and wait to set the hook.

"I'll let you think on it for a while," Stilwell said. "Just knock on the door if —"

"No, man, I don't need to think anymore," Gaston said. "Let's do this. I'll tell you everything I know."

"You sure, now?"

"I'm sure."

30

STILWELL HAD HIS head down, eyes on the text he was writing to Tash, when Monika Juarez approached him in the small lobby of the Zane Grey.

"Fancy meeting you here," she said.

He looked up. He had been sitting here waiting for her, knowing her weekly routine of coming out to the island the night before court.

"Monika, hey, did you check in?" he asked.

"About to," she said. "What's up?"

"I need to talk to you about a case. A deal, actually. Why don't you check in and I'll finish this. Get into your room and come down when you're ready."

"You sure? We can do it now."

"It might take a while to walk you through everything. Go ahead, check in, and I'll be down here."

"All right, give me twenty minutes."

"Perfect."

She went to the front desk and Stilwell went back to his phone. He sent the text to Tash telling her he would probably be working later than usual. A few moments later he got a return from her.

So who is she?

She did this often, a humorous way to hide her insecurity about their relationship. He played along.

A tough-as-nails prosecutor named Monika.

In response to this he received a green-faced emoji symbolizing jealousy, and then:

Invite her to dinner?

At least once a month they invited Juarez out to dinner. She was one of the first people they had revealed their relationship to.

I'll ask.

He put the phone away and opened his laptop, which he had brought with him in case the wait for Juarez went long. He connected to the hotel's Wi-Fi, went to the California Secretary of State website, and searched for Wheelmen LLC, the company mentioned in the *Catalina Call* story on the proposal to build the giant Ferris wheel on the Avalon harbor.

A listing of incorporation documents filed on behalf of the company appeared on-screen. He opened Wheelmen's application to incorporate, filed on February 7 of that year. This showed that the company had initially formed as a Delaware corporation two months earlier and then applied to California. The corporate address listed was on Wilshire Boulevard in Los Angeles, with a registered corporate agent named Ellen Sparks. Stilwell opened a Word document and typed in both pieces of information. The application listed the company as a public-entertainment enterprise.

Stilwell started going through the other documents on the state site, identifying the company officers. He typed these into the Word document as well.

President and CEO: Marcus Rifkin
Vice president: Stanley Banks

Secretary: Nathan Cabot

Chief operating officer: Susan St. Jacques

The attorney who filed the documents was named Bryson Long. Stilwell recognized none of the names except Marcus Rifkin, who had been mentioned in the *Call* story. It was Rifkin who had submitted, with Mayor Allen's endorsement, the design and other documents pertaining to the Big Wheel project to the Avalon planning board for initial review.

After closing out of the California Secretary of State site, Stilwell started googling the names one by one to see if anything else came up. Several references to Rifkin appeared, most concerning other cities where his company had proposed building either giant Ferris wheels or zip line systems. Some had been turned down, but most were still in play or had been initially approved and were in the designing stages. As far as Stilwell could tell, none had become operational yet. These projects were in towns in Florida, Texas, and Louisiana that depended heavily on tourism.

He plugged the Wheelmen corporate address in Los Angeles into the search engine and soon was looking at a photo of an office building in Koreatown.

"What's that?"

Stilwell looked up from the screen to see Juarez, who had changed out of her DA clothes into blue jeans and a white blouse.

"What I want to talk to you about," he answered. "You okay to talk here? Or we could go to the sub, if that's better."

Juarez glanced around. There was no one else in the small lobby, and the clerk who had checked her in had left the desk.

"We can talk here," she said. "What's up?"

"What's up is that I have a guy in my jail who admits he cut up the buffalo on the preserve a couple weeks ago," Stilwell said. "He wants to make a deal where he skates on the buffalo but gives us the man who put him up to it, and for good measure, he'll throw in what he knows about the mayor being a silent partner with that same guy in a multimillion-dollar project that he's pushing through the public-approval process."

Juarez nodded eagerly, as any prosecutor with a public-corruption case dropped in her lap would do.

"Well, tell me more," she said.

"You want to start with the buffalo or the city project?" Stilwell asked.

"Let's go with the buffalo."

"Okay, I know this made news on the mainland and you might have seen it, but two weeks ago somebody killed one of the buffaloes up on the conservancy preserve. He decapitated it and took the head. They're protected animals, and that makes it a felony. The guy in jail is named Henry Gaston. I'm holding him there in protective custody because I've got nowhere else to put him. He's a mechanic who takes care of the carts used by Island Mystery Tours, which got a franchise license from the town about five years ago. I wasn't out here then but I'm told it was controversial."

"How so?"

"The franchise owner is a guy named Oscar Terranova. The locals call him Baby Head."

"What?"

"He's got a shaved head and I guess people think it looks like a newborn baby's."

Juarez laughed and shook her own head.

"At least it's original," she said.

"Anyway, the license was opposed by other tour operators, who said there were already too many franchises in town," Stilwell said. "They claimed it would hurt all of their businesses. But Mayor Allen supported the application, saying the competition would grow the market. The town council voted, and Baby Head got the license."

"And did it grow things like the mayor said?"

"Not so much. Two of the other companies went bankrupt, but the mayor conveniently blamed the COVID epidemic for that. Tourism did tank out here back then. But Gaston said that he and Baby Head sabotaged those businesses. He said they did all kinds of stuff, from slashing tires on the competitors' carts to outright stealing them and dumping them off cliffs on the back side of the island."

"And he'll testify to all of this?"

"If he gets a deal. But that's minor stuff compared to what else he says he's got, starting with the dead buffalo. He said Baby Head ordered him to kill the buffalo so it would make news and would get blamed on aliens."

Juarez laughed again. "And of course that would bring more customers to his magical mystery tours," she said.

"Exactly," Stilwell said.

"What evidence do you have for all of this?"

"Well, last week I got a search warrant signed by Judge Harrell and went to Terranova's cart barn. This is when I first met Gaston. I seized a saw handle that tested positive for blood. I have it locked up but haven't submitted it to the lab yet for comparison to blood from the buffalo."

"Why not?"

"I've been busy with a murder investigation, and the buffalo case will be such a low priority at the lab that it'll be six months before I get a report back. Unless I have a prosecutor pushing it through. That's what I was sort of waiting for."

Juarez shook her head.

"That's a catch-twenty-two," she said. "I don't think I could press charges without results. And I couldn't push for results without charges in place."

"But now Gaston wants to cooperate."

"To save his own neck. It's not a good look if he's the one who killed and cut up that poor animal."

The desk clerk reappeared behind the check-in counter. Stilwell saw that it was Fred Nettles, the night manager he had dealt with during the eviction dustup. He had apparently just come on duty. Stilwell lowered his voice so that he would not be overheard.

"Gaston says he was also working in the cart barn when Terranova met with Allen about this proposal to build a giant Ferris wheel out on the point past the Casino. Publicly, the mayor's already supporting it as a big boost to tourism. But Gaston says Allen and Terranova are shadow partners in it. The mayor gets a piece of the action for supporting the project, and he chips off a piece for Terranova."

Juarez's body language changed. She leaned in toward Stilwell, and her face lost the mirth it had displayed earlier at the mention of Baby Head.

"Can we trust this guy Gaston?" she asked.

"I don't know yet," Stilwell said. "He's desperate. I leaned on him last week when I was at the barn conducting the search. A couple days later his wife reported him missing. I thought maybe he had lammed it, but then he walks into the sub today and says he's been hiding because Terranova is going to kill him to keep him quiet."

"Over a dead buffalo?"

"He says Baby Head's afraid he'll bow to the pressure I put on him and talk. About everything. The buffalo, the Ferris wheel, and everything else he knows. And that's exactly what he's willing to do if we cut him a deal."

"Does this Baby Head have any record that supports this kind of reaction?"

"None."

"Is he from the island?"

"I heard he came here about the time he applied for the tour license."

"From where?"

"The mainland. He's got a tattoo on his arm. Six-six-one. That's the area code for Bakersfield."

Juarez was quiet as she thought about how to handle the situation. Stilwell looked at his watch. It was getting late and he wanted to go back to the sub to check on Gaston before he went home for dinner.

"What do you think?" he prompted. "You want to talk to Gaston? I have to pick up some food to take him and another guy I have in lockup. That other one you'll deal with tomorrow. Assault on a law enforcement officer with GBI."

"Well..." Juarez began. "Sure, we can go talk to him, but this is really something I should bring to the public integrity unit. All corruption-of-government-officials cases go there. They would have to make the call."

Stilwell nodded. He knew this but was disappointed because taking the case to the PIU would slow things down considerably. An investigation of an elected official was always fraught with consequences for any misstep by prosecutors or their investigators.

"Why don't we go talk to him so you can get a sense of him and the situation," he said. "If you want to kick it over to the public corruption team after that, that's your call. We can meet up with Tash afterward and grab dinner."

"Okay," Juarez said. "Sounds like a plan."

31

STILWELL IMMEDIATELY KNEW something was wrong. The main door to the substation was locked, and it shouldn't have been. He had two deputies on duty for the evening shift, Esquivel and a man named Porter whom he had pulled off the midnight shift. He had told Esquivel to stay in the sub while Porter handled patrol duties. If Porter needed backup on a call, Esquivel was to alert Stilwell. The bottom line was that he wanted one man in the sub at all times as protection for Gaston.

But locking the front door was not part of the plan. The substation was supposed to be open to the public 24/7 and locked only when all personnel were in the field.

"This isn't right," Stilwell said.

"What do you mean?" Juarez asked.

"Esquivel's supposed to be in there and the door shouldn't be locked."

"Is he a deputy? Maybe he got a callout or something?"

"Then he would have called me."

Stilwell put the bag containing the meals they had picked up for Gaston and Spivak on the ground and pulled out his keys.

"You stay out here until I check it out," he said.

He unlocked the door and entered. He moved through the waiting area and into the bullpen. There was no sign of Esquivel, and the first thing Stilwell noticed was that the door to the tech closet was standing open. He looked in and saw that the middle shelf of the equipment rack was empty. The external hard drive was missing.

Stilwell drew his weapon and moved toward the jail section. The first cell he came to was where Spivak was supposed to be. But he was gone. Instead, he saw Esquivel lying face down on the concrete floor, his hands cuffed behind his back, an orange scrub shirt wrapped around his head and soaked with blood.

Stilwell quickly unlocked the door, slid it open, and went to Esquivel. He pulled the shirt away from his head and used two fingers to check for a carotid pulse. Esquivel was alive but unconscious. Stilwell used his cuff key to release his arms and then turned him onto his back. There was a deep gash across Esquivel's forehead, and blood was flowing back into his hairline. Stilwell reached over to the bed, pulled the pillow and blanket off, propped the pillow under Esquivel's head, and used the edge of the blanket to try to stanch the bleeding.

Esquivel started to groan.

"Eddie, you're all right," Stilwell said. "I'm going to get you help. Just hang in there."

He grabbed the two-way off Esquivel's belt, called Porter on it, and ordered him back to the sub. He then put the radio down on the floor and gently started to pat Esquivel's cheek. This produced another groan.

"Eddie, wake up. What happened here? How did—"

"Oh my God!"

Stilwell turned. Juarez had come into the jail section.

"Monika, check the other cell," Stilwell ordered. "Gaston is in there. Go!"

Juarez stepped over to the other cell and immediately brought a hand up to her mouth to stifle a scream. There was a cinder-block wall between the two cells, and Stilwell couldn't see what she saw.

"What?" he said.

"He's . . . he's dead," she said. "I think."

Stilwell leaped to his feet and left the first cell to join her. He looked through the bars into the second cell. Henry Gaston was no doubt dead. He was sitting on the cell's steel toilet, his head back, exposing a gaping neck wound and a cascade of blood down the front of his shirt. He had nearly been decapitated.

"What is happening?" Juarez shouted in a panicked voice.

"Listen to me," Stilwell said calmly. "I need you to leave the sub and go to the fire station next door. Tell them you have an officer down and he needs medical attention."

Juarez didn't move.

"Monika!" Stilwell shouted. "Go next door and get the EMTs. Now!"

Juarez seemed to snap out of it. Her eyes focused on Stilwell's and she nodded.

"Okay, okay," she said. "I'm going."

She left, and Stilwell pulled his phone. He called the sheriff's comms center on the mainland to report a homicide and an officer down. He requested that Captain Corum and the homicide unit be alerted and dispatched to Catalina.

As soon as Stilwell ended the call he heard another groan from the first cell. He went back to Esquivel and found him trying to get up off the floor.

"Hold on, Eddie," he said. "Stay down. We have help coming. Let the EMTs look at you before you try to get up."

"I think I'm going to be sick," Esquivel said.

"That's okay, that's okay. It probably means you're in shock.

Stay down and stay calm, and turn your head to the side. Help is on the way."

"Okay. All right."

"Do you remember what happened, Eddie?"

"Uh, I got hit."

"Who hit you? Was it Spivak?"

"Yeah, Spivak. He hit me. He was screaming about something, so I came to see what was happening, and I got too close. He grabbed my shirt. He pulled me into the bars and I hit my head. And then . . . that's all I remember."

"Okay. It will come back. Just take it easy. Help's coming."

"Did he get away? I think he took my keys."

"Yeah, he's gone."

Stilwell thought about Spivak's escape. He checked his watch. The last ferry to the mainland had left forty-five minutes before. Esquivel was actively bleeding from fresh wounds, so Stilwell guessed that the attack and escape had occurred recently, after the ferry's departure. That meant Spivak was still on the island — or he'd left on a boat he'd had stashed away somewhere. Stilwell assumed it was the latter. His instincts told him that this had been a setup from the start. That Spivak had engineered his placement in the jail so he could take out Gaston should he surrender or be arrested.

His phone buzzed. It was Captain Corum calling.

"Stil, what the hell's going on over there?"

"It's a mess, Captain. We've got a deputy down but alive, a prisoner dead, and another prisoner who escaped."

"Can you lock down the island?"

"I think it's too late. This was a planned assassination and most likely the escape was part of the plan."

"Who's the victim?"

"The dead man was a guy who said he could take down a local gangster and the mayor if we made him a deal."

"And you believed him?"

"I did, and I think so did somebody else."

"I'm coming out with a team. Be ready to brief us."

"I'll be here and I'll be ready."

32

ONCE THE MAINLAND team had assembled in Avalon, the investigation moved through the night. Stilwell was questioned repeatedly by two different pairs of detectives under Captain Corum's command. Even Monika Juarez was questioned extensively. Eduardo Esquivel was brought to the island's only twenty-four-hour clinic and diagnosed with a concussion to go with the deep laceration a metal bar had left across his forehead. His telling of what had happened in the jail would come later.

Corum's investigators reviewed the video of Merris Spivak's attack on Deputy Dunne the Saturday before, saw the intention in the assault, and understood what Stilwell had come to understand too late: that the violent attack was planned and that Spivak had wanted to be arrested and held in the substation so he would be in place should Henry Gaston come out of hiding and be jailed by Stilwell.

"I delivered him right to Spivak," Stilwell said.

"There was no way you could have known," Corum said. He quickly added, "At least that's my opinion."

Meaning that if a fall guy was needed in the case, Stilwell would still be the leading candidate.

The investigation stretched into Friday's daylight hours, preventing Stilwell from picking up Judge Harrell at the harbor and getting him to sign the search warrant for the Black Marlin Club. Stilwell knew it was just as well. The rule of law required search warrants to be executed within forty-eight hours of a judge's signature. That was most likely impossible now with the Gaston case dominating his time and attention. He decided he would wait until the new week, then go over to Harrell's home court in Long Beach, get the warrant signed, and come back with Sampedro and Ahearn to conduct the search.

It was not ideal to delay one homicide investigation because of another, but the circumstances were dictating his moves. He explained this to Corum and then to Ahearn, who called after getting wind of what had happened at the sub. Stilwell wasn't sure if he was calling to poke him about the situation he was in or simply to assure him that the Leigh-Anne Moss investigation was continuing on the mainland.

"We'll keep it moving," Ahearn said. "You fall in when you're clear of that shit out there, and then we'll search the club."

Stilwell and the investigators hadn't slept all night, and it was unlikely the town's residents had gotten much sleep either. Two sheriff's helicopters had been dispatched to the island to circle the town, beaches, and coastal waters in a cover-your-ass search for the wanted man. It was not surprising that Spivak was not located. He was either hiding or long gone.

What was also long gone was the external hard drive from the tech closet, and with it the recording of Stilwell's interview of Gaston. With Gaston dead and the recording gone, any case against Oscar "Baby Head" Terranova would be in jeopardy. Stilwell had taken no notes during the interview because he knew he had a recording. A reconstruction of what Gaston said now, hours later, would invite a legitimate challenge if offered in court as evidence.

"We're completely fucked," Corum said when this problem was explained to him.

"Maybe not completely," Stilwell responded.

He told Corum about the search of the cart barn he had conducted and about the saw handle that had tested positive for blood. He revealed that it had not yet been submitted for forensic analysis, and the captain agreed to personally take it to the lab and use his position to prioritize DNA comparison to blood from the buffalo.

"Even if it's a match, it won't get us far," Corum said. "It solves the buffalo caper but not the murder of our cooperating witness."

"It's a start," Stilwell said. "It gives us some leverage with Terranova. Maybe enough to flip him and move up the ladder."

Corum nodded reluctantly. Stilwell had earlier briefed him on what Gaston had said about Terranova's alleged relationship with the mayor.

"We're staying away from that ladder until we have more evidence and it's rock solid," he said.

By midmorning the media was onto the story, led initially by Lionel McKey from the *Call* but soon followed by reporters and camera operators from the mainland-based news channels and the *Los Angeles Times*. Since Spivak had escaped, the session in the courtroom next to the sub was over in a matter of minutes. Judge Harrell and Deputy DA Juarez handled a short docket of cases involving minor crimes in which defendants had been released without bail after arrest. Once court was adjourned and Harrell and Juarez had headed back to the boats, the media members were told to gather in the courtroom and await a press conference to be conducted by Corum.

McKey, the lone local reporter, was not happy about being lumped in with the carpetbaggers from the mainland. He started calling Stilwell's cell phone every ten minutes. Besides being frustrated by the repeated calls, which he sent directly to voicemail,

Stilwell was annoyed by the fact that McKey had somehow gotten his private number. Stilwell had never given it to him.

Finally, when the fifth call started buzzing his phone, Stilwell answered with a low but intense tone. He was sitting in the bullpen with several of the investigators working around him.

"Who gave you this number?"

"Uh, I...don't really remember. I think you did, actually."

"Nice try. I have no comment at this time, Lionel. And blowing up my phone with your constant calls and messages is not the way to make me want to talk to you."

"Look, I apologize, okay? But, man, this is a local goddamn story, and we've got all the heavy hitters coming in from overtown, and my deadline's in like three hours. I need something they don't have. It's a matter of pride and I need it now. I just thought you'd get that and give the hometown paper something."

"Well, you thought wrong. This is a murder investigation and there's an escaped killer out there. No comment."

"Look, we can trade. I guarantee you that someday you'll need me to write a story that helps you with a case, and if you help me now, I'll remember it then."

Stilwell let him hang for a long moment before responding.

"Is that it?" he finally said. "That's your best shot?"

"Well, what do you want?" McKey asked.

"I want you to stop calling me."

He disconnected and looked at the detective sitting at the desk across from him. His name was Crockett, like the detective on *Miami Vice*.

"Fucking reporters," Crockett said.

"Yeah," Stilwell said.

He got up and went into his office, which had been commandeered by Corum. The captain was writing on a yellow legal pad.

"Need your office back?" Corum asked.

"No, not really," Stilwell said. "What are you going to give the press?"

"I'm going to feed them shit and they're going to love it."

"Are we putting out Spivak's photo?"

"Course."

"What are you going to say happened?"

"That he overpowered a deputy, got the keys, and escaped. Clean and simple."

"Are you naming Esquivel?"

"I should but I won't. It's not going to matter, though. He's done in the department."

"He's not a bad cop. What about a suspension?"

"It won't be my call. But he let a prisoner escape and kill a guy. And Spivak may kill others. Hard to come back from that."

"What about Gaston?"

"What about him?"

"Are you going to say we had him in protective custody?"

"Fuck no, are you kidding me? He was being held for cutting up the buffalo, end of story. That case is solved and that's the silver lining in this whole thing. The guy who cut off the head of the buffalo nearly had his own head chopped off."

Stilwell nodded.

"You need anything?" he said. "A coffee or a Coke?"

"I'm already floating, I've had so much coffee," Corum said.

"Okay."

"Listen, I want you out there with me in front of the media. You're the head guy here on the island and you should be standing with me. You don't have to say anything. I'll introduce you and you just stand there."

"Whatever you need, Cap."

Stilwell took his coffee mug off the desk and stepped out of the office. But he didn't go to the break room for coffee. He walked into the jail and saw that the body and the forensics team were gone. He quickly pulled his phone and called McKey back. The reporter answered the call with an excited tone.

"Sergeant Stilwell. What's up?"

"You didn't get this from me."

"Okay."

"Say it."

"I didn't get it from you. It's off the record, deep background. Whatever you tell me, you won't be anywhere near it."

Stilwell turned so he could watch the door and see if anyone was coming in. He lowered his voice when he spoke again.

"Okay, prove I can trust you," he said. "At the press conference, the captain's going to state that the prisoner who got murdered was in jail because he had admitted to killing the buffalo up on the preserve last week."

"Was that the motive for the murder?" McKey asked.

"Don't ask questions. I'm not answering any. What the captain won't be saying is that the dead guy worked for Island Mystery Tours in cart maintenance."

"Okay…"

McKey obviously wasn't making the jump.

"So the mutilated buffalo juices the aliens-on-Catalina stories in the media…" Stilwell prompted.

"Holy shit," McKey said. "And that in turn juices business for Island Mystery Tours."

"Cause and effect."

"Did the guy who killed the buffalo admit that was why he did it?"

"I told you I'm not answering questions. But why else would he do it?"

"That's Baby Head Terranova's business. Is he being investigated?"

"Write a good story, Lionel. Just keep me out of it."

Stilwell disconnected before McKey could respond and pocketed his phone.

33

AS THE SUN set on Friday, Corum and his team of investigators piled into two helicopters and flew back to the mainland. The reporters had left earlier, as had the body of Henry Gaston, which was escorted across the Santa Monica Bay by a sheriff's boat, offloaded, and taken to the coroner's office for autopsy. The hit man Merris Spivak remained at large and it was a coin flip as to whether he had somehow gotten off the island or was still in Avalon or in the mountains hiding. Stilwell had no opinion. His attention was on how to make a case against the man who he believed had brought Spivak to the island with the purpose of killing Gaston.

Stilwell had been awake for thirty-eight hours by the time he got home. He had expected Tash Dano to be waiting for him, but the house was dark. She had not responded to his earlier texts about plans for the evening or to his heads-up that he was on his way home. The truth was that he was too tired to eat or discuss his day. He wanted to sleep. He called her, but when it went straight to voicemail, he was relieved — he was too exhausted even to engage in a basic phone conversation.

"Hey, Tash," he said. "I'm home and I'm beat. I'm going to

crawl into bed and sleep for about ten hours. Come on by if you want, but I can't promise that I'll be good company. Love you."

He disconnected, wondering if his utter exhaustion had lowered his defenses enough to say the last two words of the message. He had never said those words to her before and wondered what her reaction would be.

About a month earlier, they had reached a point in their relationship where they had agreed to let each other track the location of the other's phone. Tash had suggested this, admitting that she felt slightly insecure about being involved with a man who often left the island for work-related trips or to deal with the final dissolution of property and emotions from his marriage. Stilwell understood this and agreed to the mutual tracking. It seemed to him a modern addition to the steps of a deepening relationship, even though he felt no personal need to always know where his lover was. But now, for the first time, he attempted to track Tash.

He opened up her contact on his phone and thumbed the photo he had assigned to her number, and it opened up to her details and a map. The map showed her at the Buffalo Nickel, a bar that was out near the desal plant in the industrial section of the island. The bar was a locals' hangout away from the tourist sector — he had been there with her at least twice — and he was not surprised that she had gone there after work on a Friday evening. But under the map it said the location was more than two hours old. It would normally say *Live* under the map if it was a current location, so she must have turned her phone off, and that was puzzling.

Stilwell realized he was stumbling into the same insecurity trap that Tash had fallen into and that modern technology only served to heighten. Again, he ascribed it to his exhaustion and tried to dismiss it. He plugged his phone into the charger on the bedside table, set an alarm for seven the next morning, stripped off his clothes, and got into bed. Within five minutes he was asleep.

An hour later he was awakened by the phone. He checked the screen and saw it was Tash calling him. He hoped she wasn't going to try to entice him to come out to the Buffalo Nickel. He tried to answer with a cheery voice.

"Hey, you still at the Nickel? You get my message?"

There was no response.

"Tash?"

"So you love her, huh?"

It was a male voice that was muffled in some way. Stilwell didn't recognize it. It had a sneering tone to it.

"Who is this?"

"It doesn't matter who it is. What matters is what you're going to do to save the girl you love."

"Put Tash on the phone."

"Can't do that."

"Where is she? What is this?"

"You have something we want."

"What are you talking about? I don't —"

"The tool. We want the tool."

The fog of exhaustion cleared and he suddenly knew what was going on.

"The saw handle? I don't have it. It went to the lab in L.A."

"Don't lie to me, Stilwell. You lie, and Natasha is never seen again."

The formal use of Tash's name somehow underlined the seriousness of the call. This man had her and had read her name off a credit card or some document. Tash didn't have a driver's license because she never drove anything but a golf cart or a boat.

Stilwell stood up and started pacing to keep the panic out of his voice. "Okay. What do you want me to do?"

"We want you to get the tool out of the evidence safe and destroy it."

Stilwell thought he recognized the voice now. Merris Spivak. His neurons were firing and he broke out in a cold sweat. The image of Henry Gaston with his neck gaping open rushed into his brain.

"Listen to me, Spivak. You hurt her and I will hunt you down to the ends of the earth."

"Don't threaten me. This is simply business. A trade. We have a camera set up at the boat ramp. You go there with the tool and we watch you. There's a trash barrel there. You leave it in the barrel and go away. After that, you get your girl back—in one piece. You fuck with us, then it will be two pieces. I don't know, maybe three or four."

Stilwell knew the boat ramp was part of the Catalina Boat Yard in the industrial sector, behind the Buffalo Nickel and not far from Baby Head Terranova's cart barn.

He suddenly realized that Spivak had turned Tash's phone on to call him. Using her phone guaranteed that Stilwell would answer. Stilwell put his phone on speaker and as he talked, he opened Tash's contact to track her phone's location.

"All right," he said. "I need to talk to her first. I'm not doing this without proof of life. You understand me?"

"You want proof of life, you'll get proof of life," Spivak said.

The phone showed her location on the point behind the desal plant.

Stilwell heard a rustling sound and then his name. He knew it was Tash's voice. Her next words were muffled by a gag or a hand over her mouth. Spivak came back on the phone.

"There's your proof of life," he said. "Now, do we have a deal or should I do some work here?"

"I want to talk to her," Stilwell said.

"Impossible."

"That could have been a recording and she could already be dead. I want to talk to her."

"Fine."

He heard rustling again and an off-phone instruction from Spivak: "Answer yes or no only. Say anything else and you get hurt."

He returned to the phone.

"Okay, Detective, talk," Spivak said. "You have ten seconds."

"Tash, you okay?" he asked.

"Yes," Tash said, her voice strained with fright.

"You trust me?" Stilwell asked.

"Yes," she said.

"I'm going to get you home. I promise."

"Yes," she said.

Then it was Spivak back on the phone.

"The boat ramp," he said. "If I don't see you on the camera within an hour, she's a goner, man."

"I'll be there," Stilwell said.

The line went dead. Stilwell looked down at his phone, went to the Settings menu, and stopped sharing his location with Tash's phone. He didn't want Spivak to know when or how he would be coming for him.

34

THE SEAS WERE flat and the reflection of a crescent moon lit Stilwell's path across the black water. It took him fifteen minutes on the Zodiac to get from the sheriff's dock in the harbor to the point behind the. desalination plant where Tash's phone had last come up on the tracking app. He ran with no lights and throttled down when he cut in toward the plant from a thousand yards out. He raised binoculars to his eyes and searched the shore. The location he got from Tash's phone would not be exact. He needed to find a target. But Spivak — and Tash — could be anywhere on the point.

The exterior of the plant was well lighted, and there were several small structures surrounding the large blue storage tanks and the forest of piping and filtration systems that delivered fresh water to them. Most of the sheds and trailers were dark, but behind the window of one small structure, he saw the bluish-white glow from an electronic screen. It was a metal-sided trailer that sat on five-foot stacks of cinder block, a hedge against flooding from the occasional king tide. Between these legs were sections of breakaway lattice. Stilwell counted six steps up to a landing. The front door had a small square window through which the glow was visible. Stilwell held the binoculars on the trailer for several seconds but saw no movement. He understood that it could simply be a computer left on after the day's work stoppage, but most untended computers had timers that put their screens to sleep.

Stilwell decided that he needed to check out the trailer.

He was three hundred yards offshore now. He goosed the throttle to get some momentum and a few seconds later cut the engine for a silent approach. When the craft slowed a hundred yards out and started to drift, he dropped an anchor over the side, waited for it to catch, then cleated the line. He was wearing his dive team wet suit. He slung a waterproof backpack over his shoulders, pulled down the diving mask from his forehead, and slipped over the side of the craft into the cold, dark water. He felt the cold stab into his ears and chill his scalp. He kicked his legs and headed toward shore.

Ten minutes later he walked out of the surf and picked his way up the rocky shore toward the asphalt-paved apron surrounding the plant. There was no fence or other impediment to a waterside approach.

An old wooden equipment shed stood on the outer edge of the asphalt. Stilwell made it there first and used it as a blind to take a guarded look around its corner at the trailer he had been watching. Again, he saw no movement but decided it was still his target. He checked his watch. He had ten minutes left in the hour he had been given.

He slung the backpack to the ground and unzipped it. He removed his dive mask and stripped off the wet suit, leaving it on the ground like a snakeskin. From the backpack he pulled out black jeans, a shirt, and shoes and quickly dressed. He got out his phone and a folding knife and shoved them into his pockets, then took out his gun and tucked it under his belt at the back of his pants.

The target trailer was forty yards away across open asphalt. Stilwell moved to the other corner of the shed to see if he could chart a path with less exposure. He saw that it was a much shorter run to the nearest water-storage tank and from there a quick run to the far end of the trailer.

Stilwell took a deep breath and took off for the water tank. He covered the ground quickly and, without breaking stride, followed the huge tank's curving sidewall halfway around its circumference. He didn't stop. He kept momentum and sprinted across the final ten yards to the end of the target trailer. He huddled against the latticework and waited, listening for the door opening or any other sign that he had been spotted.

All he heard were the waves hitting the rocky shore.

He looked through the latticework to try to see under the trailer, but it was too dark. He tugged at it and found it loose, the wood rotting from long-term exposure to the sea air.

He gripped the lattice with both hands, pulled a section of it loose, and carefully laid it down on the asphalt. Again he waited to see if his actions had drawn attention but heard only the sound of the waves. He peeked around the corner at the door to the trailer. It remained closed, the glow from the window steady.

Stilwell ducked into the dark space under the trailer. It was crowded with rusting pipes and other debris. Looking up at the underside of the trailer floor, he checked for any other way in, but it was too dark to see. As he started to back out, a cell phone rang. The second ring was cut short as someone answered. He heard a muffled male voice from above. He could not make out the words but the call was a reminder that he was out of time.

He ducked out from under the trailer and pulled the gun from his belt. He checked down the side of the trailer. He was facing the stairs with the door to the right on the landing. He could not see hinges on the door, which told him it opened inward. That was a good break.

Stilwell ran to the stairs and took them two at a time. At the top of the steps, he leaned his weight back against the wooden safety rail, raised his left leg, and drove his heel into the spot just above the doorknob. The wood splintered with a loud pop and the door burst open. Stilwell's momentum carried him forward and he went in, gun up and in a combat crouch.

His eyes swept left to right, and Spivak was there, standing in the middle of the trailer. He was bare-chested and both hands were at his waist, frozen in the act of unbuckling his belt. On the desk next to him was a handgun, visible in the light from a laptop screen. The two men stared at each other for a split second before Stilwell fired.

Spivak's head snapped back and he dropped to the floor. It was only then that Stilwell saw Tash on a cot at the far end of the trailer. She was gagged and her hands were above her, tied to the metal frame at the head of the bed.

Stilwell moved toward her, checking Spivak as he passed. The shot had struck him above the right eyebrow. An instant kill shot. Spivak's eyes were still open.

Stilwell moved on to Tash and gently pulled the gag down over her chin.

"You're safe, Tash," he said. "You're safe."

As soon as she was free of the gag, a shriek came from her mouth, and tears burst from her eyes. Stilwell worked the knots to free her wrists.

"He's not going to hurt you," he said. "Nobody's going to hurt you."

He got one of her hands free and moved to the other.

"He said, 'Time's up,' and started taking off his clothes. He was going to kill me after."

"I know, I know," Stilwell said soothingly.

He couldn't break the last knot. He reached into his pocket, pulled out the knife, knelt, and carefully cut through the binding, all the while trying to shake the image that had charged into his head of Spivak on top of Tash on the cot.

Once Tash was finally free, she slid off the cot onto the floor and put her arms around Stilwell's neck in a viselike lock. Her body shook with sobs.

"I'm so sorry," Stilwell said. "This is on me. All on me."

He held her as tightly as she held him.

"I need to get you out of here," he said.

"Not yet," she said.

She refused to release her grip and kept her head buried against his chest.

"He played your message to me," she said. "You said you loved me. I knew then that you would come."

Stilwell kissed the top of her head.

"There was no way I wasn't coming," he said.

She finally released him and raised her head to look over his shoulder at Spivak's body on the floor. Stilwell stood, pulling her up with him.

"Let's get out of here," he said. "I need to call for backup."

Stilwell kept an arm around her as they approached the body to go to the door. He saw the laptop. The screen was split by two camera views. One was a view of the boat ramp and a nearby picnic table and trash can. The other was on the entrance to the boatyard. It told him that the approach on the water had been the right move.

At the desk, Tash suddenly stopped.

"Wait," she said.

There was a cardboard box on the desk containing tissues. She pulled one free and used it to pick up the gun. She then leaned down and put it on the floor next to Spivak's body.

"You shouldn't —" Stilwell started, then stopped.

He nodded and they proceeded to the door, still holding on to each other as though nothing could ever split them apart.

Before they got there, the sound of a cell phone ringing stopped them. Stilwell looked back at the body on the floor. He could see light from a phone protruding from the left pocket of Spivak's pants.

Stilwell went back, grabbed the tissue that Tash had used, pulled the phone free, and put it on the floor. It said **Unknown Caller** on the screen. He hit the Accept button and put the call on speaker.

The caller said nothing. Stilwell thought he could hear the faint sound of music in the far background.

"Baby Head, I know it's you," Stilwell said. "Your man is dead...and I'm coming for you next."

There was silence on the line for a few seconds and then the caller disconnected.

35

CAPTAIN CORUM WAS not happy about having to spend
another night and day on Catalina heading up the investigation of
another death. His team included two of the investigators assigned
to the murder of Henry Gaston, but this time they were supple-
mented by two deputies from the officer-involved-shooting team.
Stilwell and Tash Dano were questioned separately and repeatedly. Stilwell conducted a walk-through of the crime scene with
the investigators, from the rocky shoreline where he had come out
of the water to the interior of the trailer where the body of the man
he had killed was still lying on the floor.

From the start of the investigation, neither Corum nor Stilwell
was concerned that there would be any verdict other than that the
shooting was within department policy. The only issue was in Stilwell's decision to carry out the rescue of the abducted woman on
his own, without calling for backup until it was over. Corum told
Stilwell he would likely receive a suspension for this move.

At one point Corum took a phone call and stepped away from
the investigators to speak quietly. The call was short and Corum
did more listening than speaking. When it was over, Corum pocketed his phone and nodded to Stilwell to join him.

"That was Mayor Allen," he said. "He wants me to take you off the island. Permanently."

"I bet he does," Stilwell said. "What did you tell him?"

"Not much. I said I'll consider that at the conclusion of our investigation."

"He's going to be sweating when we pick up Terranova and put the squeeze on him."

"If we find Terranova."

Stilwell knew that Corum had put two of his investigators on finding Baby Head and taking him in for questioning. So far, they hadn't even picked up his trail.

"A guy like him, he had an escape plan," Stilwell said. "He was probably on the mainland when this thing went down."

"Well, we don't have much of a case against him, do we?" Corum said.

"He ordered Spivak to grab Tash, I know it. He was the one who called to check that it was done."

"And we can't prove any of that."

"We have the saw handle."

"Yes, we have the saw handle, but it doesn't prove a thing when it comes down to what happened to Gaston and what happened tonight. If we can find him, we'll see what we can get out of him."

"He'll just lawyer up," Stilwell said. "We need to charge him. Put him in a cell."

"Then we'll need more evidence."

Stilwell shook his head. He was frustrated but knew that Corum was right—and that he was just as frustrated.

"I'll get more," he said.

Corum pulled his phone and checked a text.

"Not now, you won't," he said. "You're on the bench until this investigation is over. And they're ready to do the formal interview at the substation. I'll have Ramos take us over."

Fifteen minutes later Stilwell was sitting in front of two OIS investigators, Batchelor and Harrington, in the interview room at the substation. It was the formal, on-the-record sit-down, and the story he told here would be locked permanently into the file. This would be the interview that was referenced should any legal action occur following the shooting.

While Corum watched on the feed in the dayroom, Harrington did most of the talking and questioning. It was now late Saturday morning and they had gleaned all they could from the scene and evidence. Stilwell knew from past experience that this was where things could become adversarial. Despite operating on one hour's sleep over the past two days, he believed he was ready for it.

"Let's start with the decision-making process," Harrington said. "You get this call, they say they have your girlfriend, you ask for proof of life and you get it, and then you decide to be a one-man rescue team. Can you walk us through how you came to handle it that way?"

"Sure," Stilwell said. "Time. The caller gave me an hour. In my mind, that meant I didn't have a minute to spare. I couldn't wait for anyone to come over from the mainland, even by helicopter. I had only one deputy on duty on the island at the time, and I didn't think she would be up to it."

"That was Deputy Ramirez. In what way did you think she wasn't up to it?"

"Experience-wise. We all know that deputies assigned to this island have shown some form of...deficiency in their work. I've worked with Ramirez for the past nine months and this was going to be a rescue mission, not a patrol. I just didn't have confidence in her, and I thought she could end up getting hurt herself. I didn't want that."

Harrington had a yellow pad on the table in front of him and made a check mark on it next to a written note Stilwell couldn't read from his position.

"How long have you had a relationship with Natasha Dano?" he asked.

Stilwell understood that this questioning would jump all over the place to try to catch him off guard. The important thing, he knew, was to not dissemble or outright lie. If he did, things could go downhill fast.

"We started having a few casual dates about ten or eleven months ago," he said. "I would say things started to get serious about six months ago."

"Do you live together?" Harrington asked.

"Technically, no. We both have our own homes, but we end up at one place or the other just about every night. Most often my place. There's more room and a better kitchen."

"And this was a secret relationship?"

"Not really. We didn't go around advertising it, if that's what you mean. But we didn't go out of our way to hide it. Tash — Natasha — doesn't like going to the mainland, so that meant staying local if we went out for dinner or to socialize."

"You two had been to the Buffalo Nickel together before?"

"Yes. A few times. It's a locals' place for the most part. Off the beaten path."

"Did you know she was going there last night?"

"Yes and no. I had been so busy with yesterday's work that I texted that she probably wouldn't see me. She texted back saying that was fine — I'm sure you've looked at our phones. I didn't know she was at the Nickel till I got home to crash. I checked her location and saw she had been there earlier in the evening."

"You hadn't told her about what kept you working all day? She didn't know about the Gaston killing or that Spivak had escaped?"

"There were a lot of newspeople out here yesterday. She might have seen something about it. But we didn't have a conversation about it. I don't talk about my work with her."

"Really? Why is that?"

"She grew up here on the island and was classmates with a reporter from the *Call,* Lionel McKey. They're still friends and I just never liked the idea of putting her in a position where she knew things that Lionel would like to know."

"Do you know of any instance where she passed information she heard from you over to him?"

"No, not at all. When we got more serious about our relationship, we talked about that and she understood. But I sort of stuck with the practice of keeping work stuff to myself."

"So you're telling us that she had no idea what was happening with you when she decided to go to the Buffalo Nickel last night?"

"Not as far as I know. The *Catalina Call* is the only local media on the island and it's published on Saturdays, so unless she heard some scuttlebutt about it at work or McKey reached out and asked her about it, she probably didn't know. I'm sure you've asked her this."

"Okay, well, we're just trying to figure out how they knew to grab her when she left the bar last night. Any ideas on how they knew you two were a couple?"

"Well, like I said, we didn't advertise that we were together, but it wouldn't have been that hard to find out. Since the mutilation of the buffalo up on the preserve a couple weeks ago, I've probably been on Oscar Terranova's radar as a possible threat. He could have had any one of his people checking me out, possibly following me. If he did that, they would have seen me with Tash. You can ask him when you bring him in."

That answer drew the first words from Batchelor in this round.

"We're not handling that side of the investigation," he said. "This is only about the officer-involved shooting."

"Yeah, too bad," Stilwell said. "Because that side of the investigation is what we should be focusing on."

"That side is well in hand," Batchelor said.

Stilwell looked away from them and up at the camera, knowing he was looking at Corum.

"Let's continue," Harrington said. "We want to move on to what happened in the trailer. Something's not adding up for us."

"What's that?" Stilwell responded.

He braced himself. These men had had hours to analyze the actions he had taken in a matter of seconds.

"You told us you kicked in the door and entered the trailer," Harrington said.

"That's right," Stilwell said.

"You did not identify yourself or instruct Spivak to freeze, correct?"

"That's correct. There was no time for that. But I didn't have to identify myself—he knew who I was."

"There was almost no light in the trailer. Just the computer screen. Would he have been able to see your face and identify you?"

"Good question. I don't know. I'm sure additional light came in through the open door But I identified him. I could see his face."

"You said he had just taken his shirt off and was unbuckling his pants."

"I said he had no shirt on. I don't know if he had just taken it off, because I wasn't there. You may be confusing what I said with what Tash—uh, Natasha—told you."

"My mistake. His shirt was already off when you entered the trailer. His hands were at his belt buckle, is that what you told us?"

"It's what I told you and it's what happened."

"Why did you fire your weapon if his hands were occupied at his belt?"

Stilwell was prepared for the question, although he knew his answer would break his own rule about not outright lying.

"His gun was tucked into his pants," he said. "He let go of the belt and was reaching for it when I fired."

"Tucked into the front or back of his pants?" Harrington asked.

"The front."

"And he was facing you when this happened?"

"Yes."

"Isn't it odd that he didn't remove the gun before unbuckling his belt?"

"I don't know — is it? I can't speak for what he was thinking, only what I saw."

"And you told us he was facing you."

"That's right."

"So, facing you, on what side of his body was his gun?"

Stilwell knew that Tash had put the gun on the floor on the left side of Spivak's body, but he also knew that only one in ten people was left-handed. He went with the percentages.

"His right side, my left," he said.

Harrington looked down at his notes and something about his face told Stilwell that the percentages were wrong.

"That's kind of curious," Harrington finally said.

"How so?" Stilwell asked.

Harrington glanced sideways at his partner before answering.

"Well, we've had the weapon dusted and we got a palm print on the grip," he said. "We haven't matched it to Spivak yet, but the palm is on the left-side grip, which indicates he was left-handed. But you just told us he had it tucked in on the right side of his pants. That —"

"He had the grip turned in," Stilwell said. "I think I said that during the walk-through."

Harrington and Batchelor glanced at each other.

"I don't recall that," Batchelor said.

"Neither do I," Harrington said. "So you're saying his left hand came off his belt and was reaching across his body to the weapon."

"Exactly," Stilwell said. "He was pulling it when I discharged my weapon. Then he went down and the gun ended up on the floor."

Both of his inquisitors looked at him silently, probably hoping he would add more detail, which they could evaluate for inconsistencies. But Stilwell said nothing more.

"Okay," Harrington finally said. "I think we have everything we need at this point."

He ended by officially informing Stilwell that he was relieved of duty with pay until the investigation was finished and submitted to the district attorney's office for review. There would then be a final determination of whether the shooting was within policy and the law. Stilwell would also be required to set up an appointment with the behavioral science unit and complete a psychological evaluation before receiving a return-to-duty order.

This was the routine after an officer-involved shooting.

"We will reach out to you if we need anything else," Harrington said.

"And Captain Corum will notify you when the investigation is concluded," Batchelor added.

"You know how to find me," Stilwell said. "We're finished here?"

"Done," Batchelor said.

Stilwell stood up and left the room. He believed he had handled the interview well, but he also knew that his future was in the hands of people and political forces in the department that he couldn't control.

36

STILWELL LEFT THE island with Tash on Sunday afternoon. They took the Express. Checking before they left, he was informed that Oscar Terranova's whereabouts remained unknown. With Baby Head at large, Stilwell believed it was safer for Tash to be off island with him. They would stay at a mainland resort and try as best they could to forget the events of the past two days. Stilwell also planned to show up at the behavioral science unit first thing Monday to try to get in for his psychological evaluation and a quick turnaround on his return-to-duty process.

Stilwell had been relieved of duty, but he was not planning to stop forward momentum on his investigations. There were leads to follow on the mainland and he was going to make good use of his time. He decided to splurge for Tash, and they checked into a suite at the Huntington in Pasadena. Staying there had several benefits. It was a luxury resort located far from the crowded city Tash so disliked, and it had a spa and easy access to the Huntington Gardens, which he believed Tash would love and where she could spend time while he went about his work. It was also a straight shot on the freeway from Pasadena into downtown, where he would need to go for his psych eval and casework. And finally, the last address the DMV had for Daniel Easterbrook was in Pasadena. Interviewing Easterbrook was first on his list of priorities on the mainland, and Stilwell believed that talking to him about Leigh-Anne Moss at his home was preferable to interrupting him at his downtown law firm. He wanted to confront Easterbrook when his guard was down, and there was no better way to do that than to knock unexpectedly on his front door.

But his plans went awry soon after he and Tash checked into their two-room suite and unpacked their bags. Stilwell looked up from his laptop after connecting to the hotel's Wi-Fi and saw Tash pacing in the suite's living room, arms folded tightly across her chest. It was a clear signal that this would not be a relaxing getaway for Tash and that she might have been more traumatized by the events of the weekend than she had let on. Stilwell knew that was on him. It was his relationship with her that had drawn her into Oscar Terranova's crosshairs.

"Do you think you want to talk to somebody while we're over here?" he asked.

"What do you mean?" she replied.

"Well, I have to go in and talk to the shrinks. You know, standard procedure and all of that. But when I've had to do it in the past, it's kind of helped — talking about it with a professional. I might be able to get you in to — "

"I don't want to talk to anybody. Especially a sheriff's shrink."

Her words were clipped. Her tone indicated that the subject was not up for debate. He wanted to tell her that keeping the trauma of what had happened bottled up inside could create difficulties down the line, but her answer had been so decisive that he let it go.

"I'm okay, Stil," she said. "I mean it. You don't have to worry about me."

"I know you're strong," he said. "I just thought maybe you'd want to. That's all."

"Thanks, but no, thanks."

"Okay, cool."

"What I want is to go home. Be in my own space. This was a mistake."

There it was, the undercurrent coming to the surface.

"Tash, we just got here," Stilwell said. "Why don't we just see what happens for a couple days? You know, relax, check out the spa...wait and see if they pick up Terranova and—"

"No," Tash said. "You said it was unlikely he would come after me now."

"I know. That's true. But why take a chance? Look at this place. It's like a vacation. How 'bout we just stay—"

"I don't like it here. I feel safer at home."

"Okay, okay, but there's no way we can get back to Long Beach today to get the last ferry. So let's just sleep on it, and in the morning if you feel the same way, we can talk about going back over."

She stopped pacing. "You're not listening. I'm not going to change my mind. This whole thing was a mistake. I want to go back." She started pacing again.

"Okay, we'll go back," Stilwell said. "But I don't want you going back alone, and I've got to go down to BSU first thing. You can try to sleep in and I'll hopefully get in for my evaluation, then come back and we'll check out. How's that?"

"Whatever," Tash said. "I wish we could just go tonight."

Stilwell checked his watch.

"Well, we can't," he said. "The last ferry leaves in twenty minutes and we're an hour away. That's why I picked this place. It's away from everything and it's safe. Also..."

"Also what?" she asked.

Stilwell wasn't sure how this next part would go.

"There was an interview I was going to do over here tomorrow," he said. "If we're leaving, I should probably try to get it done tonight."

"What interview?" Tash asked.

"It's on my other case. A guy who knew Leigh-Anne lives here. I could run over there now and—"

"Wait, he's here in Pasadena?"

"Yeah, I think about ten minutes from here. I was about to look it up. I'd be quick. Maybe we could order dinner when I get back."

"This whole thing, is that why we're here? So you can do your interview?"

"No, not at all. I mean, I knew it was close, but this place is—"

"Don't bother." Now she looked angry as well as agitated. "Your work always comes first. That's why I got caught up in this shit and why some gangster wants to kill me."

"Whoa, wait, hold on a second."

Stilwell closed his laptop and got up from the room's little desk. He walked toward her but she held both hands up to keep him away. He stopped.

"Tash, what's going on?" he asked.

"What's going on is that my life has suddenly changed and I don't like it," she said. "I don't want it. As long as that guy is out there, I have to look over my shoulder. And you don't seem to care. You're on to the next interview and the next case."

"That's not true. Come on. First of all, you don't have to look over your shoulder. There's no chance he's coming after you. He's on the run, Tash. He's out there hiding, and going after you makes zero sense. Why would he do it? Before, he needed you to get to me. That doesn't work anymore."

"Then, if I'm so safe, why did you take me off the island?"

"Because I thought it would be good for us to get away and be together. And, yes, I have to do things over here. I have to see the shrink before I can go back to work. I told you that."

"And you have to do your interview. What else?"

"I still have my job, Tash."

"You're relieved of duty."

"I know that, but it's temporary. And things don't just stop because I'm off duty."

"I'm never going to be first with you, am I?"

"What are you talking about? Of course you are."

She walked into the bedroom and opened the closet. Stilwell followed and watched as she pulled out her suitcase and swung it up onto the bed. She started to open its zipper.

"I just want to go back," she said. "I want to go home."

"Tash, we can't," Stilwell said. "Not tonight."

"Well, I'm packing anyway."

Stilwell stepped over and put his hand on the suitcase so she couldn't open it.

"It can wait till tomorrow, Tash," he said.

"I want to do it now," Tash said. "Why don't you just do your work. Go do your interview. I want to be alone for a while. Since it's so safe here."

The sarcasm in that last line cut Stilwell to the heart.

"You are safe, Tash," he said. "I don't want you thinking different."

"Fine," she said. "Can I open my suitcase, please?"

Stilwell removed his hand.

"Look, just go," Tash said. "Go do your thing. I really need to be by myself right now."

Stilwell knew she needed space. He backed away from the bed.

"Okay," he said. "I'll be quick and then we can talk about this again."

"I'm tired of talking about it," Tash said. "I just want to go back."

Her face was turned away from him but she sounded sad. Stilwell nodded, not knowing whether she meant back to the island or back to the way things were before she knew him.

He headed toward the door.

"Please don't be mad," Tash said.

Stilwell stopped and turned to look at her.

"I'm not mad," he said. "I'm worried about you. You've been through something pretty heavy and I want to take care of you. But you're not letting me."

"I appreciate that. Really. But I can take care of myself. I know what's right for me."

"I hope so. You know I love you."

"I do. And I love you."

He hesitantly approached her again. This time she didn't put up her hands to stop him. He wrapped his arms around her and held her in the embrace for a long moment. He kissed the top of her head.

"I'm good, Stil," she said. "You can go."

"Okay, I'll be back," he said.

He released her and headed to the door.

37

THE ADDRESS ON Daniel Easterbrook's driver's license corresponded to a mansion on Orange Grove Boulevard. The gated driveway had a call box on a metal arm that brought it within easy reach of the window of the Bronco. Stilwell pushed the button twice before getting a response.

"Yes?"

It was a woman's voice.

"L.A. County Sheriff's Department, ma'am," Stilwell said. "I need to speak to Daniel Easterbrook."

"He no longer lives here," the woman said.

Her tone indicated that she was tired of delivering the same message over and over.

"Can you tell me when he moved?" Stilwell asked.

"A month ago," she said.

He paused.

"Is this Mrs. Easterbrook?" he asked.

"It is," she said. "What's this about?"

"Can you tell me where he's living now, ma'am? I need to speak to him tonight, if possible."

"Is something wrong?"

A tone of concern cracked through the previously hard and clipped voice.

"No, ma'am," Stilwell said. "I just need to talk to him."

There was no response. He pushed the talk button again.

"Mrs. Easterbrook?" he prompted.

"I'm looking it up," she said. "I don't have it memorized."

Stilwell waited until she recited an address on Oxley in South Pasadena. He thanked her, backed the Bronco away from the gate, and headed south.

The new address belonged to a much smaller house that was not guarded by a gate and had the distinct look of a rental. No ornamental landscaping, no furniture on the porch. Stilwell parked on the street out front. There were lights on inside and this time he was able to approach the door and knock. A man in his late forties with a chiseled jaw and a full head of expensively cut brown hair opened the door. He was in workout clothes, with sweat stains under the arms of a gray T-shirt that said LAKERS across the chest in faded purple.

Stilwell was holding his badge up.

"Sheriff's department," he said. "Daniel Easterbrook?"

"Yes," the man said. "My wife told me you were coming. This is about Leigh, isn't it?"

There was a look of distress in his eyes. Hearing Leigh-Anne Moss referred to as just Leigh momentarily gave Stilwell pause.

"Yes," he finally said. "Leigh-Anne Moss. I need to ask you some questions. Can I come in?"

"She's the one they found in the harbor, isn't she?" Easterbrook asked.

"I think it would be better if we talked inside."

"Yes, of course."

Easterbrook stepped back and let Stilwell enter. He led him to a small living room where none of the furniture matched. It looked as though everything had been taken from a variety of other living rooms reflecting different fads and tastes. Easterbrook pointed him to a black leather couch while he took a chair with puffy arms and a floral pattern. Stilwell began by identifying himself and telling Easterbrook that he was assigned to the Catalina substation. Easterbrook nodded.

"I knew it was her," Easterbrook said. "When I stopped hearing from her and she didn't return my calls, I just knew it."

"You were in a relationship with her," Stilwell said. He stated it as a fact, not a question.

"I was head over heels," Easterbrook said. "I just can't bring myself to believe she's gone. Who would have done this?"

"That's what we're trying to find out," Stilwell said. "When was the last time you saw her?"

"Well, now it's been over two weeks."

"Was that on Catalina?"

"No, here. She stayed here with me, then she went back over to tell them she was through."

"Can you be more specific about the date and time you last saw her?"

"Yes, it would have been Saturday morning, the ... seventeenth. I drove her down to the Express dock in Long Beach. She took the eight-fifteen ferry."

Stilwell showed no reaction, but he knew this was likely the day Leigh-Anne had been murdered. The 8:15 ferry would have gotten her to Avalon a little after nine. It matched up with what he knew about her activities that morning before her arrival at the Black Marlin.

"You said she was going to tell them she was through," he said. "Who was she going to tell?"

"The GM at the club—a man named Crane," Easterbrook said. "She was going to pick up her last paycheck and quit. I told her to forget about the money, I'd give her the money. But she'd left some of her things at an apartment over there and she wanted to get that stuff too."

"She wasn't terminated from the club, as far as you know?"

"Terminated? You mean fired? No. Not that I know of. She was going to move in here with me. I ... gave up everything for her. I destroyed my marriage; my kids hate me. I didn't care. I mean, I cared, but I wanted her. I needed her. Now what am I going to do?"

Stilwell didn't think Easterbrook was looking for an answer from him.

"Mr. Easterbrook, when did your relationship with Leigh-Anne — Leigh — start?" he asked.

"It would have been ... three months ago," Easterbrook said. "I'd seen her there at the club before that, of course, but one night she was behind the bar and I was there alone and we started talking. You know, very casual, just banter, really, like you do with younger women, and then something ... just happened. She showed an interest in me and I felt something I'd never felt before. And I know what you're thinking: *Older man, younger woman.* But it was real. For both of us. She was funny, and she was well-read. She was a ... wildflower. She put a streak of purple in her hair. She said that was for me. It was our secret — like a signal to me when we were in the club but had to keep our relationship, you know, on the down-low."

"Nightshade."

"Exactly. I first thought the color was Catalina sage, like they have up on the hillside behind the Mount Ada. But she said it was called Nightshade. I started calling her that — it was my pet name for her. I felt this passion come to the surface in me, a passion I never knew I had. It made me rethink things — everything about my life."

He brought a thumb and finger up and pinched the bridge of his nose in what looked like an effort to stop tears. Stilwell wondered if Easterbrook had ever looked up nightshade on the internet and learned that the beautiful flower was also a deadly poison.

"What am I going to do?" Easterbrook asked again. "I know I'll never be able to fill this empty space. I can't go back to what I had before. I can't go forward."

Stilwell believed his pain was as real as his passion for the woman he called Nightshade. But just because he loved her didn't clear him as a possible suspect. From past experience, Stilwell knew that women were often killed by men who professed to love them. Easterbrook would need further scrutiny before Stilwell could sign off on his gut instinct that he was not the killer of Leigh-Anne Moss.

He let a few moments go by so Easterbrook could pull himself together. Stilwell had to tick boxes, collating what the known facts of the case were with Easterbrook's experiences and memories.

"I'm sorry I have to ask you this," he said. "But when was the last time you and Leigh were intimate?"

"The night before she went back to the island," Easterbrook said.

"And did you use a condom?"

Easterbrook paused.

"I hate to think about why you need this information," he finally said. "But the answer is no. She took care of that."

"You mean birth control?"

"Yes, she was on the pill. Why are you asking me this? Was she raped?"

Outrage was building in his voice.

"I'm just gathering all the facts," Stilwell said quickly. "We need to ask about everything because we don't know what could become important to the investigation."

Stilwell could already see the complication this information brought to the case. If it was Easterbrook's DNA that was recovered during the autopsy, it handed an easy alternative suspect to a defense lawyer representing anyone else charged. He tried to put that thought aside and continued his questioning.

"On that Saturday, what did you do after dropping Leigh off at the Express dock?" he asked.

"I just turned around and went home," Easterbrook said. "Wait—no. I stopped by my office first to pick up some files I was going to work on at home."

"Did anyone else in the office see you?"

"Uh, no, it was a Saturday. The office was closed."

"What about in the building? Was there security or some kind of check-in process? Cameras?"

"There's cameras and security but I don't remember seeing anybody. You're asking if I have an alibi, aren't you? You don't believe me."

"I'm not going to lie to you, Mr. Easterbrook. If you've got an alibi, then I need to check it. Because when we catch whoever did this and go to trial, my investigation will also be on trial. It doesn't matter whether I believe you or not. I need proof of innocence before you're in the clear."

Easterbrook nodded.

"I understand," he said. "I'm sorry."

"So, was the building locked?" Stilwell asked, pressing on. "Does it have a gated garage?"

"Yes and yes. I have a key card that opens both the garage gate and the doors to the building and my office. I'm sure that can be checked."

"It can be but it will only show that your card was used. It doesn't prove it was you. Where are the cameras?"

"Actually, I'm not sure. I've just seen the screens at the security desk."

"But no one was at that desk when you entered?"

"I don't remember seeing anyone. Maybe they were on a break or making the rounds. It was a Saturday, so I'm sure it was a short-staff day."

"And when you left with your files, did you see anyone?"

"I don't think so."

"What time did you get there and what time did you leave?"

"Probably got there a little before ten and stayed about an hour. I had to print out some documents so the originals would stay in the office."

While his instincts told him that Easterbrook was telling the truth, Stilwell knew that a further effort would be required to prove his alibi and clear him. He moved on with his questions.

"Let's get back to the relationship you had with Leigh," he said. "Did you ever buy her expensive gifts?"

"I did," Easterbrook said. "I bought her a pair of heels she wanted."

"Do you remember the brand?"

"Prada."

"And you stayed with her up at the Mount Ada on occasion?"

"Yes, that's where we would meet on the island. We'd stay there so she could work. And I would wait for her there. I used to stand on our room's balcony and look down at the club, hoping to see her when she left."

More tears came, and this time he did not try to stop or hide them.

"Do you know anyone who would have wanted to harm her?" Stilwell asked. "Did she talk about anybody who threatened her or anything like that? On the island or the mainland? Or at the club, even?"

"No, nothing like that," Easterbrook said. "That's what I don't understand. How could this happen? We were in love. I was in love for what seemed like the first time in my life. We had a plan. We were going to take the boat to Tahiti. And now there's nothing. I have nothing."

Stilwell asked a few more questions about the club and the plans Easterbrook had made with Leigh-Anne Moss. He decided he would tell Sampedro and Ahearn that they should conduct a follow-up interview with Easterbrook under formal and recorded conditions, then run down his alibi. They would also need to take a DNA swab from him. But Stilwell believed he had gotten all he could get for the moment. Easterbrook had given him his next move. Either Easterbrook or Charles Crane had lied about Leigh-Anne's last visit to the Black Marlin Club, and Stilwell was going to find out which one.

38

TASH WAS IN bed asleep when Stilwell returned to the suite. He saw her suitcase standing upright near the door. He grabbed the handle and lifted it — it was heavy and full. She was ready to go back in the morning and he knew there would be no further debate. He entered the bedroom, quietly undressed, and slipped beneath the covers next to her. If he had woken her, she didn't show it. As he tried to get to sleep, his mind crowded with thoughts about the future of their relationship and whether the very best thing he had found on Catalina was going to go away.

He knew thoughts like these would keep him awake through the night, so he shifted gears and began to review cases. This often did the trick and led him to sleep. He first went over his interview with Easterbrook and the follow-up work that was needed. Ahearn and Sampedro would be tasked with that. Though Stilwell was not overly impressed with their skills, he believed they would see what he had seen. They would perhaps put more pressure on Easterbrook and even ask him to take a polygraph test, but Stilwell believed that Easterbrook would ultimately be cleared. The semen recovered during autopsy would likely match to him, but there had been no indication of anything physical other than consensual intimacy.

From there Stilwell was drawn back to the Oscar Terranova case. Thinking about the Merris Spivak shooting and the investigation that followed, he remembered a question for which he'd had no answer. Why did Spivak — and Terranova, for that matter — think that the saw handle was still on the island and not already at the lab? As he ruminated on the question at the edges of sleep, he came to an answer that he didn't like but that he knew fit. He opened his eyes, realizing there would be no chance for sleep tonight.

Just after dawn, while Tash was still sleeping, he drove downtown. He'd left a note on the bed table telling her he'd be back by noon, and they could head down to the ferry dock then. On the freeway, he called the behavioral science unit and was told that the two therapists scheduled that day were not in yet but were booked solid and no walk-ins were being accepted. He gave his name and cell number and asked to be notified if there was a cancellation.

He kept driving. It was early enough that the traffic on the 110 was moving at a slow but steady pace, at least until downtown, where it bottlenecked as it did at any time of day. Once he was past the convention center, the freeway cleared, since he was going against the tide of commuters into downtown. He sailed on a southwest diagonal across the county to Long Beach.

The Long Beach Superior Court building on Magnolia was one of the newest courthouses in the county. The design was modern, with a mirrored-glass exterior and concrete columns. The Long Beach division of the district attorney's office was on the third floor. Stilwell identified himself at reception and asked to see Monika Juarez. He was told that she was handling the morning calendar in Judge Kyle Hawthorne's courtroom on the second floor.

Stilwell went down and found the courtroom crowded with representatives of every realm of the justice system, from prosecutors to cops to defense attorneys to defendants, and there were also family members there showing support for either the accused or their alleged victims. He slipped into an open spot on a bench at the rear of the room.

In a flat tone that reflected the routineness of the session, the judge methodically called cases to hear status reports on their slow creep through the overburdened system. Juarez sat at a table with three other prosecutors opposite a table crowded with even more defense attorneys. Stilwell watched as she stood for her own cases and sat and waited during the others. Each time she stood, she informed the judge that she was prepared to set a date for trial but that the defense was stalling through protracted plea negotiations, discovery-compliance issues, or other pretexts. The defense attorney then rose and protested the prosecutor's insinuations, and the judge refereed and made a call on how and when to proceed. It was as predictable as weekly trash pickup by the sanitation department and in some ways just as messy.

An hour into the session, Stilwell got a call from the BSU. He hustled out of the courtroom and took it in the hallway.

"We have a cancellation at one," the caller told him.

"I'll take it," Stilwell said.

"Don't be late."

"I'll be early. Who's it with?"

"Dr. Perez."

"Got it."

Over his eighteen years with the department, Stilwell had been sent to the shrinks four separate times for various reasons. He had never had a session with Perez and didn't know if the therapist was a man or a woman. Previously, he had found it easier to talk to a woman.

As he opened the courtroom door to reenter, he was met by Juarez, who was coming out. She was surprised to see him.

"Stil, what are you doing here?"

"I need to talk to you. Are you finished in there or is it just a break?"

"Finished for the day, yes."

"Do you have a few minutes?"

"Sure. Do you want to go up to my office?"

Stilwell had met with her at her office before and knew that she shared the space with three other prosecutors.

"No, I need to talk to you privately," he said. "Is there somewhere else we can go?"

"Well, it's such a nice day," Juarez said. "Let's go outside to the courtyard."

She led the way. But Stilwell thought she would not consider it a nice day for much longer.

39

STILWELL AND JUAREZ exited through a side door to a triangular plaza scattered with tables, chairs, and potted palm trees. People wearing juror tags sat or milled about. There was an open table near one of the building's concrete columns and Juarez headed toward it.

"I heard about what happened Friday night," she said. "How is Tash doing?"

"Tash is okay," Stilwell said.

"And you?"

"I'm okay too. How'd you hear about it?"

"Are you kidding? It was all over the news."

"Right."

Juarez sat down and put the stack of files she was carrying on the table. Stilwell took a chair opposite her.

"We could have gotten coffee," Juarez said. "You want me to go back and grab a couple cups from the cafeteria? They let the prosecutors shoot the line."

"No," Stilwell said. "This won't take that long."

He actually wasn't sure how long it would take but he didn't want her to have something she could throw in his face, especially hot coffee.

"Were you cleared to go back to work already?" Juarez asked.

"No, I've got my shrink session at one," Stilwell said. "And the shooting team is still working on it."

"Well, good luck. Seems like, from everything I saw, that you don't have anything to worry about on the CAPO side."

The DA's Crimes Against Police Officers unit had to review and sign off on all police shootings in the county. Such incidents fell under their jurisdiction because most law enforcement shootings involved cops reacting to perceived threats to their safety.

"I'm not worried about it," Stilwell said.

"So, what's going on?" Juarez asked.

Stilwell hadn't been sure how he was going to play it until that moment.

"You're originally from Bakersfield, aren't you?" he asked. "The six-six-one."

"Uh, yes," Juarez said cautiously. "How do you know that?"

"I did a little checking on you this morning. Pulled the story Lionel McKey wrote for the *Call* when you were assigned to the Catalina court. According to the story, you actually asked for the assignment. Is that true?"

Juarez furrowed her brow and put an uneasy smile on her face.

"I did," she said. "I thought coming out to the island would be kind of fun. But why would you check me out, Stil?"

Stilwell ignored her question and proceeded with his.

"Is that where you first met Oscar Terranova? Up there in Bakersfield?"

"What? What are you talking about?"

Both her surprise and outrage felt staged, as though she had prepped for this moment for a long time. Stilwell read her reaction and knew he was on the right track.

"You're the same age," he said. "The story said you survived growing up in a gang neighborhood in East Bakersfield to get to college and then to law school up at Davis. I figure you two knew each other from back then. Was it in high school or in a gang? Maybe both? The article in the *Call* didn't say."

It was a guess, but an educated one.

"Look," Juarez said. "I know you've probably been under a lot of stress, but be very careful about what you say here."

"Same back at you, Monika," he said. "I'm giving you the benefit of the doubt. I'm actually hoping I can help you and you can help me, and we can maybe keep this between us."

He said it but wasn't sure he could keep any of it quiet. It was all he could do to contain the fury he felt.

"What is 'this,' Stilwell?"

"I think you know what it is, and you need to talk to me, or you leave me no choice but to go down the official road with it. If I put it in my formal statement and it goes to CAPO, then you'll end up in front of the justice integrity unit explaining it."

Juarez pushed back her chair and stood up.

"I'm not going to listen to this," she said.

She started gathering her files.

"Sit down, Monika," Stilwell said. "Spivak told me you were the leak to Terranova. Right before I killed him. He said you two were homeys from back in Bakersfield. For now, I've left what I know about you out of the investigation. And I can keep it that way."

It was a bluff. Juarez stared at him from her standing position. Then she slowly sat back down. It was as good as a confession.

"You are the only one I told that I hadn't sent the saw handle to the lab yet, that it was still on the island," he said. "That's why they grabbed Tash. You told them it was locked up at the sub."

As Stilwell talked, Juarez looked off toward the other tables as though watching her career run away like a fleeing felon. But Stilwell was more interested in using her to get to the bigger fish.

"Where is he, Monika?"

"I don't know."

"Talk to me. I can help you. We can help each other."

Juarez folded her arms the way Tash had the night before. Stilwell waited. He knew she was about to break.

"Look, I made a mistake, okay?" she said. "He asked me how long the lab would take to analyze it, and I was stupid. I said the lab didn't even have it yet. That's all. I had no idea what he was going to do. It was just...conversation."

"Conversation with the primary focus of an investigation," Stilwell said. "Conversation that led to an innocent woman being abducted and terrorized by a killer who'd cut somebody's throat twenty-four hours earlier."

"You don't think I feel guilty about that? But I didn't think in a million years that that would happen."

"You're not that stupid, Monika. You gave inside information to a fucking killer."

"I *know*!"

She shouted it, causing others in the courtyard to turn from their conversations and look. Juarez took a deep breath and continued in a calm and quiet voice.

"He told me he didn't do it—kill Gaston. That it was somebody else."

"When did you talk to him?"

"He called me Friday morning and he was just as surprised as I was. He said somebody else set it up."

"Who?"

"He wouldn't say. He said it was his ace in the hole. He'd only reveal who it was if I made him a deal."

"What did you tell him?"

"I said no deal because I knew I could be the collateral. I couldn't make a deal without ending up disbarred or in jail myself."

Stilwell shook his head.

"No," he said. "Don't you see? He wouldn't have come to you if he was going to deal you in. That makes no sense. His ace in the hole is Mayor Allen. Baby Head's willing to trade him to save his own ass."

"I don't know about that," Juarez said.

"Give me the number he called from."

"It won't matter. He uses burners and changes phones all the time. It's never the same number."

"Then where is he?"

"I told you — I have no idea. This is a nightmare. If I'd known what was going to happen, I would have warned you. I would've stopped it."

"I wish you had."

"But I didn't know. Stil, you have to believe that."

Stilwell didn't answer. He was thinking about what Juarez had just told him: Terranova was willing to make a deal to give up a bigger fish than himself. It had to be the mayor.

"Who is he?" he asked. "How come he has no record? Not even a juvie jacket in Bakersfield. I checked."

"Because he's smart," Juarez said. "He stays clean and makes other people do his dirty work for him. Like me. He gets something on you and then you have no choice. It's probably how he played the mayor. He got something on him."

"What's he got on you, Monika?"

"We..."

Juarez shook her head in disgust — with the question and herself.

"We did things when we were younger," she said. "Things I'm not proud of. He has pictures, okay? Photos that would destroy me. That's all I'll tell you. That's all you need to know."

"Then this could be your way out. You must be able to get a message to him."

"What message? He'll have me whacked if he sniffs a setup—and believe me, he'll know."

She pointed to the whitish scar that ran along the left side of her jaw.

"He gave me this," she said. "When I told him I was leaving to go to college, that I wanted to be a lawyer someday. He did this to me, and you know what, I didn't even call the police. I lied about it to my mother—said I crashed my bike—because I knew he would do worse if I turned him in."

It was a terrible story, and despite himself, Stilwell felt sympathy for Juarez and her lifelong predicament. But it didn't alter the contradiction between her actions and her pose of victimhood.

"Look, you need to figure out a way to contact him," he said. "Tell him you thought about it and there is a deal to be made. He said it wasn't his play, so we'll hear him out. If he comes in and gives up the bigger fish, you'll deal."

Juarez shook her head as she thought about that.

"And so what happens to me if a deal is made?" she asked. "What's to stop him from throwing me in to sweeten the pot?"

"You said he's smart," Stilwell said. "If he gets what he wants out of it, why would he burn you? He'll want to keep you for the next rainy day."

Juarez considered that and Stilwell could read her face. She saw it as the smart move.

"And what about you?" she said. "What happens to me with you?"

"I don't know," Stilwell said. "If you help me take these guys down, I will try to move on."

"How can I trust that?"

"You're just going to have to."

Juarez shook her head.

"All of this because of a dead buffalo," she said. "It's crazy."

"It's not about the buffalo," Stilwell said. "It's about greed and power."

"I guess it always is."

"So can you get to Terranova or not?"

"Maybe. He once came to me because he needed a good lawyer. For a business matter. I gave him the name of a guy I went to law school with who does corporate law. He hired Bryson, and that was a few years ago, but the guy might still have a way to reach him."

"Bryson? Bryson what?"

"Bryson Long. He has a one-man firm down in Seal Beach."

Stilwell nodded.

"That's the lawyer on the Ferris wheel project," he said. "I was looking that stuff up Thursday night at the Zane Grey. He's gotta still be working for Terranova. He must have a way to reach him."

"I'll call him," Juarez said.

"When you get to Terranova, set up a meeting inside the courthouse," he said. "So he has to go through a metal detector."

"What if he wants to bring Bryson or a criminal defense lawyer?" Juarez asked.

"That's his right. But if they hold us up with that, he's going to be sitting in a cell until they do make a deal. Tell him that."

"And you'll be here?"

"I wouldn't miss it."

40

ON HIS WAY back downtown, Stilwell made a call to Sampedro to summarize his interview with Easterbrook the night before. He suggested a more formal and recorded interview, a DNA swab for comparison to the foreign DNA recovered during Leigh-Anne Moss's autopsy, and a hard look at his alibi.

"But you don't like him for this?" Sampedro asked.

"My take is that his grief is legit," Stilwell said. "But that doesn't mean he didn't kill her."

"Right."

"But if he was at his office in L.A. while she was at the Black Marlin Club, I think he's in the clear. There's got to be a way to confirm that or catch him in the lie."

"The DNA is going to be a problem for him."

"There was no physical indication of rape. And we have nothing else that suggests it was. A match would back up his story about it being consensual sex."

"Yeah, but maybe he has one last roll in the hay with her and then he conks her on the head and end of problem. Everything we're hearing, this girl was bad news. Maybe he found that out."

Stilwell thought of nightshade being poisonous and deadly.

"My gut says it's not Easterbrook," he said.

"You and your gut," Sampedro said. "We'll bring him in, put him in a room, and see what he says. What else you got?"

"That's it for —"

"Wait, hold on. My partner wants to talk to you."

Stilwell almost groaned. He knew where this would go. Sampedro passed the phone to Ahearn.

"Hey, shooter, what are you doing working this?" he said. "I hear you're ROD for your latest shoot-first-and-ask-questions-later escapade."

Stilwell waited until he was sure Ahearn was finished laying on the sarcasm. Nothing more came.

"For once, Ahearn, you're absolutely right," he said. "I'm relieved of duty, and that's exactly why I was giving your partner the name of a witness to be interviewed. You two can follow up on it or not. Doesn't matter to me."

"You know what I'm relieved of?" Ahearn said. "I'm relieved I don't have to work on this with you anymore."

He disconnected the call. Stilwell felt his cheeks start to burn. He looked at himself in the rearview mirror and saw that his face had reddened. He tried to let it go. He had not discussed with Sampedro his realization that if Daniel Easterbrook was telling the truth about Leigh-Anne Moss, then Charles Crane had lied. Stilwell had kept that to himself because it threw the investigation back over to the island, and that was his part of the case, whether he was on duty or not. He felt guilty about withholding salient information from fellow investigators — it was never the best way to run an investigation. But to Stilwell, it was the only way with Ahearn in the picture.

He picked up the phone again and called Tash. He told her that he'd been on a waiting list and finally had an appointment at one with a BSU therapist. He said that after the session he would come back to the Huntington to pick her up and that they should be able to make the three-thirty Express back to Avalon. Tash seemed calmer than she was yesterday and sounded pleased with the plan.

"I'll be ready," she said.

"If you want to speed things up, throw my stuff into my suitcase," Stilwell said. "Call the bell stand and have them take the bags out to the front drive. I'll give you a thirty-minute heads-up, and you should be ready for a swoop-and-scoop. It'll save a lot of time."

"Like I said, I'll be ready."

"Good. See you then."

After disconnecting the call, Stilwell thought about the tone of Tash's words and her short answers and he had to admit to himself that he had no idea where the relationship was going. Seventy-two hours earlier, it had felt to him like something that could go the distance. Now he was not sure. Tash was too difficult to read at the moment.

The BSU was located on the ninth floor of the county transportation tower, which sat above Union Station, several blocks from the offices and prying eyes of the sheriff's headquarters on Temple. At first, the session with Dr. Olga Perez went as he'd expected it would go. She asked stock questions about how he felt about taking a life, and Stilwell gave stock answers, explaining that he had had no choice, that it was a kill-or-be-killed situation and that the safety of an innocent individual had also been at stake. But then the therapist zeroed in on his relationship with that individual and his state of mind in the frantic minutes leading up to the shooting.

"You used the phrase 'kill or be killed,'" Perez said. "In a situation like that, the body floods with a chemical called epinephrine. It's a stress hormone that increases clarity, reactions, and brain speed. Decisions that might normally take minutes to make are made in microseconds. Sometimes bad decisions."

"Are you saying shooting Spivak was a bad decision?" Stilwell asked.

"No, I'm not. As you know, that's not my call or my purpose today. I'm asking you if *you* think it was a bad decision. Are you having second thoughts or any trouble with it?"

"None. In the same situation, I'd do it again."

"Okay. My purpose is also to understand whether you have any residual stress or regret relating to the incident and to make sure you wouldn't hesitate should such a situation arise again. Hesitation in a deadly confrontation could lead to your own injury or death."

"I have no regrets about shooting and killing Spivak, okay? My only regret is that I didn't see him sooner for what he was and realize that everything he did was part of a plan. I knew there was something odd about the assault on the deputy, but I didn't put it together. That's on me, but everything that came afterward is on him and I don't feel bad about how it ended."

Stilwell and Perez continued the verbal dance around the subject for a half hour longer, and the session ended with Perez saying she would sign off on his return to duty, though she would wait forty-eight hours before doing so. She said she wanted him to take at least that much time off before returning to his job should he clear the other parts of the official investigation without issue.

Back on the road to Pasadena, Stilwell called Tash to tell her that he would pick her up in a half hour.

"How did it go with the shrink?" she asked.

"Good," Stilwell said. "She'll take a couple days to write it up, but she said she'll sign my RTD."

"What's an RTD?"

"Return to duty. It means she thinks I'm ready to go back to work."

"On Catalina?"

"Yeah, of course. You want me to come back there, don't you?"

"Yes. I was just wondering because you said the mayor told your captain he wants you gone."

"Yeah, well, the mayor doesn't get to say. But you're sure you want me back on the island?"

"Of course."

"Good. Then I'll see you in about thirty. You packed my stuff?"

"Doing it now. You're lucky I'm not going to 'forget' to pack your Willie Nelson shirt."

It was a T-shirt from a Hollywood Bowl concert celebrating Nelson's ninetieth birthday. Stilwell had loved the concert and loved the shirt, although it had seen better days. He only wore it to sleep in. But Tash was a Swiftie and didn't care for Willie or the bright red shirt, even though Stilwell pointed out that both performers sang about heartbreak and resilience, just in different ways.

"I'd never forgive you," Stilwell said, returning her joking tone. "See you soon."

After disconnecting, he was encouraged. The shot she had taken about Willie Nelson felt like the old Tash coming across the call.

As he drove toward Pasadena he felt that things in his life might be falling back into place.

41

THE SEAS WERE rough on the Express ride back to Catalina but things were smooth between Stil and Tash. They sat inside and away from the spray and were so engrossed in their conversation that they didn't bother to get up with all the tourists and go to the stern deck to watch the fleet of porpoises jumping in the boat's wake. The closer they got to Avalon, the more Stilwell saw the tension ease out of Tash's face. It was reassuring in the moment, but it also reinforced his belief that a future with this woman meant a future on the island. That was going to be fine in the short term. The island felt like home to him. But he wasn't sure he liked the idea of the rest of his life being predetermined.

The thrum of the engines and the up-and-down rhythm of the rolling seas helped put him into a pleasant daze as she held his right hand, took one finger at a time, and massaged the joints. She announced that she wanted to cook dinner that night and would go directly from the dock to Vons to pick up groceries if he could handle both their suitcases and his backpack.

"Not a problem," he said. "Whose place are we going to?"

"Yours," Tash said.

Another good sign, he thought.

"What are you making?"

"Not sure yet. It'll be a surprise."

"Okay. Cool."

"You know I told Dennis I was taking a few days off. I only promised to be back for the weekend. You want to maybe go camping out at Two Harbors now that you don't go back on duty till the shrink signs your RTD?"

"Uh, maybe. Yeah, sounds good. When do you want to go?"

"Tomorrow."

"Uh…"

"What?"

"Just wondering if I'll need to be around for any final questions from the shooting team. Can I just check in the morning and then we'll make a plan?"

"Fine."

Her tone turned cold with that one word. Stilwell didn't want to lie to her, but he needed to be ready to go back to Long Beach if Juarez was successful in bringing in Terranova.

"They might want me to come over for another sit-down."

"Why? You've told them everything. What more can they ask?"

"That's how they do it. They make you tell the story over and over at different times to see if you slip and your story changes. It's going to be done soon, but let me just check with them tomorrow. If we're camping somewhere and I don't have cell service, it could be a problem. Technically, even though I'm relieved of duty, I'm supposed to be available to the investigators."

"What a nightmare."

Stilwell wanted to stop the cascade of lies and get her back into a positive mood.

"You want to rent a boat and go fishing?" he asked. "Or just stay on land?"

"We can go fishing," she said. "That'll be fun."

"Then we'll rent a boat. Or we could charter. I know this guy who works on a charter over there."

"No, just you and me. Maybe just use my kayak and a rental for you."

"That's good too."

It appeared he'd successfully weathered the rough seas of guilt and dishonesty. But like a gambler who wants to make one more bet, Stilwell pushed his whole stack of chips into the pot.

"Can I ask you something?" he said. "It's work-related."

"What?" Tash said gamely.

"Do you know who Daniel Easterbrook is? Do you ever deal with him directly?"

"I know him because he's a boat owner. Uh, I deal with him occasionally. Why? He's got a nice boat."

"He's the guy I went to see last night."

"In Pasadena? I didn't know that's where he lived."

"Well, South Pasadena now. What is your take on him? Good guy? Bad guy?"

"Well, you can hardly tell by the sort of interactions we have with the boat owners. But they generally fall into two categories. You've got your rich, entitled guys who treat you like you're there solely to give them what they want, and you've got the ones who don't. Mr. Easterbrook is definitely in the second camp. He seems like a nice guy. He always says thanks over the radio when he works with the tower or the pilot boats. Why? Is he mixed up with the girl with the purple hair?"

"He knew her. Well."

"Is he a suspect?"

"Maybe. At least a person of interest."

He realized he should not be talking to her about the case.

"What kind of boat does he have?"

"Uh, I think it's a Hylas. Fifty-plus feet. It's super-nice."

"That a yacht or a sailboat?"

"Sail."

"Oceangoing? Could he make it to Tahiti?"

"If he knows what he's doing. Those ocean sloops can easily cover two hundred miles in a day. But that's still a long journey."

A long journey Easterbrook would now have to make on his own. Stilwell wondered if he should risk checking in with Sampedro about the interview he'd said he and Ahearn would conduct with Easterbrook. He knew that he might wind up in another confrontation with Ahearn. He decided it was too soon. He had only told Sampedro about Easterbrook a few hours earlier. He would wait until the next morning to check in.

"What about Charles Crane over at the Black Marlin?" he asked. "Do you ever deal with him?"

"Oh, yeah, every now and then when there's a complaint about something in the harbor from a member of the club," Tash said. "He'll call us up and explain the member's complaint. He's definitely in the first camp I was talking about."

"Crane is, or the members who complain?"

"Crane, and we kind of laugh about it. Because he always acts all entitled, and he's just a glorified servant, if you ask me. He's not the rich guy but he sure acts like he is."

"You remember any sort of complaint in particular?"

Stilwell felt and heard the engines throttle down as the ferry approached the mouth of Avalon Harbor. He had been on the Express so many times that he knew this meant they were ten minutes from docking. Neither he nor Tash made a move to get up from their seats.

"Uh, I think the last time was when he called to complain that Judge Harrell was making too much of a wake with his boat," Tash said.

"Really?" Stilwell said. "I wouldn't think that old Viking could make that much of a wake. Besides, I pick him up most Fridays and he doesn't come plowing in."

"It's when he leaves. He's always in a hurry to get back, I guess. When he heads down the lane behind the BMC, he rocks the floating dock and the tenders. Sometimes there are members out there and they get mad."

"You ever tell the judge to mind the wake?"

"I have, yeah. But I think it only encourages him. I don't think he likes those rich guys ever since they kicked him out."

"Wait a minute—they kicked him out? When was that? What did he do?"

"He didn't really do anything. But for, like, fifty years they used to give the judge assigned to the island court an honorary membership."

"Like the mayor."

"Right, and I think it was mostly so the judge could have lunch at the club after he came over to hear cases. But Judge Harrell has a boat and that was new. I guess before him, the judges used the Express. But Harrell comes by boat, and so he really started using the club—you know, coming over on weekends, using their moorings like a real member, not an honorary one."

"And they didn't like that."

"No. So they said no more membership, and they told him it was, like, a belt-tightening move. But everybody knew the real reason—including the judge. The club members don't like outsiders acting like they belong."

Stilwell nodded as he thought about Judge Harrell's fall from grace at the Black Marlin Club. Heaven help any member who had to appear before the judge as a defendant.

People started lining up in the aisles to exit before the ferry was even docked. Stil and Tash waited to stand up until after the jolt of the vessel hitting the rubber liners of the pier. Stilwell slung his backpack over his shoulders and managed the two roller suitcases as they got off. Tash asked him if there was anything from Vons he wanted her to pick up and he said they might need coffee for the brewer at his house.

They split up on Crescent, Stilwell heading toward home and Tash going up Sumner to the grocery store.

Two minutes later Stilwell was dragging the two roller bags behind him through modest crowds of tourists when his phone buzzed in his pocket. There was a number on the screen he didn't recognize, but he stopped and took the call anyway, anticipating that he would be telling someone that he was off duty until further notice.

But it was Lionel McKey, the reporter from the *Call,* engaging in the reporter's trick of calling from a line that wouldn't be recognized in hopes that a reluctant source would answer.

"What do you want, Lionel?" Stilwell said. "I'm off duty, and if this is about Friday, you know I can't comment pending the outcome of the investigation."

"It's not about Friday," the reporter said. "It's about the press release the sheriff's office just put out."

"I don't know anything about a press release. You'll have to call—"

"They say they've solved the woman-in-the-water case. That's our story, and I'd hoped you would have at least given me a heads-up before it went out to every newsroom in the damn county."

"Wait a minute. Just hold on a second."

"Fine."

Stilwell looked around. Tourists were passing on both sides of him and it wasn't the right place for a call like this. He spotted an empty bench facing the harbor. He slipped the phone into his shirt pocket, grabbed the handles of the suitcases, and dragged them over to the bench. Sitting down, he retrieved the phone from his pocket.

"Lionel, do you have the press release there?" he asked.

"Yeah, they just put it out," McKey said.

"Okay, read it to me."

"It's kind of long."

"Just read it to me. I haven't seen it. I can't comment on it if I don't know what it says, okay?"

That was an old cop trick. To act like you're willing to comment if the journalist will reveal what he's got.

"All right, I'll read it," McKey said. "It says: 'Today the Los Angeles County Sheriff's Department announced its findings in the homicide of twenty-eight-year-old Leigh-Anne Moss, whose body was found May twenty-third in Avalon Harbor on Santa Catalina Island. Moss was bludgeoned to death before her body was weighted with a boat anchor and submerged in the harbor. In an intensive ten-day investigation, detectives from the homicide unit and the sheriff's substation in Avalon were able to identify Daniel Easterbrook, age forty-four, of South Pasadena, as a suspect in the case. Today —'"

"Ah, Jesus," Stilwell said.

"What? You want me to stop?"

"No, just keep reading."

"'Today, when investigators went to his home to question Easterbrook about the killing, they found him dead by apparent suicide. Captain Roger Corum said that there is evidence that Easterbrook, who was married but had recently separated from his wife, had been involved romantically with the victim and that she had tried to break off the relationship. Investigators believe Easterbrook, an attorney, met Moss in Avalon, where she worked as a waitress at the Black Marlin Club. Corum said that DNA evidence is being analyzed that investigators believe will further connect Easterbrook to the death of Ms. Moss. Corum said that the investigation is ongoing and further details will be withheld until its completion. He thanked investigators from the homicide unit and the Catalina substation for their tireless'—blah-blah-blah, and that's it. Now, can you tell me what exactly led you to Easterbrook?"

"No, I can't."

"Was he a member of the Black Marlin Club?"

"No comment."

"Come on, man, you said you would comment if I read it. I need something nobody else has. This is our turf. Our story."

"It's nobody's story. They have it wrong."

"What? What do you mean?"

"That's off the record."

"No, you can't do that. You can't say something and then afterward say it's off the record. What do you mean, they have it wrong?"

"I have to go."

Stilwell disconnected and got up off the bench.

42

STILWELL WAITED UNTIL he was home to call Corum on his cell. He didn't want to bother with Ahearn and Sampedro and wasn't sure he could control his temper if he spoke to one of them. He could tell that Corum was driving when he answered.

"I thought I would hear from you," the captain said by way of greeting. "Good work on Easterbrook."

"Are you kidding me?" Stilwell said. "I don't think he killed Leigh-Anne Moss and I told those two idiots that this morning."

There was a long silence while Corum digested this and Stilwell listened to the sounds of traffic through the phone.

"What are you talking about, Stil?" Corum finally said. "They told me this was your lead. They went out there, and the guy had hung himself."

"Killing himself is not proof he killed her," he said. "Was there a note?"

"No note. But there were photos of the victim—bedroom photos, I'm told."

"And, what, that's their evidence that he killed her?"

"They said she was playing him for his money. She was bad news."

293

"So we're blaming the victim."

"That's not going out to the public. I'm just saying, is all. She was playing him, he got wind of it, and he acts out and ends up killing her."

"The guy was infatuated with her, yes. He told me so. He said they were planning to take his boat and sail off to Tahiti. I told those guys that he was not the guy but that they needed to formally interview him, get a swab, and check out his alibi. He *had* an alibi. This is fucked up, Captain. Ahearn is hanging a murder on him. This is just like before."

"No, it's not, Stil, and you need to watch yourself on this one. I saved your job the first time. I can't do it a second time."

"You're going to have to eat that press release, Captain."

"Stil, the case is closed. My guys will do the paper on it and take it to the DA for a sign-off. And you go back to doing what you do on that island. You understand?"

The front door opened and Tash walked in carrying two plastic bags of groceries from Vons. She stopped in her tracks when she saw his face. She mouthed the words *You okay?* Stilwell nodded in return, even though he was far from okay.

"I want to hear you say it, Stil," Corum said. "Do you understand?"

"I understand," Stilwell said.

"Good, then I think we're finished. I just got home and I don't want to carry this shit into my house."

"Fine. Good night, Captain."

"Good night, Stil."

Stilwell disconnected. Tash had put her bags up on the kitchen counter and was unloading them.

"Grilled cheese and chili," she said. "Comfort food. Okay?"

"Okay," Stilwell said.

"What's wrong?"

"Fucking Ahearn."

"What about him?"

"It's déjà vu all over again. He's hanging the murder on the wrong guy. He's so fucking incompetent, and the captain doesn't care because he gets an easy clear on a complicated case. Meantime, somebody gets away with murder."

Tash stopped, a can of pinto beans in her hand.

"What are you going to do about it, Stil?"

"I don't know yet . . . but I can't do nothing."

He grabbed the handle of his suitcase and rolled it into the bedroom. He opened it on the bed and started unpacking, returning unworn clothing to drawers and hangers in the closet. He was halfway through when his phone buzzed with a call from a number he recognized.

"What do you want, Ahearn?"

"I want to know what the fuck you're doing telling the captain we tagged the wrong guy."

"You did, Ahearn. You did what you always do. You took the easy road. But it was the wrong road."

Ahearn laughed.

"You know what this is? It's jealousy. I thought you'd be happy that we shared credit with you, but no, you want —"

"Don't you get it, you fucking idiot? He's not the guy."

"So you say."

"Okay, your press release says she was breaking up with him. Where'd you get that, Ahearn? Because less than twenty-four hours ago, he didn't say a thing about that. He only talked about her quitting her job on the island so they could sail to Tahiti."

"So he told you. He lied to you, Stillborn, and you can't stand the fact that you fell for it hook, line, and sinker."

"Did you even try to check out his alibi? You know what, never mind. I already know the answer to that. You didn't do shit. You go to the guy's house, find him dead, and think, *We can make this case go away real fast.* You padded the press release like you padded the case. You were just hoping it was true. But it was bullshit, just like you."

"You're bullshit, Stillborn."

"No, you know what I am? I'm the guy who's going to bring in the real killer."

"Stilwell, you better not do any—"

Stilwell disconnected. He raised his arm to throw the phone against the wall but held back at the last moment as Tash walked in.

"Are you all right?" she asked.

"Fine," he said.

"What's going on?"

"Nothing."

He pocketed the phone.

"Do you still want me to make dinner?" Tash asked.

"Of course," Stilwell said. "I'm already hungry."

"Then open a bottle of wine. I need an hour."

"Red or white?"

"Red."

"You're on. As soon as I'm finished in here."

She left the room. Stilwell zipped his empty suitcase closed and put it up on a shelf in the closet, then sat down on the edge of the bed and tried to compose himself. He had to put Ahearn and Sampedro out of his mind and concentrate on the case, not on their betrayal of Leigh-Anne Moss. Because that was what it was, a betrayal of the sacred bond between a victim and those charged with finding justice. Stilwell closed his eyes and promised himself that he would not do the same.

His phone buzzed in his pocket, a short tone indicating a text. He pulled it out, expecting a text from Ahearn. But it was from Monika Juarez.

We're on. He's coming in at 10. No lawyer — yet. You'll be here?

Stilwell typed in a short reply.

I'll be there.

43

JUAREZ MANAGED TO reserve a private room for what she'd told Stilwell would be a "discussion" with Oscar Terranova. Stilwell reminded her that while there was no warrant or charges on the books for Terranova, he was wanted for questioning in a homicide. He said he couldn't promise not to arrest him, depending on how the discussion went. And Juarez reminded Stilwell that he had been relieved of duty and making an arrest would probably result in an internal investigation and discipline for not abiding by departmental orders and policy.

"We're just going to talk," Juarez said. "And he walks out of here when we're finished."

"Does he even know I'll be here?" Stilwell asked.

"I told him I had to have an investigator present."

"But you didn't tell him it was me."

"No, that will be a surprise."

"And not a good one."

Stilwell expected Baby Head to do a one-eighty the moment he saw him in the room.

"So, what's our best-case scenario?" he asked.

"He has to have evidence," Juarez said. "It can't be a he-said, he-said. We won't even file that shit."

"You tell him that already?"

"I did. He said he had something we're going to like."

"Well, he — "

He stopped when Juarez's phone started buzzing. She took the call, listened, then responded that she would come get her visitor.

"Here we go," she said as she headed toward the door. Her voice sounded shaky. She was nervous and Stilwell knew why. Terranova had already marked her for life. There was no telling how he would act if things didn't go his way in the next hour.

The room was unlike any interview room at a sheriff's station. It was used mostly for negotiations between prosecutors and defense attorneys. The table Stilwell sat at was unscarred wood that had been polished with Pledge and not the sweat and tears of accused suspects.

The door reopened and Juarez entered first, followed by Oscar Terranova, dressed in bleached white pants and an untucked Tommy Bahama shirt with blue parrots on a field of yellow. But two steps into the room, he saw Stilwell and stopped dead.

"What's he doing here?" he said. "This ain't the island."

"I told you I would have an investigator in the meeting," Juarez said.

"Yeah, but not him," Terranova said. "This ain't happening."

As Stilwell had predicted, he turned back to the door.

"Sit down, Oscar," Stilwell said. "You leave, you break the agreement. I've got deputies outside that'll grab you up and put you in a cell. You want that?"

Terranova turned back and looked at Juarez for confirmation.

"Oscar, sit down, please," she said. "I think the only way you walk free today is if you keep our deal. So sit down and tell us what you've got. If it's as good as you said it was, there won't be any problem here."

"Fuck this," Terranova said.

But he went to the table, yanked out a chair, and sat down opposite Stilwell.

Juarez sat in the chair next to Stilwell.

"So, as we agreed, we're not going to record this," she said. "We're just going to talk and listen to each other. You told me you had nothing to do with the crimes that occurred recently on Catalina and that you could prove it. This is your chance."

Terranova sat back in his chair, one arm on the table, fingers tapping the wood like he was contemplating a bet in a poker game. Finally, he spoke.

"Okay, so what you've got to know is that I'm totally clean on Gaston and what happened with your girlfriend, Stilwell. It was somebody else callin' the shots and not telling me shit. That Spivak motherfucker is his guy, not mine."

Juarez looked at Stilwell and nodded slightly, giving him the lead.

"Who was calling the shots?" he asked.

"That's my ace card, *el jefe*. I don't reveal it till everybody's all in."

"Meaning what?"

"Meaning I want a guaranteed no-incarceration deal. Like you were going to give Henry Gaston to get to me."

"We're not making a deal until we know what you've got. Stop dancing, Oscar. I know your silent partner is Mayor Allen and your corporate lawyer's fingerprints are all over the Big Wheel deal. Why don't you start by telling us how you and the mayor connected."

Stilwell kept his eyes on Terranova, looking for a reaction.

Terranova showed no surprise that Stilwell knew about him and Allen.

"Yeah, we've got business," he said. "I made a little money back home and came out to Catalina to invest it. I wanted to start a legitimate company, you know, so I did my homework and saw they needed more golf carts and tours out there. I applied for a license to operate and that was when I met him."

"Because of your application for a business license?"

"Yep. I met him pretty quick about that and he told me it could take three years or three months to get the operator's license, depending, and how did I want to handle it?"

"He wanted a bribe."

"I just call it doing business. Everybody always wants a piece of a good thing. I don't begrudge that, you know. I say go along to get along."

"You knew it was a two-way street. You pay the guy off and you get leverage on him down the line."

"That's right, like that."

"You keep any records of these...transactions?"

"Let's just say I got enough to deal. You want my help, you keep me out of a cell—permanently."

"If all you've got is the mayor taking kickbacks from a small-time tour operator, then we're done here, Oscar. This is a murder investigation, not a minor corruption case. But I can give you a ride downtown where there are people who want to talk to you."

Terranova smiled like he was the only one in the room who knew the real lay of the land.

"Oh, big man," he said. "You think you're so smart and tough. Tell you what, you didn't have that badge, this'd be a different story between you and me, Stilwell."

Stilwell just stared at him and their eyes locked in mutual hatred. Juarez broke the moment.

"Oscar, he's right," she said. "Talk to us about the killing of Henry Gaston. And remember, anything you tell us is useless if you can't back it up."

"I told you on the phone," Terranova said. "I can back up every fucking thing I say. I got documents and I got tapes. You want to hear what I got, Stilwell?"

"Yes," Juarez answered. "We do."

"Okay, then," Terranova said. "Let me give y'all a little sample."

He dropped his hand below the table to reach into his pocket. Stilwell sprang up from his chair, ready to go across the table at him. Terranova immediately raised his hands.

"Relax, man," he said. "Just going for my phone."

"Slowly," Stilwell said.

He remained standing while Terranova retrieved his phone and held it up to show it was not a weapon. Stilwell sat back down.

"What are you going to show us?" Juarez asked.

"I ain't showing you nothing," Terranova said. "Take a listen to this."

Terranova opened the recording app and played what was obviously a recorded phone call. Stilwell recognized both Terranova's voice and that of Douglas Allen, starting with the mayor taking the call:

"Hello?" he said.

"What the fuck you do?" Terranova asked.

"I told you never to call this number."

"Fuck that, it's a burner. What the hell, man? I just heard Gaston was dead in a fucking cell."

"He was going to rat you out. That was not a risk I was willing to take. I was watching out for you."

"Now you got me tied up in a murder, man. You should've talked —"

"I don't need to talk or clear anything with you. You understand? And *do not* call on this line again."

The call ended. Terranova typed a command into his phone and dropped it on the table.

"Erased," he said. "You want it, I got a copy stashed with my lawyer. You don't get it unless we make a deal."

Stilwell glanced at Juarez to see if she was going to respond, but she looked frozen. It was clear that Terranova still had a hold on her. This told Stilwell he needed to keep control of the interview.

"What about the abduction of Tash Dano?" he asked. "What did Allen tell you about that?"

"Not a thing," Terranova said. "I read about it in the news."

"That wasn't you who called Spivak in the trailer that night?"

"Not me. I never spoke to him one time. Like I said, he was the mayor's guy, not mine. I had nothing to do with that thing either."

"Bullshit. They grabbed her because they thought the saw handle was still on the island and not at the lab. That piece of information came from you, so don't try to claim you're innocent. The whole thing went down because of you."

"Well, maybe, maybe not. But if you want to go that way with it, your pal and prosecutor here is part of the chain of guilt. That comes out, I don't know how the chips will fall."

Terranova had thoroughly thought out the moves here. Stilwell would be forced to throw Juarez to the wolves if he tried to pursue him for abducting Tash. It was an impossible decision, so he put it to the side for the moment.

"Tell me about Spivak," Stilwell said. "If this was all the mayor's play, how did he know him?"

"Far as I know, they went way back," Terranova said. "The mayor used him before. He was like a bodyguard for hire who was willing to do whatever needed to be done."

"Including murder?" Stilwell said. "And assaulting a deputy to get into jail to carry out the murder?"

"For the right price, you can get people to do anything," Terranova said. "Don't tell me you don't know that, Deputy Doo-Dah."

Terranova stared at him, and Stilwell saw the threat in his eyes. Then Terranova's face transformed into a smile.

"So we got a deal or what?" Terranova said. He looked at Juarez for an answer.

"What kind of deal are you looking for?" she said. "You've committed serious crimes. You can't expect—"

"I get the golden parachute," Terranova said. "That's what I get. No conviction and no jail time, or it's no deal. You take your best shot at me, and we'll see how that goes with no witnesses and a . . . compromised prosecutor."

That brought a long silence to the room. Stilwell didn't know if he should respond, because golden parachutes were Juarez's department.

"We're going to step out for a moment," Juarez finally said. "Sit tight, Oscar."

"I'm not going anywhere," Terranova said. "Yet."

Stilwell followed Juarez out. She closed the door to the interview room and they walked several steps down the hall so their whispers could not be heard. Juarez spoke first.

"So, what do you think?" she asked.

"I can't see him walking away clean," Stilwell said. "That bothers me."

"It may be the only way."

"I don't like it."

"Nobody *likes* it. But there may be no choice. That recording alone is solid evidence, and he says he has more. We're talking about a corrupt mayor who had someone killed."

"And Baby Head's complicit in all of it."

"He may be, but he's holding the high cards and we might not have a choice."

"Yeah, you happen to be one of those cards."

"Don't you think I know that? Don't worry. As soon as we get through this — if we get through this — I'll resign and never step into a courtroom again."

Stilwell moved away for a moment to think and walk off his anger. He forced himself to concentrate on what was at hand, not what had been done in the past. He came back to Juarez.

"Okay," he said. "What will you do, take him to a grand jury?"

"Possibly," Juarez said. "But this goes way above my head. I have to take this downtown and see how they want to play it."

"When?"

"I have no court today. I can go as soon as we cut him loose."

"What will you tell them?"

"That this guy came in with solid evidence that the mayor of Avalon is corrupt and probably commissioned a hit on a witness in a developing case against him. I'll say our live witness is a criminal himself but he'll share compelling and incontrovertible evidence, including recordings, that outweighs his own crimes."

Stilwell just nodded. He wasn't happy, but this was how most cases went. People made deals, shredded their loyalties to save their own skin. There was never complete justice. But if Baby Head got his golden parachute and remained in business and on the island, Stilwell knew that he would get another shot at him somewhere down the line. And then true justice would be served.

44

ONCE HE WAS back on the island, Stilwell attempted to call Tash, but she didn't pick up. He assumed she was either still angry or outside cellular range. Or both. She had left his house and returned to her own the night before after Stilwell told her about his appointment the next morning at the Long Beach courthouse. They had just finished eating her homemade chili and grilled cheese sandwiches. She got up from the table, dropped her plate and bowl in the sink, and went into the bedroom to grab her suitcase. Her last words as she went out the door were that she was going camping without him and that if he really wanted to, he could join her later. He called after her that he would.

Stilwell did want to join her but there was work to be done first. After checking in at the sub and deflecting questions about whether he was back on duty, he took the John Deere up to the Sandtrap to see if Leslie Sneed was working. It was the middle of the lunch rush, but he didn't see her waiting tables. He finally asked a passing waitress whether she was on duty and she said Sneed was off on Tuesdays.

Ten minutes later he knocked on the door of Sneed's apartment and found her at home. When she opened the door, a waft of marijuana drifted out, prompting Stilwell to remember her claim that she'd been sober since moving to the island. Maybe to her, smoking pot didn't count.

"Congratulations," she said.

Stilwell was puzzled.

"For what?" he asked.

"You solved the case," Sneed said. "I saw it on the news."

"Uh, actually, that's what I'm here for. The whole story isn't out there and I wanted to ask if you'd help me with the investigation."

"Well, they said that guy who did it killed himself."

"That's not the full story, Leslie. If I can come in, I'd like to explain what you could do to help with the case."

Sneed looked behind her into the apartment and seemed to hesitate. Stilwell spoke quickly.

"I don't know if you heard, but the Black Marlin Club matched the reward money. So now it's up to twenty thousand. It's a pretty good chunk of cash."

"Well, shit, that is a lot."

"And I have an idea about how you could get the whole thing."

She stepped back to let him inside. They moved into the tiny living room.

"What do I have to do?" Sneed asked.

"I want you to send a text and set up a meeting with somebody."

"And where do I go for the meeting?"

"The Zane Grey."

"Am I, like, bait?"

"Yes, but I'll be there and you'll be safe. If he shows up, I'll take him down."

"And if I do this, you'll put me in for the full reward?"

"That's the deal. If this goes the way I think it will, you'll get it all."

"Okay, I'm in."

45

LESLIE SNEED SENT the text to Charles Crane at three thirty and set their meeting for two hours later in the bar at the Zane Grey, where there was always an evening happy hour and a guarantee of safety in a crowd. That allowed plenty of time for Crane to go to the bank to withdraw what her message had called a down payment on her silence. Crane did not acknowledge the text in any way, but the fact that he didn't ask **Who is this?** or respond that it was a wrong number told Stilwell that he might be taking the bait.

The two hours also gave Stilwell time to get to the hotel and enlist the cooperation of the manager, Fred Nettles, in his plan. He needed to get into the bar before it opened and hide a directional microphone from the substation's equipment room between the bottles of bourbon on the shelf opposite the barstool where Sneed would sit.

The message Stilwell composed and had Sneed send to Crane contained a clear threat: **I know it was you. She told me about you two. Think the sheriff will change his mind about the killer when I tell him? There's reward money, so make me a better offer. Bring a down payment on my silence to the Zane Grey at 5:30. Don't be late. If I don't see you, I call the cops.**

By 5:15 Stilwell was positioned in the hotel's office in front of a split screen showing two camera views of the lobby bar. Couples were sitting at two tables, and Leslie Sneed sat by herself at the bar opposite the line of bourbon bottles, a glass of sauvignon blanc in front of her. Five stools down from her sat Starkey, the writer who'd been involved in the eviction call the week before. He was now apparently back in the hotel's good graces financially and still the writer in residence.

Stilwell rolled his chair away from the desk to a window that had a good view of Chimes Tower Road as it ascended from the harbor. It wasn't the only way to the Zane Grey but was the likely route Crane would take from the Black Marlin Club — if he was coming.

The video feed was being recorded and so was the microphone hidden between bottles of Blanton's and Pappy Van Winkle. Stilwell listened on headphones connected to a wireless recorder as Starkey attempted to engage Sneed in conversation. Stilwell had shown her a DMV photo of Charles Crane so she would know who she was meeting, and Starkey was clearly not him. She told Starkey that she was waiting for someone and he left her alone.

Stilwell checked the road again and saw no cart heading up. He was beginning to believe that Crane had not taken the bait after all and had simply ignored the text from Sneed. He started wondering if he was wrong about Crane. He thought about the bar manager, Buddy Callahan. He was one of the club employees Crane said had complained about Leigh-Anne flirting with members. Was he the one Sneed should have sent the text to?

Stilwell's phone buzzed and he saw that it was Juarez. He answered.

"I'm in the middle of something," he said quickly. "Can I call you in an hour or so?"

"Sure," Juarez said. "I just wanted to let you know we're on for tomorrow."

"What do you mean? We're on for what?"

"Oscar's going before the sitting grand jury downtown."

"That soon? Don't we need time to prep? Do you know what he's going to say?"

"I've been dealing with his attorney all afternoon. And the public integrity unit. Believe me, we're set. We'll go for a conspiracy-to-commit charge against Allen, and Oscar will be an unindicted coconspirator."

"That's it?"

"We'll start with that. And down the line we'll add solicitation of murder as well as charges in the Dano case."

"What else does Terranova have in the way of evidence?"

"His lawyer played me another recording over the phone. It's better than the first one Oscar played for us. It was about abducting Tash, and Oscar tells Allen that he crossed a line and that he wants no part of it. Allen makes an admission. He says he's tired of cleaning up after Oscar's mistakes and that the only way to get to you is through Tash. It's gold, Stil. We got him."

Stilwell nodded. While the killing of Henry Gaston was the bigger crime, he wanted someone to go down for Tash's abduction. It sounded like Allen was going to be good for both.

"Unindicted coconspirator," he said. "So Baby Head gets the golden parachute. Your bosses were okay with that?"

"He walks for now," Juarez said. "Everyone here has signed off on it. He'll have a formal deal before he testifies."

"And no justice for a murdered buffalo."

"Well, not today, at least. But the greater good is served. Or I should say the greater evil is taken down."

Stilwell wasn't so sure about that. He checked through the window again and saw a cart coming up the hill. It had a distinctive maroon-and-white-striped roof that matched the awning over the back deck of the Black Marlin Club. Crane was coming.

"I need to go," he said.

"I need you here tomorrow to present to the grand jury," Juarez said.

Stilwell thought about Tash camping by herself out near Two Harbors.

"What time?" he asked.

"First thing," Juarez said. "They'll be seated at ten."

"Okay. Where is it?"

"Criminal Courts Building, room three-oh-eight. It's unmarked, so just wait in the hall for me. It will be you and then Oscar, and that should be all we need."

"What about Tash?"

"We talked about her and we don't think we need her for tomorrow. But we'll definitely need her if we go to trial. She'll be the emotional core of the case, and a jury will love her."

Stilwell understood that and knew it would fall to him to convince Tash to testify and then prep her for trial.

"Okay, and what about Corum?" he asked. "Has he been brought up to speed?"

"He's my next call, unless you want to do it."

"No, thanks. Like I said, I'm in the middle of something."

"Okay, I'll call him."

"Is there a subpoena for me for tomorrow?"

"Uh . . . no. I was counting on you appearing voluntarily. Do I really need to subpoena you?"

"It will help with Corum, since I'm supposedly relieved of duty."

"Got it. I'll have one for you in the morning. I'm going to need you to walk the grand jury through the whole case, starting with you serving the search warrant on the cart barn."

"The start was the beheading of the buffalo."

"You know what I mean. So, are we good?"

311

"We're good. I'll see you at ten tomorrow."

Stilwell disconnected and stood back from the window so he wouldn't be seen as Crane parked the BMC cart and walked toward the lobby of the hotel. Stilwell returned to the seat in front of the video screen and put on the headphones. It was showtime.

The turnout for the midweek happy hour remained low, which was to Stilwell's advantage. He could hear the banter between the bartender and Starkey even though they weren't in the target range of the microphone. There was a familiarity between the two that told Stilwell that Starkey didn't miss many happy hours at the hotel.

Nervous energy made Stilwell stand as he watched the screen. He had thought about asking one of the off-duty deputies to be at the bar as a precaution but dismissed it out of concern that Crane might know who the deputies assigned to the island were. There was no one but him, and though he was only one door away from the bar, he had to be ready to move should Crane choose to act out in any way with Leslie Sneed.

Right on time, Crane entered the bar through the lobby, looked around, and assessed the couples seated at the two tables and then the two people sitting three stools apart at the bar. He took a position between them and said something in a low voice to Starkey that Stilwell could not make out. But Starkey's response was audible.

"Sorry, pal, I play for the other team."

Starkey had taken what Crane said as a pass. Crane shrugged it off and turned to Sneed. Again his voice was too low for Stilwell to hear. The hidden microphone was pointed directly at Sneed, but Crane was standing two stools away. Her voice came through clearly.

"That's right," she said. "Did you bring me something?"

Crane moved to the stool next to Sneed and sat down. He glanced at Starkey suspiciously, and when he turned back, the bartender was there to take his order.

"I'll have what she's having," Crane said.

The bartender pulled a wineglass off an overhead rack and moved down the bar to the wine cooler. Sneed watched him walk away, and at the same moment, Crane made a move, running one hand down Sneed's back and one up the front of the loose-fitting blouse she was wearing.

"Hey!" Sneed said sharply.

The bartender turned to see what the disturbance was. Crane held up his hands, palms out.

"I had to check," he said to Sneed. "Let me see your phone."

"I'm not giving you my phone," Sneed said.

"I check your phone or we're not having this conversation. You want the money or not?"

"Fine."

Sneed opened the small purse that had been on the bar top next to her glass. She pulled out her phone and handed it to him. This was a move Stilwell had anticipated and planned a response for.

"Unlock it," Crane said.

He held the phone up and Sneed typed in a password. Crane then started looking through her apps. The bartender put a glass of wine in front of him and moved away. Crane finally found the voice-memo app, opened it, and saw that there was a recording in progress.

"Amateur," he said. "You think I'm stupid?"

He stopped the recording, deleted it, and put the phone down on the bar.

"You think you can play me like that?" he said. "Well, fuck you, honey. This conversation is over."

He stood up and kicked his stool back with his foot.

"You leave and you'll regret it," Sneed said, expertly delivering the line Stilwell had given her.

Crane stayed standing but didn't move toward the exit. He leaned down and in toward Sneed, a move designed to intimidate the younger woman.

"What do you want?" he asked.

"I told you what I want," Sneed said. "I want money. I decided I also want a job at the Black Marlin. I'm tired of waiting on tourists and sweaty golfers who think they're funny. I want what Leigh-Anne had."

"Or what?"

"Or I call up Stilwell, the sheriff's guy who came and asked about Leigh-Anne, and tell him what she told me the morning before she got murdered. I sort of left that part out when he came around."

"Which is exactly what?"

"That she was going to see you to get her money and tell you she was quitting the club . . . and quitting you."

It was another line Stilwell had given her — a guess based on what he had learned during the investigation. How Crane reacted here would determine whether there was a case to be made.

"You're full of shit," Crane said. "And you know it."

"Really?" Sneed countered. "She lived with me, stupid. I'm sure she told you that. And she was only letting you bang her so she could keep her job and hook one of those rich assholes like Easterbrook. That morning she joked about dumping you. She said you were disgusting and that you wouldn't take the news too well. I guess you didn't."

Sneed had now gone off script. Stilwell wondered if the conversation she had just recounted had actually happened or if she was just riffing. Either way, she was good, and her words hit Crane hard. Even on an overhead camera, Stilwell could see his furious reaction and knew that staging the meeting in a public place had been the right choice. It was the only thing holding Crane in check. He was tensed and ready to lash out at Sneed.

In that moment, Stilwell knew that Crane had killed Leigh-Anne Moss.

"What did she say that set you off?" Sneed said. "That must have been so hard to take after all that time when you were thinking you were in charge. Hard to find out she was running you, not the other way around. You must've been scared about what she would do next, who she would tell."

Crane leaned in again to return fire.

"You're all alike, aren't you?" he said through a clenched jaw. "The way you think you can destroy a man. Well, your little friend got exactly what she deserved and you will too if you think you're going to take from me what's mine."

It wasn't a full admission, but it was close. Stilwell felt a cold finger go down his spine. He almost had what he needed. Crane's words also revealed that Leigh-Anne might have threatened him during their last meeting—threatened to expose him, which would have cost him his job and livelihood.

"Look, I'm not talking about this anymore," Sneed said. "You know the town put up a reward. Ten thousand dollars—and the members of your club announced they'd match it. I figure I get that and then some from you or I get it after I turn you in. Which is it going to be?"

"You think I have twenty thousand dollars?" Crane shot back. "You're the same as her. She didn't just want her paycheck. She wanted more. She wanted everything I had, and I wasn't going to give it to her. You've made a big mistake here, honey. Just like she did."

"Don't try to scare me. I'll put you in jail."

"You're blackmailing me and that's a bad idea. Just ask your little friend. Oh, wait, that's right, you can't, because she's dead."

Crane's anger and hate was radiating off the screen, and Stilwell was suddenly not sure that Sneed was safe despite her being in a public place. Crane had not directly incriminated himself yet, but he had said enough to help persuade a jury. Stilwell pulled off the headphones and stepped away from the monitor. He pocketed the recorder and quickly walked out through the hotel lobby and into the bar. He came up behind Crane unseen, put a hand on the back of his neck, and shoved him forward and down, chest on the bar top, knocking his wineglass over.

"Charles Crane," he said. "You are under arrest for the murder of Leigh-Anne Moss."

Stilwell pulled handcuffs from his pocket and expertly latched Crane's wrists together behind his back.

"What the hell is this?" Crane said.

"You heard me," Stilwell said. "You're under arrest."

Stilwell looked at Sneed.

"Good job, Leslie," he said. "We got what we needed. You can step back."

Sneed slipped off her stool and regarded Crane as she moved away.

"Nice doing business with you, *honey,*" she said.

Crane made a lunge toward Sneed, but Stilwell easily restrained him and swung him back hard against the bar.

"You people don't have shit!" Crane yelled. "I didn't do anything. She's an extortionist and I was just trying to scare her off."

Stilwell held Crane against the bar as he started going through his pockets. From one, he pulled a fold of hundred-dollar bills. He tossed it on the bar top and they spilled apart. It appeared to be more than a thousand dollars.

"Really?" Stilwell said. "You were going to scare her away with hundred-dollar bills?"

"That wasn't for her," Crane said. "You have no proof of that."

"Whatever you say, Crane. Now listen to this."

Stilwell recited the Miranda admonishment. As he spoke the words, he thought about Leigh-Anne Moss and Daniel Easterbrook and how the crime Crane had committed had destroyed much more than one life.

46

CRANE SAT CUFFED to the metal arms of a chair in the sub's interview room. Stilwell had placed him in the room and let him percolate for a half hour before returning. He came in and began talking in midstream, as though they were in the middle of a conversation.

"You know what I can't figure out?" Stilwell said, sitting down. "Why you reported the statue missing and fingered Leigh-Anne for it. I mean, if you had just cleaned it up and put it back in the case after killing her, we might still be trying to identify the woman in the water and you wouldn't be sitting there handcuffed to a chair."

"I didn't kill anyone," Crane said.

"My guess is that it broke. The statue. You were so angry and you hit her so hard that it broke, and then you couldn't put it back. You had to make up a story to cover up that it was missing. That was what happened, right?"

"I don't know anything about this or what you're talking about. If you would be kind enough to bring me my phone, I'd like to call my lawyer."

"Well, that's a problem, because your phone is evidence in a murder case now. We'll be checking it for evidence that you were communicating with the victim."

"She worked for me and we communicated by phone. It's evidence of nothing. Can I please contact my attorney now?"

"Tell you what. Since you've invoked your right to an attorney, I can't ask you any more questions —"

"Thank God for that."

"But I can tell you a few things, and maybe they'll be helpful for you and your attorney to know."

Stilwell took the recorder out of his pocket and hit the play button. He had cued the playback to the most incriminating statement Crane had made to Leslie Sneed just an hour before: "You're all alike, aren't you? The way you think you can destroy a man. Well, your little friend got exactly what she deserved and you will too if you think you're going to take from me what's mine."

He clicked it off.

" 'Got exactly what she deserved,' " Stilwell said. "I'm thinking that a jury of your peers will eat that up like ice cream."

"A jury will never hear it," Crane said. "Because you have no case. You need a case to go to trial."

"I don't know about that, Charlie. I mean, you revealed yourself up there at the hotel. We have it on the hotel's camera too, by the way. The whole conversation will play in front of a jury and they're going to see into your dark fucking soul. You ask me, that's a real risk, letting that happen."

"It never will. The whole thing was a setup."

"Oh, I definitely agree with you there. We set you up pretty good with that text. And you took the bait."

"The judge will throw it out. It's entrapment."

"I don't know about that either. This is a Catalina crime, so the case will go to Judge Harrell — at least for initial pleadings and motions. He's tough, and I hear he's not overly fond of the crowd at the Black Marlin Club."

Crane blinked and seemed to have no response, the first sign that his smug demeanor might be a front.

Stilwell picked up the recorder and scrolled back, watching the counter until he got to the number he wanted. He played a shortened version of what he had already played, repeating it as an interrogation tactic, reinforcing the jeopardy Crane's own words had put him in.

"— you think you can destroy a man. Well, your little friend got exactly what she deserved and you will too if you think you're going to take from me what's mine."

Stilwell hit the stop button.

"Talk about ice cream. You're saying a woman with a bashed-in skull got what she deserved. I don't know — it's not a good look on you. The best lawyers in the state won't be able to keep women off the jury. I think if you roll the dice and go to trial, then you go down. That's how I'd bet it, and I'd bet big."

Crane had no comeback this time. Stilwell started to believe he was close to breaking him.

"So, let's review things for a couple minutes here," he said. "We have video and physical evidence that Leigh-Anne Moss's body was put on the *Emerald Sea* in the middle of the night, then taken out to the bay and dumped into the Pacific. We also know that as the manager of the club, you had access to the *Emerald Sea*."

"A lot of people have access to that boat," Crane said. "It proves nothing."

"But then somehow, like a ghost, somebody said, the body of Leigh-Anne Moss comes back into the harbor with the undersea currents. And who just happens to be in the harbor scraping hulls? Denzel Abbott. Denzel sees the body and now we have a murder. The next day you report the stolen statue and finger Leigh-Anne as the culprit. I think what happened was that you panicked, Charles, and you made up a story, but it was a bad story because here we are."

Stilwell paused to see if Crane wanted to respond. He said nothing, but his eyes were cast down. Stilwell continued.

"You then get a text from Leigh-Anne's roommate and you go all the way up the hill to the ZG to confront and threaten her. You have to understand that the prosecution is going to lay this out piece by piece to the jury, like a hammer hitting nails on a coffin. And before you get to trial, I'll still be working the case, digging up more witnesses and evidence. We'll search the club top to bottom. If you cleaned up there the way you cleaned up the *Emerald Sea,* then you're going to be in more trouble. And I haven't even begun to question members of the club and employees, other than Buddy Callahan, who you gave me to throw me off the scent."

Crane turned his face away as though the thought of the members of the club being drawn into a police investigation was a greater embarrassment to him than a murder charge.

Stilwell continued to add pressure.

"Now, you run a boating club, so you must know what Yacht Lock is, right?" Stilwell said. "Mason Colbrink installed it on the *Emerald Sea.* It's a hidden GPS transponder that helps the authorities track yachts that get stolen. So we served a search warrant on Yacht Lock and we'll be getting the GPS for all the *Emerald Sea's* movements. Once we pinpoint the spot where you took the boat out and dumped the body, we'll put a dive team down. My guess is that they'll find your missing statue — the murder weapon — and Leigh-Anne's cell phone. What we don't get off your phone, in case you were using a burner, we'll pull off hers. You know, all your texts and maybe some photos. And then we'll have everything we need to get a conviction and put you away forever."

"You live in a fantasy world, Stilwell," Crane said. "Pure fantasy."

It was a weak comeback. He said it without the defiance he had mustered just moments before.

"Maybe," Stilwell said. "But I don't think so. I think the evidence holds up, and a prosecutor is going to see headlines and glory. And you're going to see the inside of a cell for the rest of your life."

Stilwell stood up and went to the door but turned back before opening it.

"There's really only one way out for you," he said. "Own up to it. Tell me what happened. She played you, used you. She got under your skin and you reacted. Without thinking. You followed her to the door and grabbed the first thing you could get your hands on. You lashed out and you hit her. You didn't want to kill her; you just wanted to hurt her. Hurt her for hurting you. That's manslaughter and there's light at the end of that tunnel. There is no light at the end of murder one."

Crane smirked and seemed to be calling on his last ounce of bravado.

"Nice try," he said. "Can I call my lawyer now?"

"I'll get the phone," Stilwell said.

He opened the door and looked back at Crane.

"I think I like it better this way," he said. "Knowing you'll never be able to use or hurt another woman again."

Stilwell stepped out and closed the door.

47

STILWELL WAS ANNOYED with himself. His bluffs hadn't worked with Crane and now he was left with a case that no prosecutor would come close to calling bulletproof. His strongest evidence could also be his weakest. Crane's statements could easily be interpreted in different ways. He and his lawyer would only have to convince one of twelve jurors that he was simply trying to scare off an extortionist. Any prosecution would also be starting in the hole, thanks to the department's blunder of initially declaring Easterbrook the killer. Even a defense attorney fresh out of law school would know how to tee that up for a jury to view the investigation as completely incompetent.

While Crane called his lawyer from the locked interview room, Stilwell went to his office and picked up his phone. He saw that he had missed three calls from Captain Corum. He knew what they were about and decided not to avoid the confrontation any longer. He put the video feed from the interview room on his computer screen and muted the audio so he could keep an eye on Crane without invading attorney-client privilege, then called Corum back. His boss picked up before the first ring was over. Soon Stilwell was holding the phone away from his ear as Corum yelled.

"What the fuck, Stilwell? You are going after the fucking mayor of Avalon and you don't even think to give me a heads-up?"

"What are you talking about? I told you the mayor was on the radar."

"Yeah, you told me he was on the radar. Not that deals have been made and it's going to a grand fucking jury."

"Look, Captain, things started moving beyond my control. Oscar Terranova turned himself in to the DA, not to me. They cut a deal with him, and apparently I'm supposed to give testimony to this grand jury as well. But I learned of this about the same time as you."

"Stilwell, you have been relieved of duty pending an OIS investigation. Don't you understand what that means? You cannot testify in a grand jury case."

"Captain, the prosecutor said there's a subpoena with my name on it. I don't have a choice. I'm sure you don't want me to break the law. I have to testify. And it doesn't matter if I'm ROD. Court testimony doesn't count as active duty."

There was a long silence. Corum realized that Stilwell was correct and calmed down.

"Okay, how strong is this case?" he finally asked.

"It must be strong if they're rushing it in front of a grand jury," Stilwell said. "I talked to the prosecutor an hour or so ago and she said Terranova has recordings of himself and the mayor that are damning. She said they have Allen on both the murder of Henry Gaston and the abduction of Tash Dano."

"Have you heard these tapes?"

"I heard part of one. I think it will do the trick. Juarez, the prosecutor, said the other one is even better, but I haven't heard it. She was too busy."

"Are they clean? That's the important thing."

Stilwell knew he was asking if the tapes were legally obtained and acceptable as evidence in a trial.

"Juarez thinks they are," Stilwell said. "I'm sure they'll be challenged by the defense, but that's expected. It sounds to me like they'll hold up."

"I don't like that we were not part of this," Corum said. "It's not how it should've been handled. We should have had people in there from the beginning."

"I agree, Cap. But it is what it is. Terranova's a smart guy. He and his lawyer probably figured this was their best move. He's getting a good deal out of it."

While the conversation was chock-full of lies by omission, Stilwell had managed so far not to directly mislead Corum. The captain might eventually learn of the fuller role Stilwell had played in bringing in Terranova, but Stilwell hoped that this would come to light due to the successful grand jury indictment and arrest of Mayor Douglas Allen.

"All right, I want to hear from you tomorrow, Stil," Corum said. "When there is an indictment, you call me right away and we'll figure out the arrest plan. We'll need a strategy for managing the media on this as well."

"You'll hear from me right away."

"After you testify, we can send you back on a chopper. You make the arrest, and then we fly the suspect back and book him right into county."

"Sounds good. But, uh, okay if we fly two suspects back to be booked into county?"

"Two? What are you talking about? I was told Terranova's getting a pass."

"He is. But I just made an arrest in another case."

"What case?"

"The Leigh-Anne Moss murder."

There was a moment of silence and Stilwell braced for the verbal onslaught that was coming.

"Jesus Christ, Stilwell, what did you do?"

This time, at least, Corum's exclamation wasn't loud enough that Stilwell had to hold the phone away from his ear.

48

AFTER COMPLETING HIS testimony before the grand jury, Stilwell stepped into the hallway on the third floor of the Criminal Courts Building and saw Oscar Terranova sitting on a bench with a man he assumed was his attorney. Juarez followed Stilwell out after addressing the jurors about the next witness. She held the door open and waved to Terranova.

"Oscar," she said. "It's time."

Terranova was wearing a pin-striped suit and tie. He stood up, but his lawyer didn't. The attorney was not allowed in the grand jury room. Terranova headed toward Juarez while buttoning his suit jacket. The suit was sleek and expensive, but to Stilwell he still looked like a gangster.

"You did good, Stil," Juarez said. "You prepped them for the main attraction."

"It shouldn't be that way," he said. "He should go down with the mayor."

Juarez ignored that. "I'll call you when we get the indictment."

"I'll be ready."

Terranova reached them and stopped.

"Ready for what?" he asked.

"None of your business," Stilwell said.

Terranova smiled glibly and assessed Stilwell with his eyes. He adjusted his tie.

"It kills you, doesn't it?" he said. "The deal I got."

"No, Baby Head, it doesn't kill me," Stilwell said. "I know there will be a next time. A guy like you, there's always a next—"

"Oscar," Juarez interrupted. "Let's go in. They're waiting."

Terranova smirked and walked past Stilwell and through the door. He would tell sixteen strangers about how his life of crime had resulted in two of his associates being killed, an innocent woman being traumatized, and a buffalo getting beheaded.

"Go, Stil," Juarez said. "I'll call you with the news."

49

BACK ON CATALINA, Stilwell made his first stop at the sub. Mercy was at her desk and her eyes lit up when she saw him.

"Stil, you're here."

"I'm here. How's our custody?"

"Very quiet now. Angel said he was up all night pacing and howling."

Stilwell nodded. That often happened with first-time arrestees. Stay up all night, sleep all day. The night before, Stilwell had called Angel Fernando in off patrol to babysit Crane through the graveyard shift.

"I heard the sheriff's helicopter just came in," Mercy said. "Was that you?"

"Yes. I had court over there."

"It didn't take off again. Are they going to transport our prisoner to county?"

"Yes, but not right away. We might be adding a passenger."

"Really? Who?"

"Waiting to find out."

Stilwell trusted Mercy implicitly, but it was safe practice not to talk about arrests before they happened. She would learn soon enough that the highest-profile arrest in the island's history was about to go down—that is, if Oscar Terranova's testimony convinced the grand jury to hand down an indictment.

Stilwell went into the jail to eyeball Crane. As expected, he was on his bunk and looked like he was sleeping. Stilwell returned to the bullpen and grabbed a Diet Coke out of the fridge, then went into his office and shut the door. He had arrest documentation to prepare for both Crane and Allen.

The call from Juarez came in shortly before two. By then Stilwell had gone through three levels of anxiety, wondering what had gone wrong with the case and worrying that the jurors had not believed either him or Terranova.

"Go get him," Juarez said.

"Okay," Stilwell said. "What did they return?"

"Like we said. Conspiracy to commit murder, but they also threw in obstruction of justice on the abduction."

"It was more than obstruction of justice."

"Don't worry, we'll upcharge him down the road."

Stilwell would be sure to tell Tash that.

"Okay," he said. "We'll go get him and send him over on the chopper."

"You coming with him?" Juarez asked.

"Probably not. I don't really need to, and I've got someplace to be."

"Tash?"

Stilwell hesitated. It felt like Juarez was trying to slide back into the mix of professional and personal banter they had often shared before the revelation of her complicity with Terranova. He knew things would never be the same again. He could never trust her.

Juarez stepped into the silence, seemingly understanding that things had changed.

"Okay, Stil, go do your thing."

Stilwell disconnected and proceeded to print out the paperwork he had been working on. Because of the communal printer in the office, he had held off doing so until he got the green light from Juarez.

He stepped out of the office and collected the printouts before Mercy could get a look at them.

"Mercy, who's out on patrol?" he asked.

"Ilsa and Ralph," Mercy said.

"Is either on a call?"

"Uh, no, last time Ralph checked in, he was posted up by the golf course. He's the one who asked about the sheriff's chopper. He saw it come in."

"What about Ramirez?"

"She was on Crescent by the ferry dock."

"Can you get on the radio and tell them to meet me at City Hall? I'm going up there now."

"Should I say what it's for?"

"No. Just tell them to meet me there in the circle. It's not a call for backup."

The last thing Stilwell wanted was to broadcast over the radio that he needed backup at City Hall. He folded his paperwork, slid it into his back pocket, and went out to the John Deere.

50

CITY HALL WAS located on Avalon Canyon Road. Parking was not allowed along the brick-lined circle in front, but Stilwell parked there anyway, pulling to a stop directly opposite the green-framed glass doors of the main entrance. While he waited for Lampley and Ramirez to show up, he called Captain Corum. As usual, Corum did not answer with a hello.

"Are you in position?"

"Yes. Just waiting on backup."

"Backup? You think there will be trouble?"

"Not really. But I want numbers for this so nobody gets a bad idea."

"Good. The chopper in position?"

"And waiting. We'll be sending two."

"And we'll meet them."

"You have media relations working on press releases?"

"In process. Big day for Catalina."

"Bad day."

Ilsa Ramirez pulled her cart to a stop next to Stilwell's.

"Backup's here," he said to Corum. "I should go."

"Call me when they're in the air," Corum instructed.

"Will do."

"And by the way, I just got word that the DA has signed off on the shooting. We got the psych eval in too, and you are returned to duty."

Stilwell thought about that for a moment.

"You hear that?" Corum prompted.

"Good to know, Cap," Stilwell said. "But I'm going to need a couple days off after this. A personal matter to attend to."

"Not a problem. But it would be good for you to be back by the weekend."

"That's the plan."

After ending the call, Stilwell saw Lampley pull up behind Ramirez. He got out and walked between their carts.

"What's up, boss man?" Lampley said. "You back on duty?"

"As of right now, yes," Stilwell said.

"Welcome back," Ramirez said. "What are we doing here?"

"We're arresting the mayor," Stilwell said. "For conspiracy to commit murder."

Both deputies were speechless. Stilwell continued.

"I'm not expecting anything other than verbal pushback," he said. "But be prepared. He's got a lot of cronies in this building. Keep alert."

"You got it," Lampley said.

"Copy that," added Ramirez.

Built by William Wrigley Jr. in 1929, City Hall was a sprawling one-story structure that featured the same mix of Art Deco and Mediterranean Revival design elements that the town's signature Casino had. The trio had to navigate a warren of hallways and helpful arrows to the mayor's suite of offices, all the while attracting the attention of passersby with their gun belts and badges. Along the way, Stilwell pulled his phone and tapped out a quick text. He sent it just as they got to a set of dark wood doors with the seal of the City of Avalon carved into them.

They proceeded through. In the foyer of the mayor's suite, twin desks were occupied by female gatekeepers who looked like a formidable mother-and-daughter team. Matching looks of shock spread on their faces when they saw the firepower that had arrived. The elder gatekeeper spoke first.

"Is something wrong?" she asked. "Is this an evacuation?"

"Not really," Stilwell said. "We just need to see Mayor Allen."

Her eyes dropped to her desk, where she apparently kept the printout of the mayor's daily schedule, and she began to shake her head.

"I'm sorry," she said. "I don't think you—"

"No, we don't have an appointment," Stilwell said, cutting her off. "Is he in the office?"

"He's with people at the moment. I may be able to squeeze you in this afternoon if you can tell me what—"

"That's not going to work."

Stilwell moved between the two desks and headed for the next set of double doors, which he knew led to the inner sanctum. He had been in the mayor's office exactly one time previously. On his first day on the job on the island, he had been summoned there for a meet-and-greet, during which Allen made it clear that he was in firm and permanent control of the town, while Stilwell was a mere carpetbagger who served at his pleasure and convenience.

"Excuse me," the elder gatekeeper said. "You can't just go in there. The mayor is—"

"Busy," Stilwell said. "Yes, I know."

He kept going, and Ramirez and Lampley followed. Stilwell pushed through the doors, opening both wide, and entered the spacious office. There was a desk to the left and a seating area to the right. Allen was sitting in a chair on the right; another man sat on a couch to his left, and a third stood in front of an easel with an artist's drawing of what looked like a small hotel or apartment building.

The man by the easel abruptly halted his presentation and looked frightened. Allen turned to see who had entered and immediately jumped to his feet.

"Stilwell!" he barked. "You can't just come barging in here like some kind of—"

"Douglas Allen," Stilwell said loudly, shutting down the mayor's protest. "You are under arrest. Do not resist, and place your hands behind your back."

Stilwell signaled Lampley and Ramirez to move in and cuff Allen. Lampley hesitated as though they might be making a mistake, but Ramirez didn't. She moved toward Allen, who put one hand up to try to hold her off.

"What the fuck is this, Stilwell?" he yelled.

"You have been indicted by the Los Angeles County grand jury on charges of conspiracy to commit murder and obstruction of justice," Stilwell said calmly. "If you attempt to resist, you will be taken to the ground. Put your hands behind your back and surrender peaceably."

Embarrassed by his hesitation, Lampley now moved toward Allen, passing Ramirez, and grabbed the mayor by an arm in an attempt to turn him around for cuffing. Allen shook him off and raised a hand to point at Stilwell.

"This is you," he said. "You trumped up this whole thing."

"Cuff him," Stilwell ordered. "Now."

Lampley forcibly took hold of Allen's arm again and spun him around and into the back of the chair he had been sitting in. He snapped a cuff over one of Allen's wrists and went for the other arm.

"You're hurting me!" Allen yelped.

"You're resisting," Stilwell threw back at him.

With Ramirez helping, Allen's other arm was pulled back and cuffed.

"Put him in the chair," Stilwell said.

He looked at the two men who had been in the meeting. Their eyes were wide, and the color was draining from their faces.

"You two, out," he ordered. "Now."

One man headed straight to the door; the other grabbed the easel and awkwardly followed without folding its legs. Stilwell tracked them and saw the gatekeepers standing in the doorway, blocking the exit.

"And you two, back out," he ordered. "Now."

The younger gatekeeper spun around and went to her desk. The other held her ground.

"Mayor, who should I call?" she asked.

Stilwell moved toward her to push her out of the room. She saw him coming and started leaving the room while Allen yelled after her: "Dotty, call Derek Haas. Tell him to get me someone. I need a lawyer that will blow these fucks out of the water."

"On it," Dotty said.

"You've made a big mistake, Stilwell," Allen said. "I don't know what you think you have, but you're the one going down. You're finished."

Stilwell ignored his words.

"Mr. Mayor, we've got a helicopter waiting for you," he said. "You'll be booked on the charges under the indictment at the county jail."

He then looked at Lampley and Ramirez.

"Take him out to the carts."

The deputies took one arm each and started walking Allen toward the doors. As they passed Stilwell, Allen looked at him, his eyes sharp with hate.

"You're done," he said. "You hear me? You're done!"

With the deputies on either side, Allen was walked through the building, the halls now lined with city workers who'd somehow already gotten word about an arrest in the mayor's office. They saw a lot of open mouths and heard whispering as they passed. Allen kept his head down and acknowledged none of them. When they exited the building, Lionel McKey was there waiting with his phone up and ready to video the perp walk. He fired questions at Allen, but the mayor ignored these until he was firmly belted in the passenger seat of Lampley's cart. He then looked directly at the camera and spoke.

"I am innocent of these charges," he said. "I am the victim of a corrupt investigation by a corrupt law enforcement officer and I will prove my innocence when I have my day in court."

Stilwell slapped his palm twice on the top of the cart and looked at Lampley.

"Take him to the chopper," he said. "Ramirez, you follow. Don't stop for anything, and hold the takeoff until I get there with our other custody."

"Copy that," Lampley said.

"You got it," said Ramirez.

The two carts drove off, leaving Stilwell standing next to McKey.

"Thanks for the text," McKey said.

"You owe me one," Stilwell said.

"What are the charges against him?"

"They'll be putting out a press release as soon as he's booked."

"You can't tell me?"

"Conspiracy to commit murder."

"Holy shit! Are you talking about the woman in the water?"

"No. Henry Gaston."

Stilwell walked over to the John Deere. McKey followed him.

"I don't understand," he said.

Stilwell got behind the wheel.

"That's why I told you to wait for the press release. You've got video and photos. The press release will give you the words to go with them."

"Come on, Stilwell. You can't do this to me."

"I just did."

Stilwell turned the key and put the cart in drive. He turned the wheel and pinned the accelerator. The cart took off, leaving McKey in its wake. The reporter called out after it:

"Who's the other custody?"

Stilwell didn't answer. He kept driving.

EPILOGUE

TASH HAD NOT told him exactly where she was going, but Stilwell knew that her favorite spot to camp on the island was Long Point Beach. It was what was called primitive camping, with no water or sanitation stations, but that was what kept it isolated and why she liked it. There was a trail up and over the ridge to Button Shell Beach, where those conveniences were available. But Long Point remained pristine. It sat below a sheer rock face that changed colors in the morning sunlight and provided shade in the afternoons.

Stilwell took the substation's Zodiac out of the harbor and halfway to Two Harbors before cutting in toward Long Point. From a hundred yards out, he saw Tash's blue-and-green Firefly tent behind the chaparral that lined the rocky beach. There were no other boats or tents in sight.

The sun had turned the cathedral of rock that rose above her spot a grayish purple. Stilwell ran the Zodiac in, killed the engine, and pulled up the prop as the boat moved over the surfgrass onto the stony beach. He watched for sharp coral that might rip the inflatable's skin, then jumped off the nose and pulled it safely up past the tide line.

Tash wasn't in the tent, and the kayak leaning up against the rock wall behind it was dry. Her fishing pole was in place in the kayak's clamps, and her wet suit was drying on a low branch of a nearby manzanita. He figured she had fished in the morning and then hiked the trail over to Button Shell to get a shower or to visit with friends who ran the youth camp where she had spent many summers while growing up. He checked the supplies she'd stowed in the tent and found the cooler holding a nice-size calico bass on top of the Yeti ice packs.

Stilwell went back to the Zodiac and grabbed the two folding chairs he had brought with him and the waterproof backpack with his own supplies. When he returned to the tent, he saw Tash coming down out of the trailhead. He put everything down and stood ready for whatever greeting she offered.

He felt his heart lift when he saw her eyes light up under the wide brim of the old boonie hat she wore.

"You came," she said.

"I told you I would," he said.

"How long can you stay?"

"As long as you can."

"Are you sure?"

"I'm sure. I mean, if you're willing to share some of that calico you caught."

"You might have to catch your own." She gave him a teasing smile.

"I can try," he said.

She crossed the campsite and they came together in an embrace that Stilwell had been waiting a long time for. Tash leaned her forehead against his chest like she always did, and he put his nose down into her hair.

"Is it safe?" she asked.

"Yes, it's safe," he said.

"And it's over?"

"It's all over."

She looked up at him.

"Good," she said. "Let's go in the tent."

ACKNOWLEDGMENTS

MANY THANKS TO all those who made contributions to the writing of this book. They include Asya Muchnick, Emad Akhtar, Bill Massey, Jane Davis, Heather Rizzo, Tracy Roe, Betsy Uhrig, Pamela Marshall, Linda Connelly, and Dennis Wojciechowski.

Any errors regarding the geography, fauna, or customs of the island of Santa Catalina are solely those of the author. Those familiar with Catalina and the Zane Grey Pueblo Hotel will know that the bar depicted in this novel is fictitious, as is the Black Marlin Club and the Harbormaster's Tower. Catalina is a beautiful place. Please visit and support the Catalina Island Conservancy at catalinaconservancy.org if you can.

ABOUT THE AUTHOR

MICHAEL CONNELLY is the author of thirty-nine previous novels, including #1 *New York Times* bestseller *The Waiting* and *New York Times* bestsellers *Resurrection Walk, Desert Star,* and *The Dark Hours.* His books, which include the Harry Bosch series, the Lincoln Lawyer series, and the Renée Ballard series, have sold more than eighty-nine million copies worldwide. Connelly is a former newspaper reporter who has won numerous awards for his journalism and his novels. He is the executive producer of four television series: *Bosch; Bosch: Legacy; The Lincoln Lawyer;* and *Ballard.* He spends his time in California and Florida.